Electric Letters Z

Peter Cowlam

Electric Letters Z

_____cHp_____
CentreHouse Press

Published by CentreHouse Press 1998
CentreHouse Press, Totnes, Devon, England
e-mail DLittcHp@aol.com
Copyright © Peter Cowlam, 1998

Distributed by Gazelle Book Services,
Queen Sq, Lancaster LA1 1RN

The right of Peter Cowlam to be identified
as the Author of this work has been asserted by
Peter Cowlam in accordance with the
Copyright, Designs and Patents Act 1988

ISBN 1 902086 00 7

Set in Times New Roman

Printed and bound in Great Britain by
Professional Books, Oxford, England

For Sarah

Amusing, perhaps, to transpose that human geometry found in a *roman-à-clef* to the solid planes of reality, yet this is not, reiterate not, a *roman-à-clef*. Characters resembling etc. living persons etc. are an amazing coincidence ...

Foreword

Whether Zob really intended the commemoration of John Andrew Glaze's death, and a celebration of his life, is still open to question. A great deal went against it as a project, whose demands should have been eased through Zob's own profession—although that is in itself complicated. By whatever chance or accident, those of us at work on the 'inside'—so to speak in the boardroom of English letters—have come to know Marshall Zob as wholly constructed, borne up on the vanes and those many social wingbeats first tested by his father—by Zob Snr—two men inclined to act according to the scale of likely reward.

Worse still for me has been Zob Jnr's personal weather map, his London clouds (I mean his sullen brown drizzles), and at certain other times his tumble of intoxicated sunbeams (all bound up with his flight up the fastseller charts). This has made his home—or rather, my former place of work—unpredictable atmospherically.

Astonishing? No—but it is ironic, that Glaze should come under my pen, an instrument I'd hoped to keep free of any such taint. By contrast this is so unlike the golden quill the mercenary Zob is obliged to wield—this by his family's rules of fortune—practically every working day of his life, in a padded cell. In just that ramble through another man's life (and death) is an often unbearable strain on my nib, host to all kinds of opposing forces. This is the point, the sore point, that I note even now (do I feel embarrassment? discomfort? shame?) since what I have come to spawn, under the privacy of my editorial lamp, is the full revelation of not just any old diary, but *my* diary (extracts below). That document of course I kept for scrupulously professional reasons, by which I mean that it isn't my fault that it tends as its seed the full and vulgar exposé. Plus there has also been the problem: how to contend with the sheer ineptitude of John Andrew Glaze's death ...

My name I shall hardly need to stress is Alistair Wye. Apart from having been informed, by a certain ill-dressed inhabitant of a certain misty purple moor, that numerologically this is a sign of passion (my name's numerical transposition), I have been, and I admit laboriously, Zob's amanuensis. Marshall Zob, should this not already be known to you, is the perfection of the dead Andrew Glaze, PhD, whose brightest student he was. This was way back in the early 1970s, in the cloisters of Modern College, Exe University, where the writer and academic, and incidentally Blagueur Prize-winner (twice), the witty Zob Snr, had passed before him—many years ago.

So. Gloves are off. I shall refute mythologies. Shall prick that iridescent bubble, a falsified lament over Glaze's death. Shall go on saying, that this has been no loss, a passing that hardly caused me to put down my coffee cup, or extinguish my cigarette.

I drove Zob, in Zob's silver Mercedes, to the stone parish outside Exe, while over preceding nights I had smiled patiently at his oration, which somehow he always managed to rehearse with a straight face. The priest, a man in a newly ironed cassock, I recall beamed throughout, and remarked of Glaze what bookish soil that gifted peasant had tilled (that slightly sanified reference to the proletarian origins of a leading academic). Zob, whose pallor through recent small-hours liaisons I should describe as aghast, had reached that point in his 'literary' success of luring a fabulous procession of womanhood into his Hampstead lair. One, a red-haired girl of twenty (less than half the litterateur's age), sought his assistance in finding a publisher for her thinnish collection of poems—so that she, like me, had the pleasure of his funeral oration. Unlike me, she tested the tog of his duvet. Her night-long amplitude dispatched Zob throughout the next morning, to the first, then to the second, then to the third bathroom, I later deduced in search of that cream, potion or palliative for his poor sore phallus. His redhead had tongued, petted, squeezed, caressed—once too often.

I slipped away before Zob's last farewell, and with the engine running warmed up the Mercedes. By now I was pretty well versed in that mendacious act over Glaze's mortal remains, so soon to be incinerated. Zob commended his fumes to the cosmos, assured of the 'greatness' of his achievement, for had he not laid down his lucid path—through 'a continent of English culture'—for less certain feet to tread ... Perhaps depressingly that was so, but can't be discussed now. For here should end the life, work, and attainments of John Andrew Glaze, whose second journey in a void I should much rather contemplate across the street, in the Forces Inn, where I could weep into some lovely local beer.

Therefore in some sense, our latest Zob masterpiece—a novel he has tactfully called *Gimme the Cash*—is overshadowed by the demise of his distinguished tutor of Exe, a man wholly without insight. May the Lord protect his soul.

(By the way, Merle, what did you think of that capon?)

AW, Highgate

Diary

'Diary' is not a term I should have chosen, since this implies adherence to one clock alone, that remorseless timepiece of our daily lives. Time, I note with some amusement, is in the very soil of my little adventure, and is measured retrospectively (once, ineptly, and as a chance remark, by Andrew Glaze, and now on a separate occasion by me, contriving editorial amendments to everything that follows). Were I to present myself professionally, this would have to be as Zob's assistant (which post I shall shortly have to resign), not Glaze's executor. Politically Zob has partitioned me, to a small and interdependent state known as roof space. This amounts to two large rooms, with extensive views of the neighbourhood, and a hazy green glimpse of the Heath. I am equipped technically, having a networked IBM-compatible, which constellation is linked to another, the phone- with exchange- and fax-system. The central heating, which Zob thoughtfully modernised before moving from Wandsworth, extends its luxurious pipes considerately to my attic. One of my rooms I set aside—this is for me personally—its having a divan, should I work late and not wish to go home (which is another garret, this one in *West* Hampstead). Zob's father, himself once of Exe, as both student and professor (colleague of Glaze), approved my wallpaper, a plain cream with gilded crowns (as I feel is only befitting). His mother, twice a divorcée, and famous for more than twenty novelettes for the Lady's Romance market, didn't much care for the Wandsworth furniture. She urged him to sell that off and invest in fine mahogany and walnut, country pine for the landings and bedrooms (of which there are seven), and sumptuous chintz for the living quarters.

Glaze—the immortal Glaze—had shuffled off his coil (not without assistance), back in the greys of November. The millionaire Zob (or at this stage I think *near* millionaire) stamped his feet on the cold parish pavements, shuddered, and wrapped himself more snugly in his coat. In the glove of his Mercedes, I found, and avoided, his emollient.

In December that same Zob trimmed his wistaria ruthlessly, the thing having overreached the mesh of its green reticulation, and

5

having pulled that from the eastern gable. Now it was late January. From that same eastern perspective I could look down on the emerald crocus stems, and the lawns sugared with dew. *Gimme the Cash* was due to appear, and was an automatic choice for the Best-novel-to-be-published (this-decade) committee. I shan't have to add, Zob even now dreamed up something 'special' for the millennium.

Innocence is everything. Zob's with that plaything the microchip is spectacular, and can offer, sometimes, curious mishaps. Take for example that item of e-mail, addressed to me in my room, to prepare him and his agent a pot of ground coffee. They had feet up with cigars in the drawing-room. Unfortunately this was a communication the benighted Zob—novelist, columnist, critic—delivered to the wrong queue, dispatching it to his publisher's office, as a telex (point I later deduced from a honey-tanned secretary). So to my immense surprise, I did receive instructions, on 27 January, a Thursday, when the moon was auspiciously full, as e-mail—smooth as winged Mercury over cupric ether (and so sure had been Zob's touch over his keypad):

MEMO

From: MZ
To: AW
Cc: %null%
                                                    Date: 27/1

Al. Cheers for the mug of chocolate. And ta for telling Annie I was out. Some thoughts re Glaze, that is I think two months is a decent interval. The hacks have sharpened their nibs, so why not me too? Anyway I've got material on Glaze. Please make time to talk about this, before lunch say. By the way the second, as well as first bathroom, is now out of bounds to you. And please could you smoke outside. Marsy.

Why-thankyou-Marsy ...

January 28. As a matter of fact that meeting was postponed, because Annie—a redhead, with a redhead's temper—hung fire round the nakedness of a distant forsythia, and must have seen Zob step out to his Mercedes. This was to retrieve his briefcase, and possibly lotion for his phallus (though I'm sure there were several jars in bathroom one). Zob was in the doldrums all day—I know this because he kept playing that Albinoni *Adagio*—and sent me home early for the weekend.

Albinoni's somewhat Gothic for my taste.

February 1. Yesterday I didn't see him, hear sound of him, or manage to intercept phone calls. He remained in his study throughout. I smoked my afternoon cigarette over the ledge, exhaling white cloudlets into the dry, cold air. In a patio corner, where Zob's gardener Adam had carelessly left a rake, a jasmine showed its tiny yellow flowers on its dark green stems.

February 2, a Wednesday. At approximately 9.30, a Mach 1 courier delivered a padded envelope, moments before I arrived for work. Zob put it with the other mail and told me to deal with it (delicately and as a matter of urgency). I took all correspondence up and had my morning cigarette.

Later. The tireless Annie Cryles, poet, turned out to have been the co-ordinator of that Mach 1 courier, a 'lively chap', I'm told, with a cockney patois. It was someone she knew. Her covering note presumed Zob's appreciation (for what was attached. A thin collection of verse, plus a half-dozen photographs). These latter were all in monochrome, of which I select only two. A close-up, to show us an outraged snarl. Then an action shot, of a young cosmopolitan in leggings, arms wide to a low flight of pigeons— scene, Trafalgar Square. Annie's little plan bejewelled itself as divine intervention, i.e., that Zob declare his 'find' to his publisher, having himself gone so far as an ecstatic foreword. This would be in his populist style. The one other trumpet was that institutional weekend column of his, for a broadsheet whose name I hesitate to utter, and which is in no sense 'guardian' of any culture I understand. Incidentally here his social percipience ranged over all human commerce, so lending us his wisdom on—oh—all kinds of matters. For example the 'Greene legacy'—with that inevitable

Browning quotation ('Bishop Blougram's Apology':

> 'Our interest's on the dangerous edge of things,
> The honest thief, the tender murderer,
> The superstitious atheist ...')—

for example the political future of Federal Europe. Zob also once gave us 'original' thoughts on the purpose of organised sport, which pan-Europe had been an entertaining surrogate for humanity's war-mongers. In fact for these last forty-five years it had actually kept the peace. He ignored the Irish question, naturally. Graciously, at the time of writing, Yugoslavia hadn't yet devoured itself.

Annie foresaw herself heralded, perhaps in the light of these concerns. I think on her behalf I must mention Zob's debut novel, dismal prose for a dismal Western World, whose clever title—let me remind you, *Aristotle's Atom*—he claims to have plucked from a dream of blue woodsmoke. This as you'd expect, Zob as the son of Zob, was patiently received, and is retrospectively hailed, a clear prediction of nuclear cover-ups. Since then the whole panorama of Western rapacity—an ape who pales under the spotlight—has so often been the subject of the younger Zob's newspaper work. Herein Annie Cryles stepped forward centre-stage, to take her cue.

Alas intuitive as to the making of careers—Dear Annie, permit my departure from Zob's official line. Understandably, you hadn't accounted for all those satin-faced beauties—I mean your competitors—whose rise in the world was doubtful, all on that one man's initiative. What he did for you, he must for them (being, as you now know why—nothing). Her poems bore an epigraph, 'For Marshall Zob, without whose attention' &c., and had a title page littered with acknowledgements. These were to her motleys, those magazine editors, haphazardly doubled under the burden of so many Post Office sacks. For what reason I do not speculate, these had once consented to publish individually all these rough fragments now propping up a collective title—mysteriously, *Keep Off the Grass*. One short 'lyric'—'Muesli, Mondays, Electric Eels'—was a prize-winner, though I shan't defame that organisation foolish enough to part with a cheque. This I turned to, and read:

> 'Man in green suit
> Steps out at green light
> Twists my mirror
> Sez Cut me up
> like that again
> I'll fill yer face you hear
> I'll fill yer face.'

According to Annie, a critic, writing for *Poetry Review*, described the repetition of green (green suit, green light) as 'startling'.

So our plebeians of the muse, who have seldom the imagination to advance beyond a palette of brown.

A second collection—*No Ball Games*—is currently being assembled.

February 3 (a.m.). I paused before going up and slipped into the press room (basement, full of tea chests, full of unread publications. That was the far end. Better lit, and more often frequented, was the near end, where Zob kept his wine bins). I eventually found the offending article, and was able therefore to verify Annie's claims. That same critic I discovered went on to construct a complete social thesis on her tepid seven lines. In 1 & 2, the unprepared (and necessarily ignorant) reader infers Freudian levels of consciousness, the key 'Steps out' denoting transference from one to another. Lines 3 to 5 are extrapolated, to incorporate a mobile populace, conducting its business 'always in transit'. Lines 6 & 7 are a fulfilment (is that of the Freudian wish?). No. There's another repetition, which the critic either didn't see or considered unimportant. This one 'concludes alarmingly' those 'unbearable pressures' 'postmodernist' man lives life with.

Cryles envisaged one small step, to a life as critic herself, perhaps competition adjudicator, perhaps even summer school poet-in-residence. However. I had my instructions. Not to say a personal view on those flimsy leaves she had lumbered a courier with. 'Marshall,' I wrote, 'is grateful for the opportunity of seeing your work, and felt it showed great promise. He looks forward to your second collection.'

That afternoon. Another cigarette over the ledge, and the thought that technically it was unwise to talk of flaws, since this implied a good poem slightly marred. That green light should have been red, though I concede ... it may have necessitated garish effects in shading a man's suit.

Adam had moved his rake.

February 8. In two days there will be a new moon. Mrs Clapp, the Thursday cleaner, seems to have got her days muddled, and was in the laundry room hectically ironing shirts.

February 10. That new moon, and an explanation re Clapp. Today it's her brother's funeral (cancer victim). I have noted our metropolitan sky as a distant zinc, extending its cloudy arcs over the neighbouring roofscape. Chimney stacks, those at any rate I can see (being a burnt orange), dissolve, then re-integrate, through the sodden streaks of mist. Adam, a man who has rendered me two syllables only, since his appointment after New Year's Day ('Thankee'—for the mug of tea I proffered), has put down certain markers, though I can't yet see him. There are his lazy footprints over the dewy lawns. There is a barrow with tool bag. I see already the crocuses want to reveal a deep blue. Daffodil buds—one day these will be a riot—just begin to show yellow. There is a thin pink blossom on the cherry trees.

February 11. The traditional path of strife, where two roles are cast (villain equals indifferent Establishment, heroine as genius), has no appeal for Annie. She was here just now slamming doors, which shook the whole house. She had gone when I got down, having left Zob ashen in the doorway of his study, still in an echo of her valediction (which bad taste makes highly printable in a novel of his. It finds no place under a stylish hand). Farewell, Ms Cryles. ·

Ash Wednesday. That new moon ushered in new realms of adventure, for only now do I discover, in the twilight of Zob's mountain spectres, that he has tried out his electronic bulletin board, whose Stateside calendar defaults have temporarily thrown me.

Although now I have sorted it out. Here's something he posted, almost a week ago, and two weeks after that first Glaze memo:

BULLETIN BOARD

Subject: Professor Glaze
Item #: 56
Date: 2-10, 16:10:51
Reply to: Box #1, Ext. #1, Zob

By: Marsy
Chain to: %null%
Comments: %null%

Text: Al—Well done for not upsetting Mrs Clapp. More than *I* managed ... Cornelius phoned me all last night, on the Glaze project, so I think I'll resurrect it. When can you spare some time on this? Any idea why these screens sometimes lock up? Marsy.

There was another, which through an automatic generation of software pointers (so saith the user guide) encamped itself on my screen, though I had tried manfully to escape (intending to pick up the phone. Intending to tell Zob this wasn't the best medium for spontaneous communication). This was as follows:

BULLETIN BOARD

Subject: Professor Glaze
Item #: 57
Date: 2-10, 16:19:32
Reply to: Box #1, Ext. #1, Zob

By: Marsy
Chain to: #56
Comments: %null%

Text: Forget that about the screens. I had my NUM LCK down, its little red light.

February 17. A bronze sky today, without that sheen, and with patches of turmeric. A week ago, Adam—or so Mrs Clapp reports—expected 'a boy on work experience, who bless 'im only now turns up'. Adam wanted to dismantle a timber chalet, which had been assembled directly on to a concrete oblong, which over the years had meant a bad case of rising damp. The boy—or rather pouting

11

youth—arrived in denims—shirt, jeans, half-length jacket. He had, not boots, but canvas shoes—a nice matching blue. Mrs Clapp took a hand-held vacuum to the drapes. Zob was out, so I left him a note on his desk.

February 18. Zob, Wye, finally meet, to discuss Glaze. Good-time Marsy, over a glass or two of malt whisky, has been talking in the hamburger bar to Cornelius, who wears large-framed glasses, and whose bona fide nose is comic, yet seems false, and seems also attached to his shop-front specs. Cornelius (Zob's agent) having previously considered the Glaze angle, has got bored with it (so, it follows, has Zob). Zob Snr drew attention to the year of our Lord the next. This—*annus mirabilis*—would see the sixtieth anniversary of Glaze's birth, in a Cornish fishing village. Zob Snr was born in the Valleys, in a mining town, and loathed Dylan Thomas. Zob Jnr, a man immensely more successful in money matters, now tells the independent Wye—which is me—that next year is therefore a good year for a commemorative book on Glaze, a man 'who has done so much' to promote understanding of present-day letters. However. I am to forget all this for the moment. A TV anchor man, who unfortunately encountered Zob's last novel, *Hype*, was taken with its central character, or more correctly was taken with that character's absorption in televised sport, in particular soccer. That character is Tallon. Tallon seemed so 'knowledgeable' that naturally his creator must also be—and would Zob care to participate in a TV debate, entitled 'What's Wrong With our National Game?' Zob said to me, 'Well. What is wrong with it?' Should I reply, so?—it's rather like *your* trade, its emphasis on aggression, less on skill. In Zob's case, that I mean was marketing aggression. On the field of play—well, it was physique. For myself this is too gloomy a picture. I am hymned by those angels of my native Manchester, who have combined Gallic poetry with Celtic persistence, and in a season of triumph, and of double triumph (as I am now able to insert, joyously, gloriously), are the velvet contrast to the prosaic Annie Cryles, plus troupe. *Oh là là, M. Cantona!*

I told Zob I would give this some thought, and pen a script to rehearse.

12

February 21. The problem, as I see it, with Zob and the TV debate, is essentially this. Zob had a precariously wealthy father, and this had a bearing on Jnr's school life. In the particular fee-paying institutions I have managed to document, soccer is, and always was, anathema. I ought to advise Zob to contribute only on that other, that barbarians' game—i.e., rugby. Though I think Zob was always one for smokes behind the bike sheds.

February 24. Mrs Clapp placed a tray of snowdrops on the kitchen table, when she arrived shortly after ten. I say this because Zob sent her out for steaks, an avocado, prawns and button mushrooms, which she also placed on the kitchen table. That incidentally is a dark antique pine, which bears the incisions of possibly a hundred cooks, going way back to Victoria. There are, pretentiously, hanging from ceiling hooks, redundant utensils, also from Victoria's reign—booming copper receptacles, somewhat tarnished today, and iron ladles. Zob interceded as I made a mug of chocolate—this was before midday—and asked me to bring one for him, strangely on the middle landing. He sent Mrs Clapp out again, this time for a single carnation, at which she huffed, wanting, as she put it, 't'-hoove'.

On, the middle landing. Zob had opened a door into a room I had not been in, whose sash overlooked the corrugated car port between *his* house and the lower numbered neighbour's (who is a liver surgeon). Zob cradled his mug of chocolate. The sky was a patchwork of ochre and lead. The room, said Zob, represented Wandsworth. By this he meant its contents were what had padded the *lebensraum* at his previous address, a poky flat. Statistically it's not worth the trouble (papers, so many papers. A Neanderthal hi-fi, able to play tape and vinyl. A bookcase, not square but a parallelogram. Prints. Posters—one of M. Jagger. Frames, and separately pictures. Much tasteless bric-à-brac. There was a roach clip). There was a personal computer, also from the Neanderthal period, with several five-and-a-quarter-inch discs, still neatly racked in a tinted library box. I remarked on the wallpaper, whose regular pattern was an aquamarine seaweed intertwined in a violet trellis. I picked up a long-play Rolling Stones (*Around and Around*). I put that down and picked up a Telemann, an earlier starlet from a later

13

period in Zob's aesthetics.

Before I went home, Zob insisted I make a garlic mayonnaise, for the prawns and avocado. He wouldn't tell me who the 'someone special' was he was entertaining at dinner. While I did this he poured me a gin.

If you want my opinion, garlic's not a suitable dressing.

February 25. Adam and that laconic boy have at last got around to the chalet, or its re-assembly. Much of its lumber—loungers, garden tables, a wheel from Zob's very first bike (a BSA Bantam)—has been stacked for the last week or more in the laundry room. I hardly need mention Mrs Clapp's chagrin (though not Mrs St John's, the Tuesday cleaner, who having 're-considered' her position, is to return on St David's Day). As I suspected, those flanking borders, a quincunx of circular mounds, and a north-east heart-shape, are a ripple of daffodils, yellow smears against the condensation of our north European crystal. The chalet's going up this time on risers, which Adam assures his master have been treated. I have refused to work in a room draped with seaweed.

Let me be precise. That old personal computer, in this respect like present refinements, is not one the clever Marshall Zob ever mastered. This has something to do with Glaze (who had a big-bosomed secretary, a spinster who typed, typed, typed). 'Don't trust 'em,' he said (computers. Bosoms he adored, especially big, and was faddish about. Zob observed this, observing Glaze, observing Zob's then-partner playing squash). Glaze, almost two years before his tragic demise, and after decades of philosophical consideration, took a sabbatical. This was to deliver the fruit of his metaphysics, in the form of a lecture tour, not in Britain (always slow to accept revolution)—but amongst our friends across the Atlantic. The tour did in fact take place (and has not so far as I can tell changed Western thinking at all). Glaze kept in touch with his friend and former disciple continually via air mail. Zob, whose first novel had not yet attracted Hollywood, and was remaindered, still scratched for a living in Wandsworth, doing hack work. He replied to 'all' the professor's correspondence, somehow, using a proprietary word processor, mounted on a PC. I have looked, but cannot now find the

14

printer, which I expect to be a Microline.

Zob's professional vanity, if it persuades him, doesn't persuade me, that the commemoration—The Zob-Glaze Letters—will be a milestone. 'There's plenty of time,' said Zob. 'Keep it to the background. When there's nothing else.'

St David's Day. To be honest the task's not that easy. I find, having brought that old PC up to my room, that the fixed disc is unreadable. Nor are the professor's writings easily found. His letters, in no particular order, are scattered among heaps of other material. By the way Cornelius was here to shake my hand, wearing a black shirt, a yellow tie, and with a daffodil in his lapel. Mrs St John threw out that carnation, which had expired badly, and which was still in the green flute Zob had planted on the dinner table.

March 3. Explanation. Mrs Clapp I heard warbling, singing, and whistling, presumably as she cleaned bathroom three. Cornelius, who has taken certain soundings and is warmly enthusiastic on the Zob/Glaze project, sluiced his personal Niagara over the falls of bathroom two. I therefore deposited certain evidence in bathroom one, which I later flushed away, and had plenty of time to take in the new Jacuzzi (its brassy fittings).

March 4. I have found a start-up firm, under a railway arch, near my home address in West Hampstead, who will restore my 'lost' data on to a reconditioned disc. You can get excellent kebabs in West Hampstead. The bill of course goes to Zob, to include the per diem.

March 9. Now this is what I call droll. Zob, for whom the world of practical science is a blur, had created a new directory (DIR1, DIR2, DIR3 … DIRn) for each electronic letter—those not always dispassionate epistles—as were replies for the hapless Glaze. I have no doubt he referred to a section called 'Sample Setups', in what would have been the then new user guide (a document somewhere, somewhere in that seaweed room). I have coded a zippy macro, to gather them together to a single, and sane harness. That, as I patrol the environment, reduces to sixteen letters, written over a period of twelve months, occupying twenty-seven kbytes of disc space. Zob, with both Oxbridge and Exe degrees, is a man only commercially literate. That old pile of junk he laboured with myopically in Wandsworth, takes up too much of my desk space.

March 10. As usual I made my mug of chocolate (it bears the legend, 'Genius at Work', which is Zob's little joke). I overheard Mrs Clapp, in a protracted exchange with Adam over chrysanthemums. Adam, invariably, wears navy blue overalls, with a tiny pink tulip stitched into the corner of a pocket. Now that he has creosoted the chalet, Zob says he doesn't like the new colour. Too dark.

I am beginning to tear my hair out over the professor's X letters, only three of which I have so far found. Much of what's in that Wandsworth room I think would prove highly combustible, not least a purple review of *Aristotle's Atom*. This, a cutting from a risible Saturday supplement, had been penned by a Cambridge confederate, who had himself gone on to the Booker, and has not ceased since to pontificate. This is chronic among public diseases.

March 11. I am in possession now of five of Glaze's letters, all in black ink, on carmine notelets, still strongly doused in the scent of apple. The next stage is this. To recover them all, then key them to disc, interleaving them chronologically with Zob's. Zob will write a foreword. One of his cronies—perhaps that ethnic writer, Khalil Azmi, himself a graduate of Exe—will write one of those tedious introductions—fraudulent, eulogistic.

March 14. Six letters now, and, by chance, a Xerox of Glaze's lecture notes. These I have found amusing. According to Glaze—or I should say, according to what has been attributed to him, as Professor Glaze's Quotidian Thoughts on Literature—time is a spatial continuum. Moreover it is linear, extending infinitely in two directions. This makes us eternal travellers on a regal strip of carpet, a thing unfurling endlessly under a cold sprinkling of stars. (Cold showers I recommend.) The mistake—or as Glaze had it, the 'Grand Fallacy'—has been to pin our lives down cyclically (sunrise, and after a period of twenty-four hours, sunrise, and after a period of twenty-four hours, and so on *ad nauseam*). This is the *false* measure of time, recurrence being—not a circle—but exactly that, the repeated occurrence of, of, of, not things, rather 'doings'. 'Doings' he attributes discretely to men, and in some lecture halls women also. So Shakespeare finds his repetition in someone like Larkin (in itself an inexcusable flaw in the whole theory). One reason that Shakespeare can't shake hands with Philip Baboon is this. Though essentially the same product, they are nevertheless products of a different time. Time is therefore only a separation in Glaze's system (or what has been something vaguely inflicted on him by at least one mischievous commentator—AW), and is measured in terms of distance. So. Why can't I step back a second or two? Answer: each 'second' is an enormity.

I conclude that he may have read his Ginsberg, but not his St Augustine, for without the 'discrete' doings of men (and the occasionally honoured woman), there would be no time, infinitely, in any direction.

I can see. We are going to have to return to this, Professor.

March 15. I paused on my way in to work today, at Annie's forsythia, which is a bloom of fiery yellow. The first presage, to me (apart from that garlic mayonnaise), of Zob's new woman, came via Mrs St John, who handed me the mail (wanting to polish the hall dresser). I sorted it, so to speak dealt to the top its smallest envelope—white, window, self-seal, not recycled (tut). Its franking—as I later learned I misconstrued—bore the fragmented scales of a cobra, charmed in part, and had the caption 'British Open Tanka Society' (or BOTS). A glance at my society listings showed that this organisation had been conceived in 1989, and was run, still, by Fiona Trethowan, DLitt, from an address in Woodstock.

March 16. Cornelius, a big man in a sporty jacket (corn and lilac checks), and today an ash-grey silk to the top pocket, brought in his business plan on floppy disc (which he calls 'flaccid'). This was his plan for *Gimme the Cash*, which, as amanuensis, it is my job to place—among all his other business plans—in its own square mesh

17

of our network (C:\PLANS\GIMME.DOC). Thereafter Zob will expect it on his desk, laser printed. Cornelius's secretary—a delightful girl for whom it was once my pleasure to stir a Martini—is orthographically astute, though it is not always the case that these documents pass through her hands. I shall therefore run GIMME.DOC through the spellcheck.

(How's this for an afterword! an ible for indispensable, a capital C for cockney, and among the many possible suggestions for the name Philip—'phallus' ...)

St Patrick's Day. A spin-off of the Japanese Festival, which was not that long ago, is the minor academic masterpiece *Western Culture and Oriental Short Forms*, a survey by Fiona Trethowan, DLitt. In her preface she explains that the book grew spontaneously from the many readings she had organised during that festival year, usually in the open air on campus sites. Though some, under threat of our English summer (i.e., rain), were conducted, inevitably, 'in the bar' (concealed laughter). Zob was browsing through a signed copy, which I later picked up and skimmed through myself. This more or less confirmed my opinion, of Bashō et al. as literary cul-de-sac (that short if perennial thoroughfare wherein Zob also excelled). Let me propose the simple truth that those earlier, Chinese models—from which the written Japanese lyric derives—remain unsurpassed (like listening to Humble Pie when you could have Mahler).

Inadvertently, Mrs Clapp unplugged the laser printer, about 't'-hoove', while I made a salami roll. This has 'unprogrammed' my preferred font, which supports the use of italics.

March 18. Cornelius's business plan is just like the others, consisting of these points:

1) Posters, on metropolitan street corners, and in every bookseller's window, to proclaim:

GIMME THE CASH: THE NUMBER ONE BESTSELLER

2) Blurbists, to be quoted on the paperback edition, to say things

like this about the book and its author:

'A remarkable *tour de force* ...' 'Possibly the finest English writer of his generation ...' 'An important book for our times ...' 'MARSHALL ZOB! Ignore him at your peril ...'

3) Myrtle Bloge, by now famous for the sheen of her round spectacles, should agree (Cornelius thought) to chat on camera (on one of those incessant late-night media shows), possibly with Zob himself as studio guest.

4) The usual two-page splash in at least three of the weekend broadsheets.

5) All the obvious interviews (Philip Masturbile should prove indispensable here, a critic who loved a cockney yarn).

I'm supposed to make *my* suggestions, before delivering up the printed copy, but all I can think of is

6) I'm in fact working on a novel myself—I mean a good one ...

March 21. Zob's drapes are a peach velvet. Today when I arrived they were still drawn—should I speculate, to the comfort of his morning dream? (That's to say tightly on all three sides of his bay.) I have, in the past, been confided in, as to his crises of conscience. Also I know he has found his reputation 'difficult'. Reconcile, please! (A sort of exam question, Zob went so far to pose. This was under the moulded vines of a Victorian ceiling, where the light was poor, and the tables rough.) What grew warm under my restless hand was a plain Greene King—under his, of course, a London Pride (then another, and another). The question unravelled itself with each successive quaff: 'Harmonise the formal Marshall Zob, who was charm's paradigm at dinner parties, and the sluttish world of his fiction'. How often, and tenuously, he has invited a parallel in Dickens, whose humanity is, however, impossible, in the frozen soil of Zob's commercial cynicism. Answer, therefore: 'Irreconcilable' (and, for me, another failed exam). Those drapes, whose graded peach had curtailed so many rising suns, were a veil to that thin smear of ink paling the sky's luminosity. They didn't twitch. In the kitchen I found his gluey brandy glass centre table. The study, whose fug of cigar smoke I sliced through angularly (opening the blinds), awaited the remedial hand of Mrs St John (not due till tomorrow). I made no attempt to re-arrange the suite, which was of leather, and whose tone is still a perplexing acacia. I checked his desk diary, to discover today's entry sporting a matchstick man, but no appointment (though M. Bloge was penned in for the twenty-second, as was Cornelius). Later I would confirm that electronically. I removed the remaining residue of cognac, a nutty brown pool to the foot of the bottle. I spent the day quietly, mostly rummaging in the Wandsworth room. I was, I thought, able to report a breakthrough ...

March 22. ... though it had to wait. The barrel-chested Cornelius, faintly incongruous in a blue business suit, incarcerated the protesting Mrs St John in Zob's den of Sunday's solo revels. Moreover he helped with the dreadful machines of her trade (spray cans, a carpet talc, the elephantine vacuum cleaner), bringing them in. As a rule, she said, she mopped the kitchen floor, first thing. 'Rules, Mrs St John ...' he countered, and you yourself may articulate the rest (there to be broken, &c. For so England's most 'gifted' novelist had demonstrated). Frankly, that blossom of creativity was still hungover, having flirted with that hair-of-the-dog maxim, dining last night on claret (not, I have learned, a *half* bottle). This was in the hamburger bar, where I have established a network of spies. Cornelius re-checked his watch, when Zob, still in the natal wrap of his bath robe (a fluffy *café crème*), slumped down exhausted. Approximately, this was at the middle step of the back staircase. Was there, he wanted to know, coffee on the hob? Cornelius respectfully advised a shower and a shave, and, that while he was dressing, a freshly percolated cup would be brought to his room. In the meantime agent Cornelius again consulted his watch, hoping, 'Goddammit', that the small-faced Myrtle Bloge—'so incisive an intellect'—would arrive even later than she now was.

She did. By about half an hour. That gave Cornelius endless opportunities with the violet silk to his top pocket, which he repeatedly flattened on the kitchen table. Equally, he folded it to the three prongs of the trident that eventually adorned his breast. In the meeting that followed, designed to settle questions before they were asked (which would be on live television), the pertinent Ms Bloge fired salvos from her notepad. Zob—by now sober, sluggish—defended his 'art'. Cornelius, if not prompting his client, took the minutes …

March 23. … which not surprisingly have landed on my desk (for me to transfer to disc, and laser print). Instance:

MINUTES OF MEETING

From: CS   Subject: Bloge/Zob
To: MZ   interview (re 'Gimme')
Cc: MB, AW
Date: 22/3

1) MB's apologies, roadworks on Euston Rd were the delay.

2) Forthcoming studio interview, scheduled for 30th, in so far as is possible, to be based on following question/answer session:

MB: Steven Kiff, centrally lit in the belatedly successful *Aristotle's Atom*, is resurrected for *Gimme the Cash*. Is there any significance in this?

MZ: 'Resurrected' implies I killed him off in that first novel. My readers will know this is not so.

MB: And of course filmgoers too. But the point I'm making is this. You have brought back that character for your new book.

MZ: That is so.

MB: Why?

MZ: Kiff represents a social milieu. This is more deprived now than when that first novel came out. Kiff's inner city—a representative locality, shamefully English—has had to put up with further decline. Kiff has had few educational opportunities.

MB: In the precursor, *Aristotle*, Kiff was a petty criminal, with sporting ambitions. A pool hustler.

MZ: Yes.

MB: Do you feel that his cocaine empire, described graphically in the new book, is as it were a natural career progression? And realistic?

MZ: I do.

MB: Could you explain that …

MZ: In *Aristotle*, his widening circle of crime meant frequent contact with the upper middle classes. For example magistrates, solicitors. The people whose houses he robbed, whose cars he drove. Not to say the entrepreneurs he pimped for. This gave him his insight into the frailties of human life—not at street level, where he lived—but among the upper reaches, the privileged.

MB: Surely you are not saying all, or most wealthy people, have a drugs habit?

MZ: Self-evidently, there are enough to keep Kiff employed.

MB: Employment's a recurrent theme, a sort of motif, continually talked about, but only ever seen to be done by Kiff. Do you have some special purpose here?

MZ: Work's a grim affair for Kiff. For those he seeks to exploit, it's a sort of adult playgroup.

MB: Nicely put!

[Here I imagine CS, Cornelius Snell: 'Would you like some more coffee?' (Though let me quickly erase this aside …)]

MB: I don't want to talk too much about the plot, or at least its dénouement. Yet for all Kiff's slippy operations, it seems inevitable that that privileged class you have mentioned, will get the better of him.

MZ: When, in human society, we make the mistake of adopting Darwinian principles, we tend to forget that those best fitted are those who understand the machines of State. Kiff is merely street wise.

MB: If I may turn to a contemporary of Darwin, you yourself frequently invite comparison with Dickens. Isn't it the case that a text by Dickens is sanitised—page after page—by its quality of human warmth?

MZ: If there is warmth in caricature.

MB: There is comedy.

MZ: There is indeed comedy.

MB: Well. If your comparison were just, shouldn't we point to the presence of these—humanness, and comedy—in a text by Marshall Zob?

MZ: It depends what you mean by 'humanness' and 'comedy'. If, in receiving back the paucity of our age, you detect a lack of warmth, that isn't necessarily uncharacteristic of 'humanness'. A later age may come to view cynicism—or so to say an entire Zob text—as 'comic'.

MB: There have been great social strides since Dickens's day.

MZ: I am a realist.

MB: Certain, less friendly critics, have often noted your apparent indifference to the cause of feminism. One might say this seems to be borne out in Kiff's relations with his girlfriend, whom he deserts the moment he learns she is pregnant.

MZ: Feminism is as much an intellectual as a social cause, where the injustice to be corrected is an exclusion—that's to say of intelligent persons from commensurate standing. I might widen your premiss and say that this happens to many men also. But I will stick to your point. Kiff does not occupy a world of career girls and academics. His women are trodden on, as he himself is.

MB: But the company director, Piers, that most prominent of Kiff's cocaine clients, is not that much more honourable with his wife, Joanna. All masculine potency is expended largely on his PA, seldom on her. There is a point in the book where we might actually think—and here I quote—that 'he approves Kiff's ludicrous attempts to bed Joanna'.

MZ: That is quite right.

MB: Is that not fuel for your critics?

MZ: My critics may think, if they like, that I have honoured invented characters with their creator's opinions.

MB: When pressed, you have found it convenient not to give opinions. Therefore we may seek for them only in your texts.

MZ: On the contrary. In my columns, my journalism, I frequently analyse current trends.

MB: From a standpoint of detached intellectualism. But here, Marsy, we're getting off the track, and in a ten-minute interview may well get no further than this …

MZ: You want to wrap it up?

MB: Unless you think we can cover more ground.

MZ: No. It's fine by me.

3) Any other business.

CS: It's important to mention the Best-novel-to-be-published (this-decade) award, for which *Gimme the Cash* will certainly be short-listed.

MB: I'll put that in the summary.

(I happen to know that Zob returned to bed, the moment the door had been closed on the trenchant Ms Bloge. I heard her little Skoda phut from the drive.)

March 24. Her reply to my fax bore a handwritten addendum to the minutes, a caveat to her final comment. She was, she said, prepared to furnish propaganda, *time permitting*.

Palm Sunday. I am forced to acknowledge an involuntary sense of gallantry at the plight of my landlady, Mrs Isabelle Lavante, an attractive widow nearing her late forties. Her athletic son Michael—academically quite brilliant—this morning kicked out a back-door panel and headed for Dollis Hill with his football. It was the old argument. She, of course, trumpeted the virtues of higher education. He, a café existentialist, eschewed all forms of learning designed for the needs of commerce and industry—institutions which to him were beneath contempt. I'm bound to say he does have a point. Nevertheless. That does not console our middle-class mater, who wants only the best for her darling. Temporarily, I found some hardboard for the panel, since the weather was damp. I looked up, where intertwining ink-blue ribbons tumbled in our sky (as disconsolate as she). Her claw-hammer I left on the drainer, with the box of remaining panel pins, at which I invited her out for breakfast. She said no, then well maybe, then okay yes, and offered unilaterally that this was a marginally quicker undertaking in her ageing Citroën. 'Certainly less irksome,' I said, 'than my Ford,' which was a decrepit servant mottled with rust. I chose one of those pretentious little places in Hampstead, where one read the supplements and was endlessly replenished from jugs of filtered coffee (at least, had there been a waitress). For myself I ordered scrambled egg, enlivened with mature cheddar and textured with sliced mushroom. The distracted Mrs Lavante had lemon tea and a croissant. (These details I remember well, since they were repeated on one, and only one, further occasion.) Clearly I ran the risk of meeting my employer, who couldn't himself boil an egg. Understandably my lightness diffused somewhat when I did in fact catch sight of him in a window seat. His hair was impeccable (washed, brushed, blow-dried). His laptop was open on his knee (a miracle, should he record his 'thoughts'). He had with him, I saw, Fiona Trethowan, whose face was honest, naïve, dimpled. Too late to change it, Mrs Lavante preceded me to the only spare table, a pocket handkerchief of timber, whose seating was a bench (a singleton) recessed into a stone wall—and a milking stool. Marsy called out as I ducked the low beams. The litany followed. Marshall Zob/Isabelle Lavante. Alistair Wye/Fiona Trethowan. My landlady dissolved, tossing back her jet hair, to my mind a touch girlish. Later she confided, privately over the flakes of her breakfast, that while 'not exactly' an admirer, she had read both of his books. I squirmed uncomfortably on my milking stool.

March 28. I was, incidentally, sleepy. I met, incidentally, Fiona. This was, incidentally, on the back stairs—which was her *first* mistake. She had on those same leggings and pleated blouse as I recalled from breakfast on Sunday. Moreover (second mistake) she had no overnight bag. She fluttered past, and out of the front door sheepishly. No matter. Let me announce my breakthrough ... (Can you confirm, I asked Zob, that I have found the first—i.e. number one—in that series of Glaze letters? Why yes. Yes. He could.)

28a Scriveners Mews
University Place
Exe
13 December 1991

My dear Marsy,

So at long last I am going public with my theory, and I don't mind saying, am leaving behind some pretty messy domestic problems. Giles, that fool son of mine and *flâneur*, has switched to the wine trade (off on some regular jaunt in Provence), just when he'd got on his feet in the luxury car biz. Why oh why wasn't he gifted like you! How I could have guided him—and so patiently—through these hallowed halls of Exe. Jessica's no better. Wants to marry a mechanic. Rich as that good sir might be, I'll have none of it. I told her mother as much, who said to me blimey Andrew don't you ever let go! All right for her, Marsy (never! Never trust a woman!). As you know after the break-up—or perhaps I should say precipitating it—that bitch on heat fell right into the arms of New York's fattest banker. I have the virtue of not being myself corpulent. Eh, don't I just! Ah well. A life is a life is a life. Not sure yet of my exact itinerary, though first stop's not surprisingly home from home. Will write you from New England.
Loved the book. Get that weather-tanned yachtsman, whats-his-name-Snell, to swing a film deal.
The best for you, your Andrew …

It's to the exactness of my craft that I point out humbly that in December 1991, the thirteenth fell on a Friday. I do not intend by this anything sinister or ominous.

March 29. Apparently all day yesterday Marshall 'fiddled', first with an upline-dump, then with a down-line load, but just could not retrieve notes he'd made on his laptop. I put him right as ever, and found preliminary sketches to *Bust!*—his millennial piece. Slightly

27

futuristic, slightly pornographic.

In the afternoon, myself giddy under the load of cheese sandwiches (pale orange, Double Gloucester), I broached what I perceived as the problem of Glaze. Firstly by luck I'd found other letters in a shoe box. To which Zob said, Micawber-like, the rest would turn up. More importantly, 'necessary editing' raised the possibility of an over-trim, leaving little of the original correspondence. 'That's a bridge we'll cross,' he said.

March 30. Zob was in and out of bathroom one pretty much all day, and I don't think did much work. Cornelius dropped in, for a 'last' run over those minutes (at whose addendum he took issue. This was vituperatively, with little spots of foam to the corners of his mouth). Try as I sometimes, or intermittently might (to kick a foul habit), those sublunary tobacco lobbyists could still not claim the amanuensis Wye as an adopted son. Why, Wye? Well. My addiction was exotic, that fatal blend of an American cigarette. It's so-so. That I prolong a contented puff. Into the marine tints, that wash of our English season (I note: it was three days ago—Palm Sunday—that British Summer Time began).

> On my ledge, leaning,
> I saw Adam, preening.
> Tufts of grass from a corner plot,
> Are all that his stationary barrow
> Has got.

Then Adam straightened up (as I remembered not to propel my butt to the patio), scratching his head at the first blood-and-pearl blossoms of a magnolia (to his mind not advantageously placed). Sir, I envy you your simple occupational complexities, though not your meteorological terms of employment! Ash on an old man's sleeve, and so forth …

At four I got sent home. Adam, a hoe strapped to his back, had already cycled forth—so I told Zob—through a mizzle, over a brown horizon. Our master wanted womb-like conditions, and a medicinal Scotch, being the correct preparation for his appearance on TV (though this experience was certainly not novel for him). I parked my Ford, and saw that the London Pole Co had hung a sign on widow Lavante's gable. At eight, she invited me to macaroni and Pesto, with herself at the table head and son Michael at the foot. He, at least temporarily, had capitulated, and so spent what hours remained in his room, with his books. Isabelle poured wine, a repugnant Lambrusco, of which I managed a half-glass only. At around 9.30, I caught her in a huff at the local news, having adjusted her two-bay settee. She had already hollowed a round cushion (in the aureate glow, in the tasselled shade, of her standard lamp). Then at ten she observed loudly from her listings that 'leading writer Marshall Zob' was this·week Myrtle Bloge's studio guest. She decided to stay up, and yawned a lot, a certain fatigue about her eyes, a heaviness to the lids. 'May I,' I asked, 'borrow a tape, record?' Yes-of-course-by-all-means.

March 31. How I have studied ...

April Fool's Day. ... and studied that recording.
   Item one, a film montage, featured the 'work' (oh how I smile) of—it's my pleasure—a dreary sculptor, I am sure now from Plaistow. His was a social *raison d'être*, frequently manifested in a heap of household 'recyclables'—beer bottles, supermarket tins, Patak's chutney jars—which he arranged and colour sprayed in a warehouse (somewhere off the Old Kent Rd). Item two was a 'poet/dramatist', who unfortunately bared familiar pains (stigmata as presumably dignified his 'art'). Item three—an equally diminished soul, whose wearer was somehow fabulously wealthy—turned out to be an old rock-an'-roller, who by some artifice had persuaded a quite reputable string quartet 'to do some material' (which I think meant a forthcoming album). The engaging Myrtle Bloge had that harmless smile pinned to her visage throughout. She reserved, for Zob's entry (the last item), a deep, bosomy breath, which at last revealed the full circular extent of the legend on her sweatshirt. This, as a studio light caught first one, then the other round lens, read as follows ... 'WELL, WOULD YOU ACCEPT A SECONDHAND SOLECISM?' Meaning perhaps that the deity Zob

was a grammatical blunder, there to be erased. To be fair, she stuck scrupulously to that plan I had outlined in the minutes. She uttered the 'Marsy' diminutive. She even mentioned Zob's new book in the context of Best-novel-to-be-published (this-decade), as 'surely a strong candidate'. Zob could have no complaints, even as I pointed out that it was no fault of Myrtle's if—in the enforced ease of the studio chair—Zob himself had worn what seemed a shifty look. Nor did I think his choice of black suit and white shirt open at the neck made a compelling contrast. 'You can't,' I said, 'be top card in the brat pack, yet appear half respectable.' He should also consider (I thought) a haircut, being just too long to the collar.

It is pointedly so that Zob never once took my advice. Nor did his gardener, who wanted to hack down that magnolia, and to my astonishment later did so.

April 5. Isabelle, only just back from a grey Easter in Worcester, was this morning on the phone to the London Pole Co, wanting to know why there had been—as she put it—no 'action'. Zob was alas equally querulous, only in his case it was at the fellow-critic Philip Masturbile, who had not shown up. (When, later, he did, it was with a photographer—a man with a beard and perpetual smile.) The Glaze book—or I should say its primitive beginning—now had the authenticity of a second voice, but of course a third, those editorial lies so well rehearsed in Hampstead, had not been invoked. Here was Zob's first reply:

> Flat 5
> 147 Trefoil St
> SW18
> 18 December 1991

Dear Andrew,

It's bound to shake up those too many nannies in our industry, which God knows needs a prod just now. Be sure to send me a transcript of at least one lecture—this idea of yours so fascinates me. By the way thanks for those kind words. It's just a pity that weather-tanned yachtsman (yes. Snell is his name) can't find someone, in fact like you. There has been not one sympathetic review. And get this! The rampant Geraldine Crouch, that fat-faced 'masculinist' (as she calls herself), described my sober Steven Kiff as 'highly implausible'—though of course she has not herself been anywhere near a pool room. I am at the moment ploughing through her *Geishas in Godalming*, which as geishas go, is godawful! I shall return the compliment, one reviewer to another. And don't by the way be too hard on Giles. I thought immediately, on that only occasion I met him, he had got your sense of humour. (Ever so slightly acerbic.) That should carry him through. Not much I can say about the rest.

Keep in touch. Marsy …

Whereupon I conclude, it is the frailest error, and a substantial world of vanities, that Zob supposes a footnote should demand our attention.

It is mildly unpleasant to think of it as publishable.

April 6. Meanwhile a scaffold has been erected on the brown brick face of widow Lavante's, up to the ledge of my garret. The purpose, as has now been intoned by a bicephalous foreman (to his client he presents a lamb's head), is to remove those elegant, nevertheless disintegrating sashes, and replace them with uPVC imitations. For the sole member of his team, who is particularly oafish, he reserves his rhinoceros head, quite frequently ducking it down, in a preparedness to charge. I cannot describe the profound warmth I tend to feel when Isabelle wears what for me is *her* colour—a luxurious, almost hyacinthine blue.

April 9. I have been summoned to Isabelle's two-seater, now that the boy Michael has finally gone to bed (it is way past eleven). Accidentally her ivory hand has brushed my knee, but has retracted itself royally. Then I find she wants nothing more than to smooth Masturbile's two-page Zob spread jointly in her lap and mine. It's killing me, therefore I make my excuses. I spend too long in the bathroom, and hear her try the locked door, then the patter of shoeless feet. She has again I see bought toothpaste with red and green stripes. Someone, Michael, has used my blue mouthwash ...

April 10. Wind, clouds, rain, intermittent sun. A lot of greenness, moisture, not to say the wet lawn outside. I find these new windows deeply disturbing.

April 11. Auspiciously, a new moon. I shall urge on Zob the virtues of CD ROM, which as a new toy may make my afternoons a little less tedious. He glowed significantly, and made *me* a mug of coffee, even before I had opened the mail. Evidently, how Masturbile marked the launch of Zob's new book—with a career profile, of the author at forty—appealed to his exact sense of sycophancy. That bearded photographer had, also, entered the conspiracy. He gave us a reclining Zob, in sturdy brogues, backed by the marble of his fireplace, and flanked by two Victorian caryatides.

April 12. That panel the boy Michael tested with his heel has not been replaced. To my horror a wizened little mechanic, here last evening while Isabelle fried onions, superseded my makeshift patch, with—a catflap. I am assured that a cream and marmalade kitten, a 'cutie' with darting eyes, is shortly to take up residence. That I know will make me sneeze a lot.

Zob, when I got to work, was up, and had scoured the morning papers over his toast and coffee. That particular exercise rendered up a sole book review, by Geraldine Crouch—not, however, of *Gimme the Cash*. Although, her opening gambit, ringed in red marker, and awaiting me on my desk, read: 'Forget Marshall Zob. Now at last we do have something to shout about ...' In ballpoint, Zob had committed himself, so: 'Al—thought this might amuse you'. I am able to report, with not too much detachment, that the new voice, somehow sure of itself, yet with 'a youthful·resonance' (an echo, and a re-echo, in a domic canopy we have called Eng. Lit.), belonged to Justin Simms—a twenty-four-year-old. His debut novel—ahem—was, 'stunning'. Simms proved a thorn in Zob's flesh, being got up in war paint in Crouch's rival camp—which means, regrettably, more of him too soon.

32

April 13. Next in that important sequence of correspondence was a postcard from Glaze, whose ink-line depiction was of Andrew's church at Exe. Many will know its Perpendicular Gothic, that distinctive squared-off top to the tower. Myself I have also looked inside, and at the font, whose columnar motif concurs exquisitely with the church arches, windows, &c.

December 27

Refused—categorically refused—to spend Xmas with Jessica (whom the mechanic has managed to impregnate). The girl must know how I loathe Cambridge. Am going to talk to my only contact in film, about your wonderful book. A prosperous New Year. Andrew.

(To which Zob did not reply.)

April 17. Slept late, as did widow Lavante, who appeared phantom-like at the foot of my bed, and whose diaphanous, lucent négligé should prove no real obstacle to our morning of love. She had found me so hot. 'That,' she said, 'was Mr Zob on the phone,' who had invited us to breakfast. The Citroën was having its hydraulics refurbished, so, after queuing for the bathroom, and finally a hurried shave, I fired up my crock. She arrived on the doorstep—surprisingly in slacks, a jacket, a lemon bow-tie—just as my Mahler tape reached 'Der Abschied'—music I turned down. Our venue was as before, where Zob had somehow reserved a bench and two chairs in the window. Fiona, who was with him and had her briefcase, and whose small lively face I admit had a girlish intelligence, showed Isabelle a warm welcome. I asked myself what was going on. Zob only smiled, I fancy smugly. Already he had started coffee, a saucered droplet of which he inadvertently spotted on to the white acres of his woolly—a crew-neck—to which Fiona immediately took a tissue. Waitress service had been restored (there had been problems over pay, it turned out). A pretty teenager with mousy hair and a frilly pinafore moistened her pencil while the petition was gone through. Bran flakes for Fiona. For Isabelle, a croissant. Me—

33

oh scrambled egg. That's the one with cheese, and mushroom. Zob, who even at this moment checked pockets for his credit card, ordered a Scotch-woodcock. Then in the lacuna someone mentioned Masturbile, whose article Isabelle said she'd enjoyed reading. (To *my* taste, that pungency of anchovy is too overpowering, even for a pizza.)

I ummed, yet the widow (that not exact admirer) used the word 'delighted' when Zob invited us back (perhaps for sherry, one might even say lunch). There was—important to Fiona—a first hint of sunshine, if a cold wind (which induced a pinkish under-tinct to the satin of Zob's cheeks). Fiona's hair was in a not convincing bun (last night it had missed its wash), and showed us the pale rose to the flesh of her face. Isabelle, in that tumble of vernality—those pregnant clouds before, above, behind—looked less than her middish forties. I will go further, to say that her tread was light. Although. And of course. Nothing. Nothing upsets me more, than the ride she took back, not in my Ford—but listening to jazz, in Zob's Mercedes. You will say, you have in Mahler the tenacity of consolation, but to arrive, to re-park (when Fiona stooped over a plastic tray of primroses—doubtless to do with Adam), when polite laughter mutes itself only to the distant cadence of a saxophone—this is all barbaric. At noon we did as it turned out have sherry, in Zob's study, where, crossed in an intermittent sun (through the blinds), it was muggins who poured. That was not merely for our cosy quartet (or trio-plus), because now a procession of Western Miniaturists (members of BOTS, British Open Tanka Society) descended on our doors, coming in from the cold from all compass points. It meant, smiling, I exhausted the medium dry. For their majority of crones I switched to sweet, asking myself what in heaven were they (as something I soliloquise)—the room filling with hubbub. Most were greyish, advanced in years, and some even I may still enumerate (I couldn't quite close from my mind the boredom of conversation):

One, a language teacher—a somewhat greasy man who gibbered. Two, a spindly, overworked-looking female, described (first by herself, then by Trethowan) as a special-needs therapist. Three—if not their leader, then certainly a figurehead—a professor emeritus (once, coincidentally, of Exe), dumpy, and at all times wearing an enraptured smile. Four was a collective four, being a half-dozen retired dilettanti, who had difficulty apportioning equal time to the pursuit of Zob, and a sort of adulation of the professor (who remembered Zob Snr). There was, out of sorts, a curly-haired youth, a boy made pathetic in a vaunt of credentials (a dismal prize-winner in a poetry comp, all of which I can tell you are 'fixed'). One wondered whose pet he was.

So I repeat (and repent of my sins, which are too many for one man to bear), all to what purpose? Solemnly, I advise you to clutch the arm of your chair, or if travelling by train, warn other passengers—what I here disclose being likely to make sane persons shudder with laughter. Fiona is in some sense indefatigable, having moons ago proposed a postal renga (a verse structure I am not sufficiently interested in to describe). I gather each recipient pens what approximates to a couplet, and, re-stretching that tensile elastic, mails the whole job on to a next on the list. We were, ceremonially, a couplet short, the convocation in Zob's study being here for that specific *coup de grâce*. That, of course, fell to the elected hand of their guru (the professor), who brought an edge to his curved sword with Arcadian worship. All trooped out into Adam's territory, Zob's walled garden. A brown wind whipped over the roof. In central London I imagined rain, a dampness streaking the concrete. The professor, compacting the wet grass under the tramp of his feet, admired the chalet, from behind which I assume Pan kept an eye. He next took out a notebook then raised and put away a xiphoid pen. The language teacher gasped. I turned away. Fiona, with a studious grin, I suppose had seen it all before. Then the professor wrote, not that remaining couplet, but a haiku—as 'a loosener', he said. 'I saw a daisy / As I walked across the grass: / Summer afternoon.' (Huh?)

Okay, 'afternoon' would just about do. 'Spring', when I took issue, the professor claimed not to 'scan', and anyway defied syllabic constraints. As to my surprise at that solitary daisy, when a hundred others, plus buttercups, constellated Adam's turf—well, he had a mind very much for the particular (though I could question his choice of the word 'mind'). Worse followed, when the professor did, majestically, add that last masterstroke to the group renga. The resultant 'piece', which was in patches scatological, and invariably trivial—was handed to me. 'Be a dove and produce that on your laser,' said Zob.

So that was the game. I felt puce. Awkwardly, I visited bathroom one, for a splash. There I found, in a nice burnt Paisley, an alien toilet bag, overflowing with feminine contraceptives. Someone's bath cap, an olive green, nonchalantly topped a three-quarter towelling robe, hanging up. And what was that, swamped in the shower tray? Ah that, Horatio, was an anti-friction gel, so so cool in its tube. How—as I interrogated the mirror—to extricate? Solution: key renga to floppy, direct output to laser in the study. So I made my apologies, leaving Isabelle et al. to their baguettes and ham in the kitchen. A few days later I intercepted a note from Fiona, which thanked Zob for a 'lovely' weekend. Amazingly his next conquest was Geraldine Crouch.

April 18. Monday morningish. Someone in that foul assembly knew the art of laser printing. Not Zob, for sure—possibly that yellow-haired youth—who has so thoughtfully left a copy of that finalised renga on my desk. Can't help reflect, on a wiser, and Chinese parentage, which has brightened our wastes with so many fine examples. Do I see, in the fragments of its inversion, a Confucian temple, its hues reflected in a lake? A boatman? Or again, a stillness of twilit cloud, capping a purple ridge? And what is that decrescent moon, that sickle of luminescence silhouetting not one, but two distant pines?

> A chill wind lifts the leaves
> Of the one-time empire sliding behind us.
> We shall ride beyond the purple mountains
> Of the West, before the maker of our destinies
> Is ushered from his chambers.
> To be, on the flagstones
> Of his royal courtyard—once the place
> Of so much idle makebelieve, and overgrown
> With the weeds of revolution—confronted

By the zealous executioner.
We who ride toward the purple West,
Who cannot choose between ignoble powers,
Cannot intervene. We linger, though,
And watch a boatman row across the lake,
In which we see reflected autumn reds and golds.
The horses snort. A time to journey on.

(My own bit of pastiche. Highly imperfect, thoroughly honest.)

April 20. Malkin, that marmalade feline, has marked out (I think odiously) the various elevations in what has fast become its demesne. I can't much argue with that sheltered spot outside, under the bay window—where its alert, inquisitive round eyes follow every passerby. This is from under the bowed stem and greenish white bells of a Solomon's seal. What I object to is the appropriation of Isabelle's two-seater settee, which if I happen to sit there—which is rarer nowadays—attracts the fastidious swish of Malkin's tail. This is calculated to be right under my nose, while the two rear paws test the resilience in my groin. Here my eyes stream. I begin to sneeze. If Isabelle hears—in the kitchen perhaps opening a tin—she laughs. Malkin I shoo off, who returns neglectedly (finding that tin's only beans).

Tonight thankfully the widow was tired, having helped Michael with his French (an essay on life in Grenoble)—which enabled me to put Malkin out, with a note to the milkman. Myrtle Bloge was giving her full half-hour to the 'phenomenon' Justin Simms, a fact which, importantly, Zob had not pointed out to me (without question, Zob would be watching). This remarkable man (Simms) wore (note, Zob) a Cardin shirt, and a nice Italian suit. He was—and didn't blush to hear it—of gentle birth. Throughout his boyhood he tinkered with a red Bugatti, which even before he was licensed he drove direct to Vire (he drove circuitously back, upsetting the gendarmerie). His first efforts in creative writing were naturally quite brilliant, winning him a Westminster boys' prize. So I could go on (and as a point of order, so Myrtle did—and on. And on). In researching his debut novel—surprisingly not a *roman-fleuve*—

Simms had wanted to know what all this fuss was about in post-industrial Britain. He lacerated his yachting pumps, which had cost hundreds. He fished out his striped rugby socks (school wars fondly remembered). Some dungarees he had sprayed the Bugatti in served as principal garment, all enhanced authentically by a few days minus shaving tackle. The hair, bleached by a long weekend in Key Largo (where he was best man at an old chum's wedding), would just have to grow itself out. So apparelled, Simms set a course into the disintegrating streets of his, and your, metropolis. North of Oxford St, he sang (outside the Cambridge, at 'around early evening'), where people pressed coins into his open palm. He moved on to the Blue Post, offering a fabricated life story to its drinkers (or, he corrected, its drinkers outside under parasols), who urged him away with cash. For his nights he acquired a polythene wrap, into which he mummified himself, mostly in a doorway off the Strand. From that he graduated to a cardboard coffin in the precincts of Charing Cross. So on for a long three months, where such contact—a verism actually lived through—rendered the germ of his 'powerful' first novel. For Myrtle, the palm was already his, alluding to the thing so close to Zob's heart. I mean that Best-novel-to-be-published (this-decade).

April 21. As might have been predicted, a bright-eyed Cornelius, in an unusual exaggeration of gestures—with first one, then the de-pocketed shovel (or hand)—was here in good time. I mean before ten. He and his winning client went into conclave shortly after the hall clock struck, though it seemed Cornelius couldn't think. Repeatedly, that man demanded fresh *cappuccino*, while the reluctant Mrs Clapp had a preference for the Hoover. My three puffs of smoke, as they wound into grey sheets and departed from my ledge, did not, at around lunch time, coincide with any patriarchal announcement. All I saw in that line was Adam's weathered face, as it gazed up. Not at me, but doubtless the pale green fringes at the extremities of Zob's wistaria.

April 22. They attempted, and failed, to conceal their conclusions (from me). I had a call from Snell's secretary, an able girl, for whom

I hope it's my pleasure to mix another high ball. She was trying to send a fax, but got for her trouble a sequence of unintelligible error codes. I checked our software here, and found that the server had got itself in a loop (which I corrected—by halting, then re-starting it). When, techno-*naïf* that he is, Zob instructed me to output—as he called it the Snell fax—direct to his laser—he couldn't know I had read through it on my screen. It was, gentle reader, Cornelius's five-to-six-point plan, as to the problem of a dangerous rival.

1) A declaration of 'war' is inadvisable, as that could encourage what might be construed a focus on your vulnerability.

2) Conciliation is a best first step, with some public laudation of Simms, such as 'Welcome, Colleague'.

3) Open camaraderie—by that we mean friendly, professional rivalry—between you and the new boy. This, the surest principle in undermining the Crouch link.

4) Remember! Crouch is a raging suffragette, and as yet no one has sounded Simms on this issue. Ideally he'll be unsympathetic.

5) Finally. Simms was *born* with money, and could easily get bored with writing. If so, you may join others in regrets—at-or-some-such, the 'long silence'.

PS 6) Have a party. Invite Simms, and Crouch. (And me!)

St George's Day. Malkin, whose four paws prodded my duvet at precisely 9.45, alerted me to the basic facts of breakfast, mewing. Viz., that as a precedent the widow wasn't there to provide it, so could I get down and open a tin?
    Why anything you say, Malkin …

April 24. Ditto.

April 26. So, as an instance, in an acknowledged force of

serendipity, I arrive at the casual ambience I am able to saunter over Zob's landings in, with a great deal of help from Mrs St John. She, slave to the market economy, and luckless, has been unable to dust the lampshades, since someone has failed to re-charge the hand-held vacuum. I blame Mrs Clapp. Zob, with his sole suggestion, spoke nostalgically, in terms of the Wandsworth room, where a whats-it, a feathered cane, was sure to be found. I led her with my gaoler's key. Ah—and so what, Christopher Robin, did you find? Well now. In a valise. Some curious items of lingerie. (To do with the great man's research—his first book.) Would Mrs St John disguise, I thought, her peasant disgust? as I held to the light a first and a second pair of panties, swart, frilly, crotchless. Nor, I said, did I see utility in this (a cupless brassiere). I tipped out knee-length boots, to remark on the sheen of their leather. A stylised cat-o'-nine, just right I thought for the lampshades, she shuddered at. An article—'Masturbatory Deceits and the Over-forties', by Professor Hand of Edinburgh—I spared her. Why do I relate this sordid interlude? Because …

… with the wodge of transatlantic mail I found also in the valise, I am able to reconstruct the following sequence:

> 300-506 29th St
> Astoria
> NY 11102
> 22 January 1992

My dear Marsy,

A slight detour, as first lecture (about which I'm strangely nervous) isn't for a few days. Samantha—rather that bull-necked sugar daddy she's somehow ensnared—has rented above address, whose furnishings I loathe. She says 'for the kids'! for oh how she lapses into Americanisms. This is on the off-chance they would like a break. For Christ's sake what about me!

I MUST have it out with her about this mechanic—I mean, can you imagine, a grease-monkey grandson! She couldn't seem to care less. By the way that contact I mentioned is filming in Toronto (for another six weeks), which I can coincide with. Promise to have a word.

The best for you, your Andrew …

Flat 5
147 Trefoil St
SW18
2 February 1992

Dear Andrew,

Please don't fly to Toronto on my account, though that is such a clean city. Certainly not begrimed like this one. Speaking of which, the fatuous Crouch, despite my best efforts, has somehow got her suburban geishas on to the shortlist [Best-novel-to-be-published (this-decade)]. It's rumoured she once lit a cigar for Sir Maxwell Hayste, who as you know recently took over the chair. Her advocates are probably many, those numerous friends, whose CVs all list at least a year on the committee. You know. All those TV journalists she hangs in with.

By the way your banker friend made a splash in the news here, having bought, and sold, a tyre company. Lots of redundancies. This he defended in an interview on the Plymouth Hoe, for which, ancestrally, he feels an affinity.

The best, Marsy.

1655 Sherbourne St
Apt 1313
Toronto, Ontario
13 February 1992

Dear Marsy,

Really it's not out of my way. In any case Shayle and I go way back. Shayle's my film man (who for other reasons is a joy to talk to). Samantha, as I suppose I should have guessed, has proved intransigent. Some ideal in New World denial (to put a youthful figure with that empty, middle-aged head), has made her infinitesimally short-tempered. She allowed me five minutes in her apartment. This is in Fifth Avenue, from where, when she isn't jogging through it, she trains her binoculars on Central Park. I tried

41

to raise that not inconsiderable problem of Jessica, to which she said 'Goddammit Andrew you're—so English ...' This is how she lives. She dialled for her escort, who turned me out on to the cold street. And I mean, of course I'm English!

Shayle's had his own problems (low budget equals low cast), but I'm delighted to say has read, and enjoyed, your book. We talked about it over a fish supper, which the restaurants are very keen on here. I attach his card. Get that Pantalone Snell to call up his office.

Don't ever talk to me about the bull-neck.

Yours ever, Andrew.

> Flat 5
> 147 Trefoil St
> SW18
> 19 February 1992

Dear Andrew,

Snell has been hospitalised, with quite literally a balls ache (a virus, which they say got up through the vas). Thanks for the card.

My cheeks have been warmed by a many-headed monster (Crouch and friends), whose multiple halitosis I find unbearable. I am accused and found guilty of anti-feminist activities. Sentence: my *Atom* will not share space with those short-listed geishas.

Doesn't she know the cold war's over?

Marsy.

Glaze wrapped up this particular conversation via picture postcard—a pale view of rounded hills, 'Little Rhody'. I quote in full:

'Providence, 26/2. As I said, you can't trust these women. Andrew.' As a postscript he sent another (sunset, Narragansett bay): 'First lecture delayed—but watch this space! Report coming soon ...'

April 28. Mrs Clapp, whose waxy complexion I watched slowly metamorphose—to a shade of aggravated nectarine—tossed down Mrs St John's note on to the kitchen table (though had laboured to read it). This of course was to do with the miniature vacuum, and the importance of re-charging—which was a slight, I might say, on both ladies' professionalism, which to that point had been exemplary. In reality Mrs St John didn't wish to repeat the Wandsworth experience.

May 2. Bank holiday. More trouble with Malkin, Isabelle having left her bed early, and not returned till noon. For a change, tried to read a 'good' novel (*Love in the Time of Cholera*), but Michael, rehearsing low hard penalties against a back wall, instead has got me anticipating the thump-thump, thump-thump. Elect to go out and keep goal, which prompts an ironic smile (one of the glories of English football). He will learn otherwise, but doesn't think I can play.

May 4. I have concocted a melodrama—*The Guilt That is Hampstead's*—or at least Act One:

Scene: Balcony above. Below, patio. Enter, at balcony, bored office worker Wye, who lights cigarette. Stares out wistfully. Enter, below, Adam, chief of ground-staff, taciturn. Stares up at thick fringes of green at wistaria extremities.

WYE [flicks ash]: There are plans, I hear, for that magnolia.

ADAM [leans on rake]: That's as may be.

WYE [heated]: I tell you I don't like it, this—conspiracy!

ADAM [unmoved]: Folks should mind their own.

WYE [stubs cigarette]: I'm not going to allow this, Adam!

ADAM [surly]: Don't see as 'ow.

WYE [passionate]: I'm going to save that magnolia …

ADAM [saunters to rear]: 'S not as the marster sez.

43

WYE [as vow]: Well let me tell you one day you'll have a NEW master. This can't go on.

[Exit Adam, shrugging]

WYE : All of them, fools! [Exit]

The earthy R. Quiggly-Walsh I should cast as Adam. Wye plays himself.

May 6. Zob, I think, has been depressed, and at the moment suffers more than usually from writer's block (not a condition medic Wye acknowledges). He spends more and more time in the hamburger bar, drinking coffee and Marsala. But. Even the deepest human flaw may at times be assuaged—Wye is the man with cheering news. This is in the form of correspondence, from (what shall I say?) a sole continental admirer—a Miss Overmars from Amsterdam. Amazingly her envelope bore no finer detail than this, in a capitalised hand: 'Marshall Zob, London, England'. Her note, with photo attachment (a sunny blonde, freckled), was appropriately dated April 30, which according to the diary was Queen's Day, Netherlands. Miss Overmars is determined to make her pilgrimage, with rucksack and sandals. I expect Cornelius will advise against a reply.

May 8. Malkin, as I spy through my one open eye, is a cat ermined, in the sleeve of my dressing-gown—which is draped on my chair. As usual it's Sunday, and the widow is absent. Time to get up, get down, and rattle tins. There is a note for Michael, who has taken up tennis, pinned to the kitchen notice board: 'Bacon in fridge, eggs in basket, bread cut for toast'.
   I'm going to nail up that catflap.

May 9. Morning. A brown drizzle dampened my hair, which is badly in need of a trim. There might be time to see George, a corner-shop Greek, who is very safe with his scissors. This shows me, in its process of opposites, that I have lived at all times in a pellucid dream of the South. A yellow sun. Vineyards. The dapple of eucalyptus leaves. Sadly my reality's abrupt—also the northern hemisphere is most of the time cold. This doesn't deter Zob's merry English postman, a man I met in Zob's border country, the broad drive. His boots had been polished. There was, fellow-jurors, a super-sharp crease to each trouser leg, a shiny charcoal. Sky blue (I mean by that a British sky), with little maroon insets, his shirt had its sleeves rolled up! I exchanged a pleasantry, I took the mail. Much of this was uninteresting, being marked PRIVATE (Wye, keep out!), although a package, from the Miracle Book Club, has proved entertaining. A Mr Tom Corbiere, Miracle's marketing director, pinpoints Zob as (allow me to compose myself) 'perhaps the most socially astute among our leading intellectuals'. He takes a bold step, enclosing 'sample material'. This, a *nouvelle* (a modest eighty-thousand words), is by a 'bright new talent', in whose concoction of art is a reflection, a photo on the dust jacket. This takes the latter of the two available options—smug, or genius in a frown. It was, I warn, a dull book (I read it, yes), professionally turned out. One of those fretful tales of life in the basement. It ends with a poor cleaning contractor cuckolding a dealer in rare ceramics, who is—and this is the book's subtlety—despicably rich. Mr Corbiere sees 'top writer' Zob as his organisation's figurehead, at least to the point of an autographed portrait. This would appear as persuasive advertising in the Sunday supplements, glossing those much embossed spines of recent publications, and all to a jingle: 'The miracle of Miracle!' One could easily under-estimate what price Zob might otherwise pay for the name—Zob, the mighty Zob—permanently before his, your, my public (I like the sound of 'my'). This, incidentally, raises that long contentious issue, of Zob's entry in *Who's Who*. Cornelius wants to see the address c/o the Snell agency.

May 10. I cannot say what murders the earthy Adam now could contemplate. Nor, in a cross-hatch of rain, can I see what lights his face. Is it manic? Benign? I do know he's examined the first fruits of a fig tree, which at the moment are small. They're visible through a sparseness of leaves.

May 11. It's the same with a clematis, whose wonder cascades up and over the reddish brown wall of a pound (for compost).

May 12, Ascension Day. We leaden mortals I'm afraid are rooted in earth, still with our petty tropisms. Cornelius, who phoned at ten, said he'd be here at noon, then, arriving at one, wanted to go straight into a 'luncheon situation'. I reserved a table at the hamburger bar, which was deserted when we strolled in urgently. A short, hirsute waiter, whom I knew as Andreas, had set aside a shaded recess, under a winding stair, a solo ceiling spot for light. Cornelius flatly rejected that, choosing instead a prospect to the front. Here I switched off to his drone, and followed the contours, etched in a frosted hexagon of window glass, of a Twenties' belle (head and slender shoulders of), with a coy little smile for her cocktail (its cherry impaled on a stick). Cornelius removed the following to an adjacent table: 1) a glass ashtray, which Zob retrieved, 2) a white carnation in an aluminium vase, 3) a chili sprinkler (being allergic to capsicum). The big man Snell was voracious for information (quite apart from his peppered steak. That came with *pommes frites* and a cole-slaw salad). Affable Marsy was a lot less ravenous, chewing his Mexican cheeseburger only intermittently (emphatically without fries). The miracle was Miracle, about which he hadn't been sure, though under the aegis of Cornelius's grin he could now, we thought, be certain. 'Why of course go for it! Eh, Al?' Why-of-course-yes. I myself ate ravioli, so extending a long arm for the chili (to which I am partial. It's the spice of my professional life). Cornelius was resolutely against Miss Overmars, a name that Zob intended to put on his guest list. This prompted a good many paternal observations, which I am able to condense: 'Why Marsy she could be a nut, out to knife-shoot-blow-up a celeb. Five-minute fame.' That had to be thought of, Zob conceded, though he had done nothing to upset fundamentalist Hollanders.

So to dessert, and (Snell) a strawberry sundae, (Zob) the lemon sorbet, (Wye) 'I'll pass'. Cornelius left his hologrammed plastic on the saucer, getting in return (and declining the ballpoint) the chit, a shock, some peppermints. He would, he said, unscrewing his fountain pen, negotiate with Tom Corbiere. As, hurting his hand, he signed, he left me with a commission. 'Liaise,' he said, 'with Merle,' my Martini girl. 'What we need's a proper guest list. Get her to show you the mailing package—software, whatever-you-call.' I'd be delighted.

May 13 (Friday the 13th). Merle has this morning had a tooth extraction, and is feeling too numb to talk mailing lists. It's no matter, I said. 'I shall call in on my way to work, Monday.' That leaves me in company of Glaze, whose next batch of four I have sequenced—though I can't be bothered with that. I considered, over a pot of Assam tea, *The Guilt That is Hampstead's*, and now have an Act Two.

Scene: 'Top writer' Zob's study. Mahogany, walnut. Somewhere a PC plus laser. Hangings: on white, a red sun; cranes; a lake. Books: *Dictionary of International Biography, The Zen Book of Bedtime, Aristotle's Atom.* 'Miracle' price-list open at p2. Enter Wye, bearing flattish glass bowl of magnolia petals.

WYE [puts down bowl]: I'll fix *him*. [Wye goes to computer, types. Enter Zob]

ZOB: Ah, Al, hi … What's the buzz?

WYE [hammers keypad]:   That—gardener … does this! [Indicates magnolia bowl]

ZOB: Does what?

WYE [prints page to laser]:   The magnolia! Adam has chopped the magnolia!

ZOB: For a moment you'd got me worried …

WYE [takes printed page from laser]:   Oh come on, wake up, Marsy! Where's this going to end! The fig tree? Clematis?

47

ZOB: Al ...

WYE: The last thing I want's trouble. But when I tell you there's a laburnum.

ZOB: Of course that *would* be tragic. This is so unlike you.

WYE: Call him in. I want you to call him in.

ZOB: Al.

WYE: *Now*, Marsy.

ZOB [shakes head]: Okay. You insist. [Goes to door, calls Adam]

[Enter Adam]

ZOB: Mr Wye laments the magnolia.

ADAM: Can't say as some folks 'as noticed.

ZOB: And is concerned for the clematis (which one's that, by the way?).

ADAM: As grows up the—

WYE [flourishes paper]: That's quite enough!

ZOB: Oh come on, Al.

WYE: This is *not* gardener's question time! Here is your resignation! Sign! [Presses paper to Adam]

[Adam, astonished. Zob, astonished. Wye, perfectly serious]

Zob is played by any fortyish male accustomed to sitcom. R. Quiggly-Walsh as before. Wye, again, Wye. Incidentally a note on my Assam tin has this to say: 'Tea animates the intellectual powers', it 'maintains or raises lively ideas', 'excites ... sharpeneth the thoughts', tea lends 'vigour ... to invention', it 'awakens the senses', 'clears the mind'. This is an extract from *Discourse on Tea*, by Dr Thomas Short, published in 1750. 'Nother cup, please!

May 15. Widow Lavante. It's Sunday. You know how I groan. I woke to the sound of what, I suppose, was your Citroën. I'd follow—yet ... where are my keys? Malkin-*gesund*, that's Malkin-*gesund* (that's a poor chap, hah-*heit* in a sneeze).

One sorry result of Isabelle's Earl Grey, which I have had a small china mug of.

May 16. Snell's leafy neighbourhood, in whose graceful deceptions your *jongleur* sings his suburbia, can actually be enchanting on a day like this. I admit there's a drizzle. Admit that as usual I have had to wrap up. Yet in no sense is it irksome (switching off my Szymanowski. Parking my Ford). Listen. That's the chirrup of a blackbird, whose now vacant gatepost has a fresh smear of chalk. Added to which there are no ground staff, no sinister Someone, whose master's saw has plunged him into the destructive manias of open-air life. There's a laburnum, whose sap shall be spared—its incipient gold (so on as I strode to the door) ... Merle, pearl, received me. Cornelius, puzzled, recrossed the hall and took off his glasses, wiping them. He remembered. 'Al ...' he said, which meant, we *will* see Marsy through. A client called him on the phone, a television chef. I, in the drug of Merle's scent—that touch to her delicate ears—found myself led (or a dab to those opulent wrists), misled, in the breeze of her opium. This was into the dry dust of her office. Here I loved her filing cabinets, a chipped grey—Snell's cast-offs, she said. Adored the floor-to-ceiling shelves, whose dipping contours bore the weight of innumerable dead histories, pretty well all the Snell agency's ring-binders. (One showed the faded stamp, 'Zob'.) Her small iron fireplace was, I suspect, elegant, though I worship that too in its lacquers of cream paint. Or the view—her, Merle's view—which is through french doors (with scroll handles, and a security lock, doors in need themselves of paint). Here was her lawn, which at 9.10 was still laved in dew, and here her pear tree. There shall we sit on its circular seat (and is there honey still)?

She wore—what did she wear? A knee-length skirt, that this morning she'd touched with an iron (her colour is black. Black). A hooped blouse, piratic. She smiled and laughed irrepressibly. She raised eyebrows, those very same plucked in a hand glass on her commuter train. Not, she insisted, Snell's special lure, 'Oo such a fidget to work for', and quite indiscreet with those great tactile paws (the firmness of her rump, rumpf, romp). I said to her, 'How is that tooth?' (so young, such wisdom). At coffee time she shared her doughnut, which sugared her fingers and oozed strawberry on to her chin. By twelve, when Cornelius went out, I'd browsed through her mailing lists. How many editors? (I forget.) Publishers? (Too many bad, too few good.) All right. Name me three reviewers. (X, Y, Z.) Writers. (Oh, they're such a bore.) In that case other agents, the criterion 'politic to meet'. (I don't deal in subspecies.) I wrote a little program, its tune goes SELECT_IF_THEN_ELSE (which Merle said was clever). That has refined her multiple lists to one, which I have copied to 'flaccid' disc, and this afternoon will load on to Zob's network. Merle, when she'd finished on the phone (or had quit that silly drone) went to work on the invitation card, which will be printed and framed in albata. She got so far—'You are cordially'—which she scrapped. 'Have you,' I asked, 'an idea when the party will be?' She had—'Cornelius fixed that days ago.' No one tells me anything. 'May I, as the time gets on, buy you a sandwich for lunch?' Sorry, no. She was too busy running Snell's agency.

May 17. Now to submit my first and lasting premiss apropos of the 'professional' life of Zob, and a recollection, for which I need only a handful of props. First, a pub sign, to render the Golding Hop (why we were there, I no longer know). This I authenticate with two pints of beer, placed on an iron table. That, is in a garden, high on the green precipitous slope of an escarpment. Then if I may just summon the first orange flame of a Kentish sunset ... There! That will do! Now to proceed ...

It was, I don't doubt, a break—in one of those long drives back from the spires of Exe (a quite tiring detour from the A2. It would not have been my suggestion). Zob defended his 'English' novel, which can mean only I'd annoyed him with car talk—naturally upholding Dickens, and of all people Lawrence. 'It's precisely my point,' I said, implying that the English, turning to books (to write them), are motivated by the gain of social applause. He told me I smoked too much, yet demanded an explanation. 'Exe is a long drive without a fag,' I said. 'Anyway. You know what I mean. "Applause" is something you elicit from a class you are trying to enter. A desirable clique is, by definition, other than that of one's origin.' His dash had, and still has, a NO SMOKING sign. 'I'm afraid your "English" novel, even at the millennium, hasn't got free.'

May 18. It's a premiss I now demonstrate, in the printed guest list I placed on Zob's desk for ratification. 'I see this as falling into three strata,' he said. 'Take away. Rework.' He supposed I should know what distinctions he had, provocatively, got in mind, though cared nothing for the addition of filters, as a kind of extended coda, to that merry jingle, my SELECT_IF_THEN_ELSE. Grade I persons, who were to receive invitations two days before Grade II, rejoiced in (strictly my elaborated) roll:

> Masturbile, a sickly smile,
> And Crouch, who hates a masculine slouch.
> Simms, Simms (an effigy, pins).
> Snell. Well!
> Bloge, Myrtle (attractive skirtle).
> Professor Emeritus, once of Exe
> (A man whose renga looks a mess),
> Then, my stars, Miss Overmars!
> The last—man's—dead!

Grade II consisted mostly of authors and agents he considered subordinate to Simms and Snell, who were to receive their invitations one day before Grade III. To the latter he penned the name Lavante, and to which I appended Merle's and mine.

May 20. Snell, it now turns out, has been 'entertaining' the 'young',

51

'exciting', minimalist composer Royston Flude (let me apologise now for all these silly, upper middle-class names). That has involved cards at the Ritz, and has gone on late and many gins into the night, not to say costing perhaps a fleet of indirect cabs. Snell is gentleman enough to see his charge up the flared steps to his door, which I am told is under a Georgian fanlight, somewhere near Randolph Ave. Why I am instructed to add his to the Grade I names, I hope will become clear. For the moment it leaves me groping for a rhyme (crude, Bude, rude, nude. Pseud). The same can be said of Shayle, that master of the low-budget clapper, and the fizzy Tom Corbiere— two other top-drawer afterthoughts?

May 22. To whom I owe the relief of Malkin in a purr round Mamma's morning bedroom, is the precocious backhand Michael, who has progressed to competition tennis and is due at 9.30 in Weybridge. That's an anti-clockwise whizz round the M25—'one of those nice blue roads': Isabelle.

May 25. I do, still, refuse your modern coat, that quilted gaberdine, purveyed by the ubiquitous Despair Bros, Oxford St. Yet, and yet. For one, vertiginous moment, I have allowed myself to stand on volcanic earth, that 'time' within the geographer's palm (I see, at at least one North American latitude, this is called 'Glaze country'). The sky here, a crepuscular turquoise, is lit by decaying stars, with just the occasional jet of flame, a mauve, or a vermilion, edged with blue. The ground shifts and is basalt, fringed in its fissures and its flattish towers of stone, in a cinerary grey. Why should I follow Glaze here especially? Well. I have no respect for that man's death. Anyway my accusation is impersonal (please, Sam, don't go to litigation: there is no scope here for your New York attorney). I charge Glaze with the worst deception, seeking not to define those irretrievable grains of time, but to reverse the trends of posterity. This is of course to do with quality, in art, science, in fact in all original thought, and is a spell of fine weather. Our English suns shine haphazardly. They assert themselves counter to the winds of their provenance. What Glaze inspires, with his sempiternal macadam, is the construction of a monolith (inscription: 'Here was a man'), visible from all points on that extensible vector, the future. It's a notion he has passed to his protégé, for whom I have spent all day backing up to tape his disc system, after which—tomorrow—I must drive to the bank, whose vaults he has begun to use for his off-line storage. When I yawn at this, incredibly bored, Zob argues that the computer salesman spelt out the problems of disaster recovery.

(Marsy. The only disaster's this. That someone should consider printing, publishing, promulgating what today I have had a hand in preserving so religiously.)

May 26. Labelled the tapes (red flashes, lilac windows to write in). Made corresponding entries in log. Drove, in an atonal swirl—the violin concerto, Berg—to Zob's bank, which for historical reasons is in Brent Cross Gardens. Not a journey I recommend. Further, the fool clerk beheld me blankly, never having heard of Mr Zob, and not apprised of the bank's data-storage facilities. I called for the manager, who did eventually take him aside, no doubt telling him to wake up. The poor boy took out a pocket handkerchief, to wipe, from under the blue tufts of his fringe, the silver sheen that had filmed his brows. It wasn't, I remarked, particularly warm that day. Handed over this, in return for last month's tapes. Manager was unctuous, vulpine. 'Mr Wye, I think I can clear up this slight misunderstanding. Adrian here wouldn't have been expecting you. Our arrangement's, you'll recall, for the last Tuesday in every month.'

Suddenly remembered: consented to pick up Malkin, who is now at the vet's for the second time (being wormy and prone to vomit). This makes me late back, which seems to have irritated Zob. He's in a lather over Royston Flude, who, according to Snell—who has again bought lunch in the hamburger bar—is actively seeking a librettist. Coming shortly is the Free City Festival, for which Flude has a commission (from the Coliseum). I sat down with Zob for over two hours, excessively worn at what importance he attached to this. It amounted to a showcase, 'for new work,' he said. Flude was contracted to compose a short operetta, which, as an artistic descendant of Offenbach, he envisaged in satirical terms, a slant on our times. Could I, 'Al, give this some thought—perhaps draft a synopsis?' Mercilessly Zob meant now. Worked late and, finally switching off his desk lamp, saw moonlight barred through his blinds and etched on my moving hand. Zob poured me a beer before I went home. Refused to show him my synopsis, 'until I have slept on it.'

May 27. Have slept on it (to Zob, I would not have had to offer the following preamble). It recalls elements of the uneasy conversation that ended our interview (and signalled, I thought, failure to get the job, as Zob's assistant). This took place in a grimy café off the Portobello Rd, where research had taken him to a snooker hall. I stirred my coffee. He reviewed, prosaically, his first impressions. A peppered yellow, in the truncated isosceles of light, over that green oblong, the baize. How he had made his cue ball, dotted in a battery of overhead spots, bend with the lie of the nap. 'It's not a game I've played,' I said. He apologised, meaning that his life had not always been so leisurely (for now he lived in the expectation of royalties, advances). Nevertheless. Hack work had bent him to a thousand impostures, and at one point the adoption of a *nom de guerre*—his Marcia Esbaroz, a fiction my synopsis would shortly, indirectly revive. 'Marcia' was Zob's frustrated attempt on the world of women's magazines, that web of emotional deceit. It cost him pains, with an editor (and one only) taking pity. She had noted the name. She had rejected a sixth trite story. Her view, I may guess, can be paraphrased: No lack of potential, etc., haven't quite understood the genre, etc. Suggest following reading, also these useful courses ... Happily there was no need, because at this time his friend Andrew Glaze stepped in (having a quiet word through his connections with a paperback firm). So, now, if Mr Royston Flude has tuned in and is listening, that is how we have come to the following scenario:

Genevieve Purefoy, sole issue of Sir Walter Purefoy, wealthy industrialist and sometime government adviser. Mother, deceased. Enjoys sweeping views of South Downs from family home near Hailsham. Sir Walter has long been generous contributor to Tory coffers, and has mapped out career for Genevieve as party worker. But. Genevieve falls madly for Daddy's driver and protector, Lobridge, who is blond, tanned, virile (and nocturnally a student—

of chemistry). Won't on that secret ground move to Ealing, where Sir Walter has given her the keys to a house (in Montpelier Rd). Sir Walter blunders in on their night of love. This is in the stable, where the buck, in a ripple of moonlit buttocks, is up on his toes. Miss Purefoy, whose knees are spread, is perched on a sill. Later, in daylight, and fully attired, Lobridge refuses to be bought off. Sir Walter's hand is forced. Decides that he will risk a scandal. Fires his man. Only now does Lobridge reveal a political identity, which is nondescript, but vaguely Liberal. He campaigns for electoral reform, but at a rally has his foot crushed under the wheels of a pantechnicon. The foot is amputated. Lobridge, convalescing, completes his degree (I don't need to stress with distinction). He acquires work and limps in to the office each day. This is with a petroleum firm, from which platform he invents, patents and markets a miraculous new plastic. Now a millionaire, Lobridge hobbles back to the South Downs, where, high on a green hill, and with the wind in her hair, Genevieve has all this time been waiting. Lobridge goes down on the knee of his bad leg, weeping. *She* proposes to *him*. Tears escalate, to a deluge of joy. There's a no-fuss wedding, which Sir Walter, who is aptly heartbroken, misses, not having survived surgery. A last word goes to Sir Walter's obituarist, who is certain an elevation to the Lords was likely. The house is shut up and sold, while the dream couple move south to Antibes, where Lobridge is determined to overcome his handicap.

(A note on the cast. Lobridge, is a tenor. Genevieve, soprano. The problem of Sir Walter gave me an interrupted night. I prefer a baritone.)

May 30. A quiet weekend, bar that marmalade Malkin, the arch of whose back and lazy tail I saw silhouetted through the thin mulberry blind in Isabelle's laundry room, late on Saturday evening. Michael and the widow zoomed in and out with the Citroën, whose lugubrious grille is spattered with fly specks. It seems that the boy is a difficult left-hander. What's current—timed for the bank holiday—is an under-seventeens tournament, located somewhere 'between Reading and Slough', whence he's progressed to the quarters. This has involved an occasional return to wash, dry and iron his tennis whites, which Isabelle insists must at all times be impeccable. She did not thank me—in fact was disparaging generally of what she called my 'awareness'—when I, and not she, had failed to encounter recent confirmation of Malkin's green malady. I didn't offer to scrub the affected carpet tile (in the malodorous laundry room).

May 31. Zob, in a distant grin, has had time to think about the synopsis, sharpening his focus to matters that don't concern him (notably staging). He is adamant on one prop in particular, being a *trompe-l'œil* (seen to be a *trompe-l'œil*), of three birds on a wall, very English in their grading—small, to medium, to large. For an adopted Hampsteadite, this is the proper emblem of Lobridge and his working-class origin. Zob, at home with the status quo, does not seriously believe in reformers drawn from any other stratum.

June 1. He committed one further indiscretion. This was some sample dialogue (predictably the stable scene), over which he and Cornelius chortled. In a meeting scheduled for tomorrow, Snell will put this, the synopsis, and a proposal, to Flude.
  RIP.

June 2. Mrs Clapp I feel has developed a dangerous rapport with that insane gardener Adam, who has cut three peony stems in exchange for a mug of soup. I watched her myself arrange their white tissue of flowers in a round vase (gently, while she hummed). I am afraid I shattered that equanimity, with the news that Zob, Snell, Flude, had been in conference all morning, and would appreciate tea. Or rather, that Flude had brought his own—a peppermint and limeflower bag—which I dangled from its thread. The others would take whatever was in the caddy. She huffed. I stepped outside and lit up, with just a glance at Adam, who eyed a bank of irises tragically. The surgeon's hawthorn capped their backing wall, with a wild breeze of crimson in its flowers.
  Took my time driving home, enchanted at the chestnut trees (there is a superabundance this year of red candles, that burn brightly in their boughs).

June 3. I see it was as long ago as May 13—a fortuitous Friday—
that I numbered the professor's series of four, in its following
imperfection:

c/o 'Biltmores'
Empire Street
Providence
RI 02903
5 March 1992

Dear Marsy,
I least expected first-night nerves, which is as well I opted for
yesterday's dry-run—in particular a non-specialist audience. I was
overwhelmed, beforehand, adjusting my necktie, with that sudden
absurdity—that tincture of human doubt—I know has accompanied
great ideas.
I am indebted to a man called Spinks, from the *Providence
Phoenix*, who had assembled three collaborating workshops,
together with a writers' group—though the hall was gloomy. I got
over my attack, emphasising purely the literary aspect of my theory.
Surprisingly, few latched on to my examples, not having heard of
most models I mentioned—Huysmans, Jarry, Nathanael West (to
name only three). One dear boy had come across Proust, and
Bergson, but muddled the flighty tart Mnemosyne with my, strictly
desolated cherub.
Did anything happen? I threw the whole thing open to questions,
permitting myself a smile (you know: the fidgets, consumptives,
chair scrapes). A tatty, malnourished, New Age-looking creature,
whose day job was evidently in the electronics business, thought he
knew what I meant, having himself the perennial toss-up between,
and I quote, 'synchronous and asynchronous switching'. I told him
not to talk gobbledegook, which raised a laugh.
There is a postscript to all this. A short piece appeared in the
Providence Journal, then a few days later, in almost the same
column, an open invitation—for me—to a lecture on McTaggart. I
suppose I shall have to go. News to brighten my path is that Jessica
insists she won't marry the mechanic, or so Samantha says by phone

(our one, civilised means of communication). That leaves only one problem. How to dispose of the orphan, when it comes.

Has that clown Cornelius got in touch with Shayle's office?

Hope all's well, your Andrew.

Flat 5
147 Trefoil St
SW18
14 March 1992

Dear Andrew,

McTaggart's a killjoy—unlike Snell, who needs only the least success to drag off his clients to the wine bar. He was fine, once on a course of pain-killers, and tries to laugh off the indignity. This was the green-coated specialist, a man who compressed his scrotum with an ultrasound scan, while Snell himself pinned back his pinkie in a thumb and index. Nor could he quite see the funny side of the invoice, which listed his genitalia as, I suspect appropriately, 'small parts'. The sort of thing Burgess does so well, whom Crouch, in an interview, has claimed to out-drink in Monaco. She gets around. And yes. Cornelius has passed papers to Shayle's office. There will be a meeting. The best, Marsy.

1422 Sayer St
Providence
RI 02903
24 March 1992

Dear Marsy,

Absolutely right about McTaggart. It tells me, that I don't intend to get embroiled in a cosmic wrangle with philosophers or physicists (but think I can probably just about handle computer people). Last night's lecturer reserved, when glancing away from the lectern, his self-assured looks for me, which is comic. How do I accept a premiss—McTaggart's I assume—whose vocabulary of time can't be abandoned in the denial of its reality? This only affirms my belief that 'time' is a function of the way we think, and that therefore we

58

are its progression. Have you by any chance bumped into Giles? I write and I write. No reply. By the way I'm moving on tomorrow, so mail me at following address &c. ...

Yours, Andrew.

Flat 5
147 Trefoil St
SW18
1 April 1992

Dear Andrew,

As a matter of fact I did bump into Giles, though before your letter came, and in none of the usual places. Snell's arranged for one of Shayle's assistants—Gloria Punch—a bubbly little red-head, who seems to be here every other day. Should the project go ahead, and should I decide to write the script, she has gone over—thoroughly, tediously—what amounts to Shayle's specification. Somehow she'd got a trade invitation to a wine tasting at the Strand Palace Hotel, where Giles chinked my glass several times, 'to the ebullient Mr Blass'. A nice '87 Shiraz. Gloria had to be taxied home.

What the high-profile Crouch incessantly sees as war attracts its recruits to both sides. Blandford—you know his magazine well—has signed me up for a regular column, with no particular job description, but this aside: 'Pull no punches.' Speaking of which, Gloria's been re-arranging my flat. Can't find anything.

The best, Marsy.

4143 Bay State Rd
Boston MA 02215
9 April 1992

My dear Marsy,

Forgive an old man his wonder. Don't—entertain other than a work relationship with Gloria, sumptuous though the girl undoubtedly is. The next step is conjugal. Then it's homemaking—furnishings, curtains, a dishwasher. Babies follow, and are not of our species. These let me tell you smell, are noisy, require food

59

(even at night). They grow. They learn infallibly to upturn porridge plates on heads. This is irritating, if it's you who has to clear the mess. Then there's the whole business of education, which is costly, and is no guarantee of adult life as learned, as accomplished as your own.

How many times during Jessica's teething did I long for a sabbatical like this ...

Be warned. Andrew.

Flat 5
147 Trefoil St
SW18
17 April 1992

Dear Andrew,

Have decided to go ahead with the script (Gloria doesn't convince me it's that difficult a job). Snell's doing his bit, throwing his (not inconsiderable) weight about—not with Shayle, with the publisher. He suggests that rather than allow my *Atom* to be remaindered, an important book like this should have had its sales performance predetermined. Of course, authorial hype is at the moment reserved for whores.

Best. Marsy.

Glaze's blessing came on another of those postcards, this time sunrise over Cape Cod, 23/4. 'If,' he said, 'you can't beat 'em ...'

June 5. It's usual for Isabelle, when not in transit over Michael's tennis, to arrive home Sundays around noon. I have come to set my watch by that. Figuratively. (It's years since I've worn one.)

June 6. Snell, in tasteless checks, made all the more hopeless by his two-tone shoes, with golfer's slacks—in my opinion earned his reprieve. This had everything to do with outmoded gestures at his passenger door, which had the result, when opened, of admitting light—a tall, bright-eyed, refulgent Merle. Merle had the document case, which she handed to Zob in his study, and as a matter of priority ascended to bathroom one. Here I'm sure she powdered that freckled little nose. No Clapp, no St John, ergo 'Al will make the coffee'. The fourth mug, mine, did not join theirs. Nor, at one, did I share their table at the hamburger bar.

June 7. Zob's diary had one entry, 'British Library', where he seeks obscure references to a physician called Golde, to be found, he's been told, in a Renaissance tract on alchemy. Someone has asked him to write a small piece on the divergence of science. For me, he has left the following item of e-mail:

· M E M O

From: MZ
To: AW
Cc: %null%   Date: 6/6

Al. Snell's got a lovely little girl, but a bit scatty. All of us knew I'd overlooked Corbiere, but, great though her smile is, she has managed NOT to get him a printed invite. This occurred to me after they'd gone. He's a Grade II, so, if she can get one made in the next couple of days, the Grade I's can be mailed, as planned, this morning. Please phone her. Marsy.

The (expanded) date/time stamp pinpointing this particular memo's inception (it appeared on the queue as MEM001), was, according to the system log, 94-06-06.20:24.49.MON.

June 9. Another (94-06-08.18:56:31.WED. MEM002):

M E M O

From: MZ
To: AW
Cc: %null%   Date: 8/6

Al. Thanks for giving Merle a shake—that problem's sorted. Snell's giving this some thought, and I'd like you to too. Have agreed to read, South Bank, as part of promotion, new book. Consider the usual format a bit bland. Any suggestions on how to pep it up? By the way I see you're 'invited' to the party. Would like to talk to you about dress. Marsy.

I discussed this with Isabelle over supper (noodles, courgettes), but got nowhere there.

June 10. I shall have to admit, that approximately fifteen years ago, mid-summerish, usually in a liquefying ray of sunshine—usually early evening—I considered the solution of practical problems as no more involved than acquiring the right degree of detachment. This I pursued through the discomforts of the lotus, a posture I abandoned—also its associated pattern of automatic respiration. That, I am prepared to accept, is a mystical afflatus that *perhaps* is a mode of consciousness. For me, the floor didn't rush away. I can't candidly report an elevated perspective of what was then my room— a rectangular plan, with further oblongs shaded in (bed, desk, drawers). The manual, which I have kept and refer to, describes the next stage so: 'a headlong rush into the astral dome'. I was supposed to see the bluish charcoal in the slates of the roof. The whole terrace of houses. The winding street. An aerial projection of the Hertfordshire village I at that time lived in. Then the cold brightness in that canopy of stars. 'It shall be granted,' the book says—though not, alas, for me. So, and therefore. Does, eventually, the Westerner return to the gurus of his own hemisphere? It is, I think, most often the case, though in mine I rejected Freud quite early (on the ground that his aspect is seedy, and that I was not after something so potentially tyrannic as his 'id'). Jung, of course, has an appeal to literary minds, in his construction of psychic meaning, that tapestry of coincident mythologies. I deal, don't forget, in the fiction of Zob's life, that flimsy, virtual structure he has floated his existence in. I recall my dream days, now, with the flux of activities that, frail mortal, I spatially coordinate as a South Bank reading. Nor do I necessarily attribute to that wedge of Brie I scoffed with a water biscuit before bedtime, the Gothic extravagance my sweet dreams imparted. It is, nevertheless, that Jungian habit of fifteen years ago that prompts me to draft it. Shall I redraft? (Note. Fifteen years ago

62

I was twenty and a stripling, having triumphantly, and finally resisted, the formal notion of education. However. In those breezy days, the detachment I prized as an intellectual position could not be accomplished through the Jungian discipline of dream evaluation. My dreams had much to do with high-performance cars—the sensation of speed—and poor Tom's *erhebung* without motion—the levitation I hadn't achieved through yoga. On one occasion I veered my shiny red Lotus into a swamp. The next moment I hovered over a revolving planet, whose sprigs of green intermittently flecked an unending acreage of black-to-purple vegetation. O we who eternally travel.) What follows is my draft. What precedes that is a pre-emptive apologia. The grey sleet this miserable oneiromancy delivers itself through, is due to two things: the inordinate influence the gup of Hollywood has had on our time; the monochrome receiver that the son of science, as a boy, absorbed it through.

Late afternoon, early evening. Scene, Zob's cellar, a location geographically broader, with accordingly a higher ceiling, than I encountered awake. A barred, thickly glassed arch, high to the rear, admitted the last, almost horizontal rays of the June sun. There was—and here I assume tiny chips of ice, random in the bloodstream—a hollowness of echoes, at any slight noise. I recall a heel on the stone flags. A human voice. Above all, the rattle of chains. The walls, in a dampish black stone, are lit by flambeaux, whose tongues of orange flame are edged with blue. There's a rope, hanging, for strappado. There's a table with thumbscrews. Then that vermilion glow, in the perforations of an iron brazier—ensures, does it? a white heat in the embedded tip of a poker, whose brass-handle I can still see. Enter, to the rear and left, Adam, in a friar's gown and open sandals—the hunchback Adam, bearer of a surgeon's tool-roll, who shambles into a circle of jaundiced light. The patient Zob is etherised on the table (and is strapped). Cornelius, whose terms are strictly ten per cent, has scrubbed up, and is currently representing the surgeon Alistair Wye. [So far I resist a second draft.] I have, as I am now forced to this subhuman view of myself, a green cap, white mask, a medic's freshly laundered gown. There are Teutonic overtones, a lost Englishness to the way I speak. 'Tsob, ja, iss here?'

Zob, yes, was here—dark-eyed, supine on the table. Small, circular contact pads, dotted on his torso, chest, on his upper arms, and to the cheeks and forehead, are connected to copper wires. These I see snake over the cold stone floor, then up to the terminals of (I have a straight face) my Dr Wye's 'unpatented' thought machine. This, is a Victorian monster, whose analogue dial calibrates its voltage output. 'Svitch on, svitch on …' My famulus Snell, a man tremulous in the newness of his task, passes a large, gloved hand over a stalk marked ON, and marked OFF. He looks at Zob's chart. A valve, pear-shaped, lights with a blue, electric zigzag. The Beast Adam, on a secret sign, shuffles to the light of the operating table, tugging at his chin, which is carbuncular. I turn the dial, just ever so. There's a twitch to Zob's ankles, Zob's wrists. The Beast cowers (a freakish mechanical, who's simply too slow), and with Snell's intervention avoids, narrowly, the depression of my rings. I have my hand raised over the arch of his back, which I lower as the tools unfurl themselves (mostly razors, one or two spiked chains). 'I vont more umph!' Snell, perspiring and limpid, turns the dial. This satisfyingly puts Zob's entire being in a spasm. 'Ja! Thed iss it! OOMPH!' From a vial, of orangy brown sludge, I fill my hypodermic. In the machine's flicker, I test its syringe action (this is a touch sardonic). Snell protests, but this I won't have. In what's now the thrash of Zob's poor sedated body, I steady the writer's forearm, and choose a green vein. I jab, pump, the patient shrieks, though of course can't sever the bonds of his strapping. 'More off thed umph!' So Snell turns, unsure yet obedient. The Beast groans. I, in this mania, pull a paper from my Doktor's gown, while the machine begins to spark. 'Ah, zo,' I say, 'to dis Sudbenk. Ver I vont you NOT to read off dat new buch.' Zob's eyes open, saucer-like, streaked with blood at the whites. His hair is on end. I want his confession—his writer's confession. Snell says the machine is too hot, which observation is borne out by the helix of sooty smoke from its backplane. Zob vibrates. The Beast crumples to the floor. Snell at last accuses me of insanity, at which I cackle, reading from my paper. 'Tsob's buch, nein' I say, over the noise, the heat. 'Here! Here!'—the 'here' being the Herr Doktor's lecture, of which my Jungian pencil recorded only six key words. The machine arced. Zob's cellar filled with electric flames. The floored brown habit that was once the Beast Adam, shrank away, as a liquid down a drain. Snell, would turn no more. My phantasmagoria, which was once Zob's cellar, rolled itself up, and in a tight ball of biblical smoke receded over my nocturnal horizon, in what was otherwise a peaceful night. In the morning, having failed to slice Zob's frontal lobes, these words only were on my bedside pad: 'subterranean', 'refracted', 'peaks', 'mapping', 'confession', 'razors'.

Zob—late afternoon, early evening—asked me if I'd had any thoughts. I said I'd give it some consideration over the weekend.

June 12. Isabelle's birthday, which means her secret Sunday morning breakfast liaison on this occasion is cancelled. Michael had no luck at all boiling an egg, a failure he told me of just as I had propped up my pillow and was about to read (a biography, by Brian Boyd). He seemed rather pathetic in my doorway, still in the candy stripe of his pyjamas. I helped him, reluctantly, starting with the saucepan, whose light brown, slightly speckled egg, had cracked along the long circumference of its oval. This had caused seepage, a mingling of white and yellow slime into water that, I considered, had boiled too vigorously. 'Throw away, rinse,' I said. I produced toast, lightly buttered. A nice little egg in a nice china cup. From the garden, a half-dozen moon daisies, which went well in a slim green vase. To these I added Michael's card, and the morning paper, and placed all on a tray. The boy, of course, got all the glory, backing in to his mamma's half-lit boudoir. Here the mistress hitched herself up on to the brassy vines of her bedstead. This I know, because I brought up the rear with a small pot of tea. Malkin turned full circle—twice—before re-sinking into the hollow of (in my view a shame) the unused pillow.

June 13. I now know why Zob was so interested in the physician Golde, since I have had to dust down that (rather pointless) article of his. It is couched in his professional journalese, for one of those semi-mystic science journals. Its topics, typically, are UFO sightings, or remarkable acts of clairvoyance. I am told that once it carried a two-pager on Watsonian pyramids (the kind one sharpens razors in). Ironically, Zob's little piece is an assault on our present age of cynicism, which, according to him, has its origin in the current remoteness of science, its 'practical unintelligibility' to ordinary, educated men and women. Golde is Zob's sample of mid-world man, a being capable of grasping all essentials in the total of human knowledge—a feat which is impossible today. In my opinion Zob then performs a stunning volte-face (in the space of two sub-clauses), positing for Golde a universe that had still not lost its primal magic (even though, for the physician, all things knowable—were known!). Golde—whose sublime, symbolic approach to the cosmos, was to change his name from Orr—believed in the transformation of base metals, devoting much of his talent to that alchemical pursuit (cf. Jung, a post-Newtonian). I pointed out the inconsistency.

'What inconsistency?'

Marsy! That to Golde, in his confident awareness, there should have been no scope for conjuring tricks. And that for us—or for most of us, with no grasp at all on the sub-atomic—our present age of science looks like hocus-pocus.

'Pedant!'   ·

June 14. More about that journal. Zob has a back issue, whose glossy cover is a blue illustration of the sapphire Earth, subtending a low sickle in darkness. This is 'home' as photographed over the moon's silver horizon. There is a caption: 'Is this a figment of God's mind?' As it prevails in one campus, physics and theology are parallel lines, bent to a single point in a distant shade of eternity. Besides. Zob has thought about my objections of yesterday (and says, to the contrary, they 'prove' his point). Golde, for whom no schooling remained, located our common mystery beyond the bourn of epistemology. That puts the kicking boot on Zob's flat foot, which gives him renewed courage on the South Bank question. What had I thought of? I can hardly relate my dream, and the flummery I later composed (remember those key words? Well, here:

These medics, pale and subterranean,
Unbending in the shafts of refracted
Daylight, have considered the febrile peaks,

The loops, troughs and coy inversions mapping
The fevered patient's chart. A confession:
That is the object of all those razors.

Ah, noting the moist brow, what confession
Is likely? Our patient's of Alpine peaks,
Ethereal. His fiction's for mapping
The savagery of urban life—razors,
Chains for the dispute—subterranean
Motives—life's glow horribly refracted.

Don't flinch. The swish of long coats—the razors—
The keen blade on cold flesh—the new mapping
When blood's let—prefigure the confession.
Don't flinch or be foolish, decry the peaks
Of surgical knowledge. What's refracted
In steel—a mind—is subterranean.

You know the patient's history. His peaks
Of fame. The base of learning refracted
In a low populism. The mapping
Out of friendly reviewers (blunt razors
For a long career—it's *their* confession
Next). Fiction *from* the subterranean.

Fiction is *for* the subterranean,
He says. He plunged from his Alpinist's peaks,
Flailing, but avoided *this* confession:
Gone, all my bright mountain light, refracted
In a crystal whiteness; my bright razor's
Intellect; my joy for a new mapping.

Anaesthetised, what *is* his confession?
Well. I look where he's lost those cloudy peaks,
And see through the filth, or the refracted
Motes, cankers, tumours, nothing the razor's
Poised to restore—hear subterranean

67

Laughter—re-draw the chart's crazy mapping.

You know the patient's history. His peaks.
He says he plunged from his Alpinist's peaks.
Likely? Is our patient of Alpine peaks?

a few lines I shuffled away among my morning's notes). I suggested to Zob two, possibly three speakers, and a selection of pages thick with dialogue (of which in a Zob novel there are always many, this technique forming the prop of his rudimentary 'style'—a word I use inadvisably). 'With a duo, or trio,' I said, 'do it in the round.'

That brought a smile.

June 15. I am suspicious. The rough texture of everyday life, has, for one of those rare, brief moments, worn its surface of sandpaper to a plane of (I am certain a) supplantable smoothness. My sweet widow has somehow learned whose genius it was behind her birthday breakfast, and for once, in her overcrowded kitchen, showed no menace at all in that serrated flourish of the bread knife. In fact a Proustian intensity glazed the sunny reflection in its blade, whose pale transparencies oscillated in the grainy pine of the cooker hood. I am sure I blushed, when she planted a little coy kiss on my cheek (though at this point could not intimate conspiracy. She told me I should treat myself sartorially). I wore the same old denims, the same yellow jumper. Later, to the shrug of Zob's black-shirted shoulders—this was to the middle of my office—I encountered something new (for him)—a first dramatic sign of indecision. Was this, was this not, a soliloquy, and our own Marshall Hamlet? Well, not quite. Adam outside, topping his ladder, passed the time of day with his master—with his trowel, I saw, in a new window box. This would give me: trailing lobelias ... petunias ... a geranium ... a sprinkle of alyssum (white). Adam, who saw me over Zob's buttoned epaulette, I think said 'How-dee-doo-dee'. He turned the peat, once only with his trowel, before descending. I'm sure I could smell honeysuckle.

Zob smiled pleasantly. I couldn't pretend not to notice, with an adventurer's eye over my décor, his two plain eyebrows converging in a wavy line. 'It's dreary,' he said (here was the rub, Horatio). The news was this, that Marsy, whose preferred decorator was a man from Purves Rd, in Kensal Green, had tormented himself with the remaining question—a soft peach or apple white? 'Anything,' he said, 'but gilded crowns.' I happened to like them, but the subject changed, politically to books (you remember, Marsy, how you scanned my shelves?). He knew I liked to quibble—therefore the thesis—to my mind Exeish (and why this moment?)—on the disciplines of reading. To him it was so, that those who professed themselves 'bookish', went cover-to-cover mechanically, dutifully, its 'thrill' occurring no more than a dozen times per life. I said his success had jaded him, and that, while I had no real objection to soft peach, I needed to see a colour chart. 'So you shall,' he promised, and took me to one, spread out in his study on his escritoire. The other thing was hair (meaning the fuzz that was mine), and clear precautions against the Greek barber George (whose creations were only partially inspired). 'Remind me. We'll drive to my club—what about tomorrow afternoon? They've got a decent *coiffeuse*.' It didn't end there, the point being the role he'd planned for me at his party. There were, he said, doubts about my wardrobe (as an aside, I said to him this need not be constructed in the language of international diplomacy). Quite. So then couldn't I spend the day in Bond St? while the decorator was here …

So that was it!

'Exactly. Do bring me the receipts. And remember. Smart casual.'

I tried to have the last word. 'There's a shade here called Perfect Peach,' I said.

'Al, that is just—perfect …'

Episode Two. Have realised suddenly what a perfected art is the rigmarole of tube travel. Here I concede to loss. I am not, friends, that platform athlete of yore, a man whose condition—not to say all-round alertness—honed itself in the bustle of my commuter days. Then, point A was a moving co-ordinate (my various west London garrets). Its corresponding B, whose recollection tinges itself with sentiment, is little more fixed (I call it my 'environs' of Mortimer

St). That goes back to my leisurely life in the theatrical properties business, a brief personal history I shall some day write an anecdotal book about. Meanwhile today, it's a catalogue of eccentricity, starting with a grey pigeon (which in a kind of boredom at the newspaper headlines I attempted to shoo, several times). The little silver train, coming in with a glum face, as a consequence opened its doors just where I wasn't. A fact that brings me to the seat I got, as has placed me opposite the world's only morning drunk, a man with a loud shape to his mouth (a phenomenon carefully avoided in the wall of tabloids erected over the seats around us). One poor girl, who seemed to have too bright a spark in her eye, had been reduced to the nth hundredth page of a blockbuster—an activity I realise it's impossible to imagine. The drunk combed out the dry curls in his mattress of brown hair. He told me what kind of society this was (he thought I didn't know). He went on, one hundred per cent counter to the rhythm of the train, to spill lager on the green dye of his shirt, asking me, now fully bathed in madness, what kind of bloke I took him for. 'A musician,' I said, seeing his guitar. 'Play.' That was a service he told me I'd have to pay for, and held out a hand. 'You should,' I said, 'get those eyes seen to'—they were rounder, redder—which stumped him. I got up—'Alas, the factor is time'— and got out at Belsize Park, rejoining the train where there were no seats.

I withstood my commission conscientiously, rejecting the countless man's shop (on the recurring appeal, revulsion), what with those dummies (white, expressionless faces—and such a resemblance of humanity), whose limbs you see bent to the conceivable pose of the cocktail lounge. I found eventually a talkative Jamaican in a store for the plainer man, who nevertheless wished to sell me a white tuxedo, a bow-tie with zebra-style chevrons, of all things a lime green fedora. These he saw neatly contrasting with a pair of snake-skin shoes, and trousers perhaps an olive green. 'I don't,' I said, 'wish to take the wind out of your sails.' I tried to attract his senior colleague. 'But.' The older man was like myself, a cool, monochromatic Caucasian (such thoughts spark solutions to crossword clues). Under that man's guidance, we arrived—happy trio—at a plausible outcome. That's to say beige slacks (I'm assured à la mode), with just the hint of a flare, and narrow turn-ups. Brushed suede shoes, a ruddy brown. And because I foresee a night oppressively warm, a short sleeved, floral shirt, whose autumn tints are the subdued golds and russets of apple and chestnut. Certain other incidents found their way to my scratchpad. For example the round, rosy burgher who asked directions to Marble Arch, yet who smiled and shook his head (apparently in disbelief) when I told him. Then in Oxford St, under the pale sentinel of Centre Point, a girl in baseball boots, who kicked at the polychrome panels of a photograph booth. This was to the competing strains of Orff (his *Carmina Burana*, from shopfront X), and an 80s' crooner (*I'll Be Watching* &c., adjacent shopfront Y).

I passed my old office in Mortimer St, now in the hands of a telematics firm. No personnel. Merely a populace of modems and multiplexers, whose open chassis of racks, shelves, struts, ensnared itself in the loops and coils of their cabling. Hard to think, eh, Wye, of a time past, in this glassed, golden front, posing on the telephone for passers-by (behind—not a hypertrophied S, as now—but Thespis's logo) … Such-and-such remembered: 'One horse's head, for a panto, Stratford East (will see what I can do). Rapiers, *Hamlet* in the Park. Difficult. We've had a run on rapiers. Will ask round. And how's this! A Broadwood piano, for a première, Hammersmith Lyric, a three-acter the resourceful playwright has penned under the simple heading *Ludwig Van*. Surprisingly I've just the thing …' I stumbled away into the metallic azure and chalky white street, not really humming to myself. In a basement off Castle St I bought a finger roll with frankfurter, whose amber garnish, a surfeit of stringed onions, was just that little bit cautious—in fact insipid, bar the mustard I added (hot, because English). So, on, and outside Foyles, where the smug Zob beamed from his posters. Here I caught sight of the blond crown and striped shirt of a man I thought I knew, though when he turned, to the puzzle of my expectant face, it was a stranger, bearing no resemblance. This had happened, oh so many times before.

Got back about two, having found, then lost, then refound the receipt (which Zob raised a theatrical eyebrow to). 'It's cheap,' I said, and lied about the snake-skinned shoes: 'They were my

71

preference.' How else to make him aware, as that man raised a finger for hush, that discounting them, I had effectively halved his bill. Shush! His radio you will see is marked ON. In an interview (the broadcast foam of those interminable women's magazines), Geraldine Crouch said yes, she did expect men to hold open doors … I went out, and shut Zob's securely.

June 16. Our man from Kensal Green has got this far precisely: my books are in boxes, the shelves are dismantled. My DTE—which he hasn't dared disconnect—is all in the middle of the room, under a sheet. Mrs Clapp says 'It's shockin' luv'—Zob can't say when he'll be back. 'I am also,' I add, 'profoundly unsure about that peach.'

June 17. Between 2 and 3 a.m. It emerges only now that, at approximately 5.30 yesterday afternoon, Michael, overstretching himself—attempting a left-hand smash over his innocent right shoulder—fell awkwardly behind the service line. This was not on a grass court (whose surface, he protests geometrically, is too unpredictable). This had the painful consequence of a grazed elbow, which puckered his lip (I don't doubt), and a turned ankle (which slight twinge he was able to walk off at the time, but is excruciating now). My dear, lovely, sleepy, unwinnable Isabelle (though she did touch my arm only yesterday) is not at her best in a crisis, particularly so, she informs me, after the loss, by drowning, of her husband. I have never pressed her to complete that tragedy. The light from her landing below, filtered through the deep plum of its orb, a voluminous paper shade, stencilled its mystical blue in all three dimensions of my open room. That—to the tune of a high, and a twangy voice that woke me—streaked itself in a refrigerated yellow, when the bathroom globe was turned on. In the hullabaloo— as I calmly put on my robe—I should expect, should I, what? Um. I went down. What I found was Michael, in that same candy stripe, semi-supine on the pedestal, with the afflicted ankle perched over the bath's plastic gunwale. The pain of it contorted what was the usual moroseness in his usual teenage face. Here too was my nubile widow Lavante, whose contours—I again had that chance—left nothing to doubt (the thrills, the frills! And oh that diaphanous négligé!). She tested, in alternate palms, the weight of a rolled bandage, against that of a jar of paracetamol. I swear, as I advised something stronger, I had not consciously noted the brownish pink in what I now know to be stupendous areolae. It's the same with that dark, inverted equilateral, such as frequently inspires a priapic interest in trigonometry. (I'm just not that sort of guy.)

She followed me—'Shall I call,' she fussed, 'a doctor?'—to my room. There was (you students of Glaze) an imagined future, where a Y-fronted-Wye made his bedding seductive for two. Woe, Wye, is flesh. I shall be, and was, and am, oppressed by a non-fictive present. I opened a drawer, to—not a bottled aphrodisiac—but painkillers. Next she followed me to the kitchen. You ask me, why go there? (She asked that too.) Well. Omitting for the moment that long-nosed tap on the outside brick, here was the only prospect of water from the main. In Isabelle's case, it was already known how solemnly I urged against drinking the bathroom water, which came via the tank. This, for the boy's pain, was a dictation I didn't repeat—though I did point out the rampancy, slung in a pot attached to the lintel over the window, of what she called her string-of-hearts. Botanically I can't hazard a nearer exactness, though in any case the description will do. Its leaves are cordate in shape and thumb-nail in size, are a paler green with darkish mottles, and grow endlessly in chains. One replanted its occasional corms. (Of course, this is all voluptuous in its irrelevancy.) On returning up, we found Michael hopping (mad, bad, sad), although by three my paternal morphine had him tucked up and soundly to his dreams. Isabelle, to her own sumptuous boudoir, followed shortly, where for seconds only I hung about in the doorway. This, in my mind, was no more than an inconclusive debate—whether or not to leave her my pills. I remember she winked, switching off her bedside light. That is what I said—winked, switching off her bedside light. Shall I repeat? Winked … whaddya know … (I shall was, I be—I therefore am.)

Coffee, mid-morning. A situation to which I am forced, indifferently propping up the kitchen freezer, which hums and tinkles its incessant, electric medley (polar ditties I am in danger of learning). Grey Kenny from Kensal Green, in applying his peach overcoats, warbles to a synthetic brand of misery—one our radio

73

goops, O they of the Corporation, rashly term entertainment. Between plaints, there's a frenetic overvoice (a man's—his chin held high to the challenge of a broadcast smile). This somewhat forces my retreat behind the closed door of the Wandsworth room, where with renewed reluctance I shall extend my purview of the Glaze débâcle. Zob does not yet suspect (and I shan't disillusion him), that the private letters—these notelets in the life of a son of Exe—are of no public interest, and certainly little value.

At and around noon. There was one high shelf I hadn't tried, because it required a step ladder, which the warbler loaned me (while devouring a bacon roll. Still, incredibly, warbling). Here, a box—cardboard, flimsy corrugations—yielded depressingly more than its superficial contents, which were the pen trays and ink cartridges of Zob's previously abandoned desktop. Incidentally this now helps, cheaply, to furnish my room.

I detected the decaying scent of apple, immediately putting my hand on a perforated sachet, assuming in this the legacy of Gloria Punch (the bubbly redhead). A car, with the reflective angle of its windscreen, edged my arm in pallid, mobile outline, as it went by, and as I lifted the box. You have, friends, guessed. Herein another wodge of the professor's tormented outpourings.

As is usual I couldn't much be bothered, making sure only to put them aside. What they had got themselves shuffled with—a handful of old photos ... well ... these did have a certain power to detain me. (Genius the late Andrew Glaze continued to lack.) His society of mutual handshakes, which were across a closed circle, had built its reputation on the precepts of internal consent, and had its own tabernacle. That was established where I—and I suspect most others—were hard-pressed to find an oasis. Take a specific example, that ephemeral (because already dated) *Companion to Writers Writing Now*. This is a questionable document, whose many hands in its making have, of course, co-operated in raising up the professor's (editorial) chair. You won't be surprised, that in his 'Preface' he cites Marshall Zob as among those 'who offered critical suggestions or tolerated a thousand tedious questions'. Zob's entry itself, a good two inches deeper than Mr Burgess's (whose *œuvre* is perhaps best trussed in some non-contemporary strait), is outdistanced by Glaze's own, whose only contribution to English letters is as flatulent commentator. The fine poet Shay (that's Bim Shay) gets no mention. (What should one expect, from Exe University Press?) Not to worry. My cool summary shall some fine day see light, ten per cent of which I shall shine on a man very like Snell (*his* terms).

In the meantime I have got these photos. The oldest is inscribed so, 'Jasmine, '69', which I see from her pose is nothing to do with that coital variation. Jasmine's a little bit plump, is stretched out alone on a stripy beach towel, and is wearing frumpy, old-fashioned underwear. She represents Zob's first goodnight. Another is dated 1974, and is one of three which feature the Glaze children. Giles, approximately seven, is wearing turquoise shorts with a tee-shirt, whose imprint's a domed Shakespeare (inappropriately, as it now turns out). I shan't dispute, that at a perspective of twenty years, you can identify the germ of failure. I look as the professor would, in hereditary terms. Yet. The Giles I see here, his hands behind his back, wears the contented grimace I imagine still persists. For Jessica, Glaze had no ambitions, other than planned introductions, whose rosy culmination, naturally, was nuptial. One hardly envisaged it, other than meaning the mixed seed of two 'good' families—or as the professor might say, 'sturdy', meaning 'middle class'.

Now, please, permit me to point out the gloved mechanical, lolling on the departed's tombstone. His diction is comic, although he's dependable, bearing my message. 'Sir, the living, breathing, Alistair Wye, has studied these portraits.' The word's this, that Jessica's liquid fire (there is mud on her denim dress. Her little red boots are on the wrong feet). That impish grin for the lens is her prefix of reform, to which end she subsequently traded pens for swords. Nothing Glaze instructed her is possibly sanctified. He is—I think I can hear her say—that clueless un-family man, who years later can't bear her sardonic frown—a plasticity reserved for Exe's voluted interior. I shall contradict that insubstantial ghost (Andrew's), to say she's a clever girl. Didn't she decline, on grounds of health, to scan his shelves? and pluck out those embossed tomes?—great slabs of parasitic English life. His trade, after all, approached its zenith in the glorification of what was English and mediocre. (He taught her to recite names. She uttered them all with a lisp.) She has insisted since, in the shrugs and tobacco stains of her adulthood, that a working girl hardly need reiterate, in deprecation of her daddy's 'importance', to what extent she has despised 'the book'—its spawned professorships, its dead industry, its stifling symbiosis. She will I am sure drink Zob's champagne, and perhaps even raise a glass to that one contributor more (or Zob himself) to an already overflowing trashcan.

There is also (Marsy, this is strange) a family portrait, minus the professor himself (do we assume Glaze the photographer?). Here in the professor's wife is the slight over-weight of resignation. (In our proletarian grandmothers, this is also called 'character'.) Samantha has never worked. 'Character'—en famille—is mid-life loathing, even if an impish Giles has a winning smile. Jessica, whose fingers pull at the corners of her mouth, is a round-eyed monster. So on and on. Our trio of snaps, completing itself in 1982, centres tall Professor Glaze in full regalia. This time it's Samantha's hand at the camera, who just for the moment has frozen the breeze in her husband's gown. The sandstone, after twelve years a faded yellow, is anaemic in the gargoyles, is just a little less so in Exe's castellations. Giles, in mid-flight as song-and-dance-man, is a swaggering teenager. Jessica's mobility has turned to a pout. This is a quad outside the library, on a ceremonial day. No tourists. This is the way it will end. There shall be no domestic bliss.

Hum …

Afternoon (afternoon of a writer). The last of us, from Albion's golden shore, to see those gilded crowns, ever more rare under the remorseless hand of the Celt (Kenny: those advancing, glistening tracts of peach), was a man called Zob, who leaned over my sanded sill, to see … what? The blue denims, the yellow jumper, the frizz of their possessor's hair. This occurred as I inhaled from my American cigarette, at the same time gazing into a wall niche (in the garden), the only man at home to appreciate the mauve bells of Adam's campanula. Zob said he had a spare moment (so, he saw, did I), and 'what about that haircut?' (which sounded rhetorical). Unavoidably, this was my opportunity to be driven by him, where I noted slight anxiety in that way, that knack he had, of shifting gear from fifth direct to second. He ummed a lot, about, but failing, to speak. He switched radio stations, settling, moronically, for news. He was I believe courteous for a Bentley. For a three-wheeler, nosing into the traffic stream, he reserved weary hand gestures (terms of abuse, properly understood), and had the face to match. Finally parking up, he did hint at what was on his mind. Zob was surprised—not, to have heard from Flude ... 'given the project's timescale', which was limited. (That was it, the operetta?

Apparently.) The sign on his health club door was a circle, meaning wholeness, pierced at its centre by an arrow, meaning death (actually fleetness, he corrected). The receptionist was a ruminant. She chewed gum. This was in the shade of an oversized yucca. For Marsy, she smiled. To me, she handed the guest book, and pen, disconsolate. Was it the hair, or the garb, or what? Well, it's been a long day. I signed. I followed Zob to the hospitality lounge, where he brightened. This was because, ahead of a perspiring squash celebrity, he got himself smothered by Madeleine, or 'Maddie' West, whose youngish flesh was a shade of solarium bronze. You will know this girl, famous for her sequinned leotard (whose fullness she pressed to Zob's elbow). She I held responsible for the exhaustion, and perhaps the despair of millions, via her breakfast-show aerobics (video to follow).

'You must,' she urged, 'try the new flotation pool. It's the "outer space experience". Do you have trunks?'

It has been, as I say, a long day.

'The *coiffeuse*, may I ask?' They headed off for a dip.

'Oh, she's that way' (indeterminate hand signal).

Evening. One grave question, which the restyled Wye can't answer: 'Où est Malkin?' Malkin, who hasn't come home, even for the rippling entrails—even the chopped head—of Isabelle's fish supper.

Malkin. Here puss puss.

Night. Not surprisingly the sweet potions of sleep, that my Morpheus has soothingly administered, before so kindly primping up the quilt at my newly naked ear. Did I say, it was oh such a long day?

June 18. Isabelle, who now maintains she has always taken a second liking to me, after a haircut (but a pity about the jumper), has got me, maddeningly, reflecting on that wink (a soft lid closed for a blissful short eternity). She has, she said, after a lapse of many years, joined an art group, whose leader gave her—insistent despite polite refusals—a walnut whip. This she has placed where the radiant gilt of a carriage clock, off-centre over the fire, douches its chocolate pyramid in a yellow veil of cellophane. 'Please tell Michael.' Michael is being coached—this will go on, and on, for successive Saturday mornings—by a man called Moncur. 'An ex-pro,' she said—who once covered ground over the outer courts during the early rounds of Wimbledon. He had had quarter-final potential, though never overcame the glaring predictability of his cross-court forehand. Majestically his lob, though tirelessly accurate, lacked pace. Moncur, alternately sullen, jolly, sullen, was fiftyish, and now pear-shaped. That was the *gravitas*, from which he was able to flash winners (after a sidestep perhaps) past his best of students—who was called Michael (whose ankle is strapped).

Still no sign of Malkin.

June 19. No. I am not your father. Trust you to turn up when Mamma's gone. And take that tail from under my nose. I'm going t', t', t'... snATISHOO!

June 20. Isabelle has torn a page from an infuriating supplement (Saturday's, I think), and has left it on the kitchen table just where I'm trying to digest my morning toast. It is therefore no fault of my own, compelled to fight back my nausea, that the complacent Marshall Zob now invades my breakfasts. Here's that surly grin, with its inventive caption ('The miracle of Miracle'). The good widow Lavante it seems to me is duped by its cynical ploy (that, friends, is the miracle), and has ringed the Jane Austen complete as the free inducement to join (even though it exists, in unread paperback, on various shelves round the house). Concerning Miss Austen, Zob supposedly has this to say: '... today's readers still find in her letters certainly a wit, and that occasional coarseness that has so surprised some admirers.' Coarseness, he knows about (knows how it sells).

June 21. Mrs St John, who has refused to phone the wine warehouse (in West Ealing, where Zob, through Giles, 'knows' the management), has filled her translucent green watering can, and has taken its enormously long spout to a basket of white fuchsias. This is something Adam has thoughtfully provided in that angular shade of the patio wall, just outside her ironing room. There is also a bench, a trellis for a climbing rose, and a terracotta tub with a cane and red fuchsia, in whose orbit I see there are both mauve and pink petunias.

June 22. The party's on Saturday, in three days' time. Tomorrow, there's a full moon. Zob, who's in a twitch, suspects that Giles's friends in the trade have let him down. He begins to contemplate, to retrieve the situation, a selection of supermarket wines. Oh what madness.

June 23. Oh what joy. (Thanks to me, of course, who knows how to word a fax.) Mr Pagliari, who had been attending to Mr Zob's order personally, apologised profusely. The fact is he has had a couple of days in Burgundy, with M. Ramonet, because he likes to stock his own cellar from source, having tasted in barrel. The van followed shortly, though I did not supervise its unlading. Some cases I saw. A Louis Roederer Cristal champagne, a bottle of which I persuaded Zob to put aside. There was a 1989 Château Latour. Then some of Ramonet's white Burgundy, a selection after Mr Pagliari's heart, which thumps ecstatically. There was, too, some mid-range Rioja, and a 1982 Meursault-Perrières, at least one bottle of which Giles later discovered had oxidised. As a token, which assured of his best intentions, Mr Pagliari gift-tagged a 1978 Bâtard-Montrachet, which Zob did place in his private rack—and which would be followed by another, when on the Monday Giles took up that glitch in the Meursault-Perrières. Mrs Clapp glanced over the invoice, and in consideration of wages viewed the whole spectacle as a shocking waste of money.

June 24. The caterer, a Mrs Obernau-Ombercrombie, is a reliable

Finchleyite, and is used invariably by Snell for literary buffets. She comes recommended, having gorged the Conservative Club at three of the last four Tory election victories. Snell, who invents epithets, tells me she's an acquaintance of—and I quote—'the harridan of Number 10 (RIP)'. She prefers to be called Olga (though I call her Agent Triple-O), and is here to finalise the menu with Zob. Agent Triple-O is not that attractive, being lined, a bit brassy-looking, and too obviously old—viz., for the intimate use of that triad of mirrors crowning Zob's dressing-table. He seems to me gloomy, and offers, as explanation, Kiff's moustache. Kiff he has resurrected for novel number four, and the monumental problem is this: had that moustache grown, way back at Chapter 5, or was that merely the point at which he stopped shaving? This leaves Zob with the depressing task of re-reading his work (and leaves me with OW, I mean OOO, of Finchley). She's quite a girl (Daddy was *Luftwaffe*), and has a categorical style. She marched to the kitchen, opening her heart, mouth and nostrils to its facilities. On the patio, she told me yes-very-good-SO. Then in the drawing-room, whose oak partition opens to the TV/music lounge, she suggested a rearrangement of the furniture, if, as she understood, the buffet would be served ah-so-here. (I wasn't sure Zob would approve this.)

So, over to Obernau-Ombercrombie, who was (you'll excuse me) yes-down-the-middle certain, to be here, in the morning at ten, having shopped. Her codas were symphonic (oh how long I held open doors for her). She professed there would be dips, as an artiste, who so objected to the easy option—such as tortilla, which being too dry just didn't perk up the tastebuds. She conceived, she said, on an exquisite scale, and even now envisaged (let us say) chopped Parma ham in a creamed whisk of avocado. Nor had she failed in her 'creation of chick-pea' (recorded, with variations, in innumerable vegetarian cookbooks), whose quintessence was garlic and lemon, and a hint of root ginger. I was surprised when she re-inspected the patio, and sat on the bench with a cigarillo. This she inserted into a smoke-coloured holder. Then, friends, she pressed, did agent Triple-O, an elbow, brazenly into my ribs, on accepting a light. Ah so! If the weather held, she said, she would bring her assistant Peter, who could set up her gridirons—anywhere here—for the one or two morsels she had 'inspirationally' thought to barbecue. Shish kebab, in perhaps her 'famous' marinade of oyster sauce—and banana, possibly peach, in a sprinkle of muscovado sugar. 'That all sounds fine,' I said, although later, when Zob instructed me to be here, and receive her at ten, I was not inclined to that view. It also meant showering, later, in bathroom three, and changing in my new peach, and unsugared room, into my party garb.

June 25 (plus appropriated small hours of following morning). No doubt in some distant circumstance, with the grey-haired Zob's hilarious memoirs (a sad waste of paper I wouldn't at this stage bet against), I shall perhaps persuade myself to share the joke, me with a crooked stick (when I am not, that is, in the mobile rage of my Bath chair). He rang me at nine. Rather he rang me in a panic at nine (so that my poor damp Isabelle, enfolded in the soft pink wraps of her ablutions, replugged her bedroom phone into the point on my landing. That's her nice blue phone, whose receiver bears the sweet imprinted scent of *eau de fleurs*, from her wrists, from her little white lobes). I rolled out of bed. I planted that exotic instrument to my still dreaming ear, and begged him what, what was that he said? Miss Overmars?

Indubitably. That leggy lass had arrived from Amsterdam, not at this eccentric hour, but several days ago, whence—sandalled and rucksacked, and with her impeccable smile—she had hitch-hiked to Oxford, to Cambridge, and staggeringly to High Wycombe (in that triangular order). Now, after an early start, she had encamped herself on Zob's doorstep, having left it late, but not she hoped fatally so, in replying to his invitation (all of them went out RSVP). This in itself I am certain did not unnerve him at all (I am looking down through the part-open bathroom door at the nakedness of Isabelle's ankle, and now as she plants herself backward, at a sumptuous thigh). So that, the juncture an awkward one, I learned suddenly how my deluded employer had assumed professional status, and if not, bellitude in his hundred-thousand readership. Only now do I recall a frosty morning, complete with vibrant exhaust, that silver Mercedes of his, whose warming carbon monoxide corrugated the crisp November air. I had sprayed a cloud of chemical vapours on to the windshield, while Zob, the huddled passenger, awaited the heater (still at this point as it exhaled the breaths of Siberia). When we drove—I expect to a bleary meeting—he must have imagined that most of his readers did this daily—smart executives equipped for the week with the insights his books gave them. Miss Overmars, who proclaimed herself his 'number one fan', with such charmless grace seemed likely to shatter his myth (not to say mirth).

The girl was gankly frangling. Let's try that again! The girl was frankly gangling. She wore shycling sorts, I mean cycling shorts, in black and lime-green stripes, a tight fit, rather longish to the knee. The inky, circular imprint on her tee-shirt attested to union with Georgia Tech, where she confessed she'd never been. She was oh so tall. Teeth, tombstones (with gap for feeler gauge between foremost two incisors). The flesh of her face was a lactic white, and at the hems of her shirt sleeves, in graded hoops, a rare to medium roast. When I got there—moments before agent Triple-O—Miss Overmars was all leg, somehow concertina'd in one of Zob's cane patio chairs, chane catio pairs. I put her at twenty-five, six, no more than seven. Zob himself fumbled over the kitchen drainer, with what courtesan still abed I don't know. He was scything through the foil seal in a newly opened jar of decaffeinated coffee (Miss Overmars had left undrunk the orthodox sludge the surprised host had previously made). On the table, humble gift, was a packet of Dutch crispy toasts. This was paired by another in Miss Overmars' rucksack, which before tossing on to the back seat and folding herself up in my Ford, she produced and presented, with a 'Zen-k'you'.

I am not a man for Wagnerian explosives (sometimes unfortunately). My tape had wound itself not that far forward into its opening lento, that is I mean Górecki, third symphony, opus 36 (1976). Okay I know. Our classic broadcasters can press little more to over-do (Miss Overmars) this piece. For you see, in that reverberating cocoon, I was not able to stifle whatever conversation our lank soprano might embark on (ergo better to gabble myself). Here was my subject (and aside: I did, Scylla, I did, Charybdis, have the presence of mind—to wind down my window and issue a cheery wave. This of course to Obernau-Ombercrombie, whose puzzled approach crested itself in the flash of metallic blue, plus tinted glass, of that person's new Espace). 'You like music?' I asked, to which I got a 'Yar, Dire Strades.' 'Never mind. You'll soon feel better,' I said, and got on with the lecture. Let us put this utterance in context. (I am talking about this symphony—yes at the moment it *is* quiet.) Dawn, imagine. September 1st, 1939, imagine. A sly old battle-cruiser, in open emulation of 'exercise', coolly departs its anchorage outside Gdańsk—till then a free city—and caddishly opens fire. Caddish? To us English that means ungentlemanly conduct—very very serious. But to go on. This meant that Europe was at war. Now I shall skip some (since I wasn't actually present). A half-century later, I want you to imagine this time that event's fiftieth anniversary. A faceless mass, the media-man's dream, notionally linked itself up through its multiple television screens—this was for a relay from the Opera House, Warsaw. The schedule, inevitably, included Beethoven. Also Mahler, also Schoenberg, also Penderecki. There was, too, the commentary of a survivor from Auschwitz. That is what I said, Auschwitz. And why, Miss Overmars, Auschwitz (or as is said in Poland, Oswiecim)? Because. Oh now you've made me miss the lights! It's because what you are listening to is in fact a prayer, we might say a prayer for the whole of humanity, who knows no end of oppression.

I pulled up on Isabelle's drive, next to the low-lying Citroën. I chaperoned Miss Overmars in, even to the point of bearing her vigorous rucksack, and debarred Michael on his way out. My un-merry widow, clued up to the day's changing arrangements (according to the guru Zob), left her milk and her cat tins and came to the hall with a newly laundered dish cloth. I told her I had lent Miss Overmars the privilege of all my acquired knowledge apropos of Górecki's *Third*, over the whole car ride, *in extenso*—to which Isabelle said 'Poor girl'. Then I addressed the entire amphitheatre, saying if Miss Overmars liked tennis at all Michael would be more than happy to give her a knock-up. 'Isabelle will lend you a racquet.' Yes yes this by the way is Isabelle. Now I must officiate, you'll excuse me, in Master Zob's castle. At which locale, when I re-arrived, a tarty blonde wiggled under the portcullis and stepped into a waiting taxi.

Obligingly the tyrant Olga (in the van of her tyro Peter, who was yet to arrive) had left visual markers as to her rampage through Zob's ground floor. Zob, one guessed, occupied a higher elevation, perhaps naked under a cone of diamonds from the nozzle of his shower. Here on a wire hanger, slung at a perfect horizontal— though asymmetrically from an end peg (the hall dresser)—Olga's short jacket, to which I later found the matching skirt, proclaimed itself in a residuum of eau-de-Cologne, and, more strikingly, a tangerine blaze of velvet. Her colours were autumn. In the kitchen, on that famous table, over which the light matters of Zob's estate had so often been discussed, Olga had parked her supermarket parcels—one had Greek olive oil, in another a bunch of celery (its overflowing green coxcomb). A breeze, intermittently gold—as through sun, then cloud, then wind—lifted the nap of the carpet, here where I now stand in the drawing-room. A Limoges perfume boule, in a blue porcelain decorated in wild roses—one of a pair the strident Annie Cryles had a liking for—had been moved from a low table to a niche. Some similar transference had visited Zob's bone china trinket box (a gift I recall from Fiona), whose gilt fleurs-de-lis I eventually located in the prismatic glass of an ashtray. These were the first superficial precautions our in-residence caterer, whose beringed hand I now saw round those oak panels to the TV lounge, had fittingly explored. The panels slid open. She wanted to know, she said, how best to deal with her client's semi-precious egg collection. She of course meant those exquisite samples—some in jasper, others in spangled quartz, one in alabaster—as details one might rightfully expect, though never come across, lighting the grey monolith of a text by Marshall Zob. It was the same with his chiming exercise spheres, whose principle was acupressure, rolling them in your hands (so massaging the palms). These, she pointed out, were in *cloisonné*, and a long way from their brocade presentation box. 'Perhaps remove these delicate things to the study,' I said.

Her assistant Peter, a dejected man in a white shirt and grey flannels, somehow wedged a small refrigerator on an extended hip while braying at the front door. I allowed him over the threshold and led him to the kitchen, where he humped the thing down. His station wagon—a mauve with punctuating rust—had its hatch door

84

yawning, out of whose maw he produced folding buffet tables. Then the gridirons. Then those one or two priceless utensils his mistress could never be without (for example a giant slotted spoon. For example a late twentieth-century pressure cooker). I thought I might hazard a precarious catalogue of further edibles—this from both cars—though having noted sardines in a bed of ice chips, our crinkled auburn-ash-to-blonde, to a flourish of culinary trumpets, shooed me from the kitchen. Symbolically I washed my hands, informing Zob, through the interdict of his closed bedroom door, that 'all' was under control, and that I could no longer prevail on mother and son Lavante for the diversion of a gauche Miss Overmars. 'Come back at five,' he said.

'Come back at five.'

Home again. (Is that a crooner I hear, from Isabelle's radio, through Isabelle's open window?) An autumnal russet splintered the jet of her hair, through the many angles she wielded her manual shears, whose oily blades also occasionally glittered. What had to be done, she did (oh how she scowled, expecting me!—yes me to help!). I protest! I am just not the home-owner type, whose decisions, precisions, excisions (those tufts of grass fringing the rope-twist edging to her path) are the contamination of good minds through popular mires. 'Your birthday—no, that's gone!' I said. 'Christmas! I'll buy you an electric strimmer.' I stepped inside and switched off that crooner, to which she said illogically she wanted the news: 'Switch back on!' And Miss Overmars? I asked. Well. Apparently. That perinatal gazelle had seriously understood my imitated Thespis, and had propelled the innocent Michael—each bore a racquet—to the local courts, which to his mind were hopelessly substandard, being potholed. For Miss Overmars ... Well ... Hers—was not naturally a tennis nation ... One thought, and none too profoundly, perhaps of Betty Stove. Perhaps of Tom Okker. Nevertheless. I shall be fair. My approach through the park was no more eventful than a first, spontaneous pause for a white fuchsia. So far my distant matchstick figures only bounced on elastic in and off the net. Next I saw clearly the demarcation in the stripes of Miss Overmars' shorts—the black to lime-green—and at this point plucked and tossed back a ball from a rose-bed, whose yellow fur (I now recall, as I re-palm it reflectively) had scarcely been ruffled. Michael served (a gentlemanly underarm). Miss Overmars caught her return on the rise, in a zigzag of limbs, scooping her racquet under the ball, without (as Michael stood there, arms akimbo) that flick of the wrist whose transmission is topspin. The ball found its own angle over the perimeter fence, and joined, as I tramped to discover, a half-dozen others in the flanking boscage. Carved on a bench, I learned that the prime minister—or someone who shared his name—was a *souteneur*.

Lunch (at Isabelle's). This consisted of cheddar, of ploughman's pickle, of crunchy Dutch crispy toasts. Miss Overmars told us her daddy was a dentist, and that she too wanted to work with people—though with rather more than their mouths. What she felt strongly about (Zob, please note) was adult illiteracy. And youngsters with learning problems.

Four-forty p.m. Have left Miss Overmars—unfurling, unfurling, unfurling an endless unfurling gown from her rucksack. For which Isabelle had prepared a cool iron.

Five (-ish). Zob—with more or less permanent prehensile fingers and thumb round the eraser end of his phone jotter pencil—is feeling tense. He paces a lot. Agent Triple-O has run the dishwasher several times. She explains she has made her dips (and plugged in that baby fridge). I imagine she has therefore racked them, in all three dimensions, at a cool degree Celsius. She has, I see, prepared four salvers of trout, each in a simulated sea of cucumber. There have been carrots, and there has been, Captain Cook (see below), celery—though these have suffered one fate. That is to say, we have amber and chlorotic three-inch oblongs, arranged in tumblers. (We have crunchy Dutch crispy toasts.)

The assistant Peter was having his coffee break in the TV lounge, where the buffet tables were erected, dressed, and adorned with china (also with cutlery, also with serviettes, in a paper ponceau). He has the TV tuned to Teletext, and takes issue—mawkishly, retrospectively—with its weather forecast. This I have no particular opinion on, but am concerned at how close his elbow is—gift courtesy Zob's plump ma—to an Alexandra vase. This is in reproduction creamware, moulded with leaf and bead borders. Its six sides are hand-pierced in open, symmetrical petal-work. Its lid is crowned with an oak-leaf finial. 'May I draw your attention to this,' is what I say, and precede that sullen man, whose empty cup shakes in its saucer, to a low marble table by the door (out of which I hope he will progressively go). 'An amusing pastime ...' Blank looks, so let me just take his coffee cup. 'Prima facie it may seem simple, and is in point of fact cleverly strategic. It is called and I'll explain that, 'The Captain's Mistress'. I urge on you the spectre of our own Captain Cook—those long lonely nights in his cabin!—after whom, for so I perpetuate our English legend, the name is gamed I mean game is named' [see above]. 'What you have to do is line up four of these hardwood rounds—there, I'll start—ahead of your opponent. As you can see, in its finely styled cabinet, with its burlwood inlay and brass fittings, the whole is not without ornamental value, as is the case with so many objects here. Well. I see you're pondering your move, wisely I might say. I shall of course allow you to pink in the ace I mean think in peace' [away, typographic sprite!] ...

The phone rang. When, friends, I lifted the hall receiver, Cornelius was already babbling, so to speak in a smother over the staccato responses of his client Zob. He said he would be here early—'at around eight'—and would help receive guests. When Zob next saw me he was in pursuit of a pencil. Olga expressed it so—'Dat's nerfs, so relax!'—when I pointed out the one he clutched, though by this time he had forgotten an important name, or aside, gleaned from that phone colloquy.

Eightish. (Snell, good as his word, is here.) In a slight *crise de nerfs* myself, I find I am in the bachelor's den, striding self-consciously into those beige slacks. No adjustment I can make to Zob's minimalist cheval-glass quite dispels the late rush of sartorial doubt (almost overwhelming when I button up that floral shirt). It seems author and agent have secretly conspired, each in his hired tuxedo. And get this! Snell's cummerbund is in a drowsy shade of poppy (his fluorescent white shirt has textured stripes). Zob's is a palace mauve. The bow-ties are complementing, my master's having a sort of *chevaux de frise* design, in a staid navy blue, with white. Snell's is a riot of Sixties' psychedelia, during which decade he was sent down (from Oxford).

At 9.02 Cornelius placed his outsize paw on the knurled knob of the Yale, and with a plasticised grin prepared himself for the first guest(s). That (or these) happened to be Miss Overmars, who found herself ushered over the threshold by a dissenting Isabelle, whose intuition told her that the party was some way off its start (she wanted, she told me later in bed, to drive around the block several times more). Zob had run away (ostensibly not having heard the door bell, and for a final dab, he said, of kohl to his nervous eyelids). At 9.30 Cornelius, prowling in the kitchen, had demolished a remaining half-packet of peanuts. Olga, noting a can of Pilsner—this her slobby assistant had perched at his naked elbow—told him to get up and check the barbecue. This had been lit at 7 o'clock, had reached its correct cinerary pallor at around 8.30, and probably now needed more charcoal.

It's 9.31, 2, 3. The door bell (faintly evocative of those quaint old Respighi airs). Cornelius opens up, to find in the reverberant porch light that flesh-and-blood rotunda, Mickey Blandford. This was a man distracted by the qualms of politics, that twilit arena his editorials had long, and impossibly strayed into. I never tire of telling Zob, that the man's common, and dubious Leftism, is already *passé*. For some reason he hadn't properly read his party invitation, having brought a bottle (of middling Champagne, beribboned). He passed this to Snell. He grinned through—and one day I shall tell him this—those highly inelegant brown whiskers. Zob was of course overjoyed, because this let him slither off Miss Overmars' microscope plate, who as social fanatic warbled to a much reprised chorus (called: 'juvenile crime') ... Zob squared to his friend (beams, guffaws, handshakes) and in particular rounded his vowels.

Isabelle had sneaked a crab vol-au-vent, and was ticked off by Triple-O, for these had not yet been 'pud owt'. Blandford, who had just come from his club in Shepherd Market, apologised for Sir Maxwell Hayste, who even at this hour was transacting pressing commercial business there (with his stock broker).

I have this empty-to-full queue theory (and am tempted to take it up with a software engineer). It operates empirically on the simple principle that once you have decided to step into an empty shop or vacant railway carriage, it fills up immediately. A procession of

Zob's guests, as it were heralded by the apricot-jowled Blandford, tripped in over the threshold. 'Maddie' West, with effeminate, and only slightly madder escort ('But darling!'), each with dewy spangles in the same solarium shade of hair. Her poncho was 'parfictly nase', which in its black and white checks—rather rhombs—matched her partner's waistcoat. 'Actually wescot', he corrected ...

Shayle I found had an endless capacity to depress, having a jaundiced tan with accompanying spleen. The in-Gloria Punch—found the right words elusive: 'Where's that flunkey for coats? Oops! Here! O well, ta, ha!' Merle uplifted me (said I was looking 'sharp'). Zob undid me (his finger and thumb to my elbow). Confidentially, *sotto voce*: 'Al. Be a whizzo. That lovely boy Andreas promised to come and serve drinks, but alas ...' No sign of Andreas. 'Why not start with Gloria there. Now. You won't let me down ...'

Marsy. One day I will.

Gloria's vogue in the aperitif line was at this time a sickly orange liqueur, whose shade, in the wrong and tinted glass I served it in, was only a touch darker than the sunned exterior of the Glaze boy, Giles, whose carroty hair and complexion tended to metamorphose instantly under the beat of his favourite, Provence *soleil*. He and his partner—a dark-haired girl with frightened green eyes—had a Pimm's No. 1, and respectively roared and shuddered to an after-dinner *faux pas*—this the raconteur Blandford had recorded, and who now, looking every inch a salty dog, related. He, incidentally, clutched a cold beer, though I had offered him rum.

Jessica—sister to Giles, in love with the 'mechanic'—entered stage left, Act One, Scene Two. As to points of restitution, the despised, prospective son-in-law (as it relates to the literary goop, now deceased), was a charming Mauritian, whose name was Vic. He I discovered (once an engineer, and *not* a mechanic) ran his own electronics firm (Cambridge Science Park), in the manufacture of asynchronous signalling devices (and thought there might be something in my queue theory). Their lovely twenty-three-month-old, Amanda, was at home being baby-sat.

Time presses. Zob has told Olga to tell her slob to tell me to open

wine, so here in a blur of integrated polychrome is my whirligig—
what remains of the guest list. The cynosure Justin Simms, who
arrived with the 'masculinist' Crouch, and got chatty with the
minimal Royston Flude ... The pugnacious Masturbile (fist semi-
permanently clenched). He in the tireless probes of his newspaper
work had persuaded the bruiser Crouch to the pillory, strictly on
'poor Tom's' turn to be manacled there (meaning Eliot). Today,
Crouch's 'poor toms' were overripe Jerseys, for whose plop and
dribble of orange pips she had a pristine new target (the Anglican
Church, meaning death). Another Tom—Corbiere—kept a more-or-
less constant, uxorious arm to his wife's attractive waist (rose-
coloured dress gathered to a broad green belt). Haphazardly Myrtle
Bloge walked in, with a much older, and balding man in a business
suit. Khalil Azmi sported a joke tie-pin (which depicted the head of
Lenin). He had long wanted to write a travel book, based on the real-
life sojourns of a cricket captain (this is a tedious game. Therefore I
fail to remember all but its most famous English names). What did
Myrtle think? (Nor is her answer something I'd remember.) There
was one other, the liver surgeon, oh and another, that hobbit of
BOTS (Professor Emeritus, once of Exe), plus motley authors and
agents now only a whirr of half-remembered, and anyway
misleading conversation.

Cleverly, I put that 1989 Château Latour among the boxed, floored
debris (as represented the aftermath of Olga's day in the kitchen),
and placed the bottle I opened insignificantly in the shade of Zob's
cooking sherry. This replenished my glass. For Giles, naturally, in
tandem with his green-eyed beauty, I reserved the Meursault-
Perrières (which had oxidised)—with the result that he got on the
phone immediately. For the Philistine horde, I uncorked that mid-
range Rioja, and perambulated with a tray. At this stage Crouch,
who quaffed and knew no better, had got Simms and Azmi in a
huddle, under a bluish pall of gunsmoke (those disgusting English
cigarettes of hers). 'No,' she corrected (at which Azmi bit his lip).
'The fact of a popularised following. Is that growth. Especially
world-wide growth. Is achieved ... Through an attendant
bureaucracy. This has been a disaster for Christianity. Its original
thrust was secularised ...' Bloge, in the adjacent circle (Bloge,

Masturbile, Blandford, Flude), drifted over on the sound of that salvo, Simms's cue (who couldn't help but finger his glittering Rolex) to give up and exchange his place.

Zob, extending white cuffs, and as I now noticed iridescent links from sleeves, somehow entertained Bloge's sirocco-blown escort, who had heard—indirect from mindful Myrtle—that Crouch had only yesterday been appointed to the committee (Best-novel-to-be-published (this decade)).

Snell (who had only himself to blame) had got himself *in camera*, and at each newly imparted detail, found that 'that was not quite so'. Merle, bright droplet of jewels, centre to my pagan altarpiece, put her boss and giant panda right. He was telling the widow (one wisp of hair over her face; for the moment a smile that had set), and the impatient Miss Overmars, that having swung a recent TV deal, a ninety-minute adaptation of Zob's second novel *Hype* would soon reach the nation's crepuscular living-rooms (barring mine, the discerning Wye's). Miss Overmars had read, and of course re-read, and of course re-re-read, and of course of course etc. double-re-re, that masterly Opus Two. To her mind here was one of few genuine works of 'literature' 'cohesive' enough to tackle the underlying 'ethic' of capitalism. And how ingeniously—for not in so many words—his implied stance was firmly *per contra* to that of 'monarchy'. ['Gone, all my bright mountain light …'] On which Merle, proceeding gently: 'How so?' Answer (if I may précis it): The function of hereditary monarchs, is to encourage, in the individual citizen [misnomer: we should say 'subject'], reverence for the State. Yet the State is a complex organ operated by, and in the service of, a powerful élite (ergo hereditary monarch is highest symbol of that). But let us not sermonise. Particularly as the night is young, and the Rioja's so, so, so … middling …

Prosit, Miss Overmars.

'Woss iss dis middling?'

'Prosit!'

Isabelle followed the laden tray. The laden tray was in my hands. Together we found out Corbiere (symbiotically attached to wife. Wife's pretty dress. Rose—shade I like). He was telling Maddie West and that sylph's animated twin how that miraculous jingle—

'the miracle of Miracle'—occurred to him in a four-second burst of genius.

'Incredible!'

The sullen Shayle took one of the last three glasses on my salver. Symbolically Zob turned up then apologetically turned down the central chandelier (via dimmer switch). An escaping, cramped ellipse of light from a table lamp, in a burnt hue of burnt sugar, illuminated an eye, a sallow cheek, an ear lobe, as Shayle began to speak. He'd had a problem with extras—this on a 'shoot' in Exeter. I shan't have to make this clear—that his job is largely low-grade entertainment, that his lode is a television enterprise I shall have the foresight not to name. 'It's what you get,' I said, 'for falling short of Equity rates'—because, brothers and sisters in servitude, picture the scene:

Director circles that particular section of (supremely pointless) script where hero, an Italianate youth, whom ignorant author has named Sancerre, enters private casino. Silence. Action. There are six extras seated at each of three round tables, above which gaffer has suspended lights on makeshift gantry. Dealers deal cards on to green baize (this is draw poker, rules of which are not entirely grasped by all the eighteen). Other props are: a Churchillian cigar, numerous cigarettes, cold tea in whisky glasses, water for gin with genuine quartered lemon, low-alcohol lager (none to be drunk, as no top-ups between takes), an imitation haze, several thousand pounds sterling in bank notes (there, gentlemen, is the rub). There is one camera only, and this means that an interesting interplay of angles to the scene—is, well, frankly troublesome (and in the end a little nicety Shayle—already over budget—decides to abandon). Sancerre strides to table where great rival Anjou (I'm sorry, that should read Andrew)—Cut. Move table, this one here. Makeup, and silence, and action. Sancerre strides &c. [I am down to one glass only, Isabelle, I am sorry if this sempiternal Shayle does seem to go on], and because the scriptwriter has no grounding whatsoever in mathematical probability theory, Sancerre fleeces his opponent, first with a full hand, then a straight flush, finally four of a kind. This—as I yawn—does not conclude the story. The casino is folded up and put away. The players break up for coffee. Those bank notes are counted. They

92

are re-counted. Then they are endlessly re-counted. Here we arrive at the brink of an accusation (though which one of the eighteen, or perhaps the star Sancerre feels he is underpaid?)—and here I turn to the liver surgeon, whose surprised left eye socket seems momentarily monocled. 'Do please have this last glass.'

I retreat to the kitchen, into the welcoming glow of my private Château Latour, and am unfortunately observed by Gloria Punch. The professor is here too, moistening a pencil, and with an open notebook, and has something to say, on 'the pleasance of sodalities' (!).

How shall I wrap up this dismal scene? My departing muse, in a lightness of tread, and with that cool air of exile she fans to my brow, has preached detachment. Gloria finished my bottle. Giles—who stumbled on my semi-hidden stocks—suddenly usurped my promotion to major-domo, at least insofar as these Orphic revels needed to be supervised. Ms Crouch and Miss Bloge processed through the buffet lounge, where the former delivered her new tractate, *Women and the Priesthood*. Here I cannot take issue (without, that is, looking stupidly solemn)—i.e., that the whole charade was essentially fun and games for the male of the species, a 'poor chap' who sought to dignify his work-horse status with the magic rain of mysticism (there I go: solemn). Flude, Snell, and the impeccable Simms picked at a raspberry-coloured pâté, and were otherwise in conclave. Merle—star of my studded heaven—had got Isabelle and Blandford into the laundry room, and needed only the unsuspecting me for a hand of solo. Merle, my precious Merle! How could I disagree with your *abondance* (or agree with your *misère*)? It's no matter. By 2 a.m. I had had enough, therefore dissolve, I say, inebriate diplopia! The smiling Wye could find no right bid ...

... for a twenty of diamonds ... a duopoly of spade queens ... a quartet of black twos ...

... and was it you, was it you who put me to bed, shoes by the door, beige pantaloons overhanging my chair, shirt on a hanger?

Merle!

June 26. Am I, or am I not, that floating cloudlet, a whitish with suffusing blue, scorched, brindled at its fluffy fringes ... or am I in a doorless dream, about four feet, about a yard, above this mattress?

Bump (of course the dream)! Here is that perfect peach (gone all my bright gilded crowns). Through there's my DTE. Amazingly shoes by the door—and what! beige pantaloons, overhanging my chair—that Tropicana shirt on a hanger ... Aw now Merle, my pearl! For these things, yes, a double-, a treble-, a multiple affirmative (why yes, why yes, why yes yes yes) ... Then for one sodden moment (for nor do I suffer common hangovers, merely a tiredness about the eyes), as I and my many morning identities trooped to bathroom one ... briefly I caught the spectre of Geraldine Crouch, attired only in an oversized pair of Zob's cricket Y-fronts, returning—not to a ring with awaiting heavyweight—but to the *auteur's* lair, whose bedroom door she closed quietly behind her, shutting out the blare, the thunderous cascade of water from the cistern.

Moreover other regions of the cosmos have suffered disturbance. I find when I get home Isabelle still abed (not on her regular Sunday morning jaunt). She insists I sit by her. She says 'heaven' when she has me massage her shoulders (one sharp scapula slips the hook of its négligé, then the other), then she collapses, prone. 'To think,' she purrs, 'I wanted to drive round the block. Such a party!'

Here is a sudden thought: I shall open my encyclopaedia, to the entry 'cockchafer'.

I go to my room, I find Miss Overmars—a sack of limbs—who all night long has pummelled my duvet. Categorically no, I shall not massage, Miss Overmars, your shoulders.

June 28. Mrs St John, put out finally in Lutheran disgust (these empties, all these catholic indulgences), hopes sincerely I will clear the kitchen, the laundry room, and get me to a bottle bank. Obernau-Ombercrombie, a surprise visitor, checks in in a banana trouser suit, having reasoned that her lost slotted spoon must be somewhere here. I had occasion to think she was right, recalling the maladroit Blandford, with that obese chuckle perfectly adapted to Saturday's self-conscious sport (because someone suggested charades). He had had the purloined utensil, with which he swatted the party's acrid air. This did not mean 'Bane', as would have been logical, but

'Lord', *Lord of the Flies*. A rosy Gloria Punch, who at that late hour secreted musk to her underarms, triumphantly guessed it, and followed on—in my view this was apposite—with *Diary of a Nobody*. I found it—the spoon—down the back of a leathern settee, though the double-dealing Triple-O could not reciprocate with a trip to her nearest recycling centre.

I shall look out dutifully for her invoice, ensuring its longevity in the heaps of number three in my grading system, that is to say the least urgent correspondence pile.

June 29. I have puzzled on one curious fact concerning Miss Overmars, that her left profile tends to a scimitar, while the right is more inclined to be gibbous. She has spent these last nights on a zed bed, in the spare but really Isabelle's utility room. Table with typewriter. An easel, now replaced. The games, jigsaws, and a dumper truck, that have outlived Michael's abbreviated childhood. There is a desk and secret effects, these being under lock and key, of the late Michael Lavante. There is, I add, his portrait, a full, smiling face in the vigour of its manhood (this was avoidably extinguished in the port of Zeebrugge).

Happily Miss Overmars is re-shod in those sandals, and enjoys the benefit of newly laundered shirt and shorts. She has left her address, and herself has promised to write. Having so much enjoyed talking to the professor (on Saturday night, 'pleasance of sodalities'), she is setting off now on a pilgrimage to Exe. I have agreed, among the sonorities of a fugue, to drop her on the West Way, where with her map and her rucksack, I can see, in the departing mirror, that she has stuck out a thumb. Bon voyage!

June 30. Mrs Clapp—who finds everything back (almost) to normal—has been run ragged by Cornelius. His incessant demands for *cappuccino* she tells me detract from an extended assault with the oven spray.

I was myself called to the meeting (Zob, in his study, reclining; Snell poised with clipboard plus fountain pen). I drank Earl Grey. Snell could not resist the raw laughter of commerce, observing, that now that the harpy had been bedded—by Zob—a place for *Gimme the Cash* on the short-list—Best-novel-to-be-published (this decade)—'of course' was assured—for had not the winged, taloned, 'man-hating' Crouch been appointed to the committee? Zob, darkish, shifty—a mien reminiscent of its screen manifestation— said only this, that for a misogamist the pugilist Crouch had an expert hand in all aspects of erogenous electrification. Excuse the coarseness in Snell's guffaw. That, he said, in a multitude of exclamation points, was exactly the colour of present business. I finished my Earl Grey.

The 'colour' was purple, 'present business' was: Zob's, and now Cornelius's plan, for that South Bank reading ('By the way thanks Al for that excellent suggestion'). Snell had marked his preferred passage from *Gimme the Cash*, which as I subdue vipers, the turmoil of my stomach, goes along following lines—

Scene, rambling Edwardian house off quiet lane in Cookham. Kiff, a street entrepreneur and supplier of all cargoes, has trawled a King's Cross *trottoir*, and has brought to client Ambrose (a bored lawyer), a teenage brunette. He has brought also a sachet of yellow powder. Also a camcorder. Events unfold in the drawing-room: thick pile carpet, heavily woven drapes, the latter drawn (though it is daylight outside). Certain theatrical arrangements have been introduced, notably a foil-lined umbrella, fully open, and a desk lamp, which has been turned on, and which is craning its neck. Ambrose emerges from a Chinese screen, where he has exchanged his daytime garments for two items only (one, a pair of surgical gloves. Two—pinched, squeezed—rolled to its owner's throbbing rhapsody—a priapic overcoat). Kiff co-ordinates his client's home movie show, whose male lead jokes that this is what makes of him that hungry *Homo erectus* (organ probes pimply-cheeked rectum of lily teenager, who is obliged to stand and not turn round). One of those gloved hands caresses a thigh, her groin, massages her clitoris. As such it's a scenario I don't mind stating is not for myself that easy (I fear the public, I fear my public blushes). For that alone (and oh how I loathe that Victorian tone), shall I ... shall I contain what is inherently a squirm of liberal toleration? (Shall there be floating dust in the atmosphere? cigarette smoke? a blue filter for the lens?) The cast is read (dye is cast). I object. Cornelius bellows,

'Intransigent!'—because (and this is the silvered gloss of my chivalry) I won't see his pedestalled assistant so routinely defiled. Patient, gentle, sympathetic reader (alas me) ... That walrus Snell fabricates our fictive trio, plus narrator, so:

Cornelius Walrus, Kiff (an Ealing-ish, South London patois—v. comic). Al, Ambrose (because I'm so stuffed-up, just like a filthy lawyer perhaps). Zob, introduction/sundry interpolations. The teenage brunette, my thirty-ish, dark-haired, light-skinned Merle. It's a human tragedy, on a scale I can't overstate, that the climax is ours:

NARRATIVE: Lubricants, insertion.

SHE: Cor blimey mate wotchya think I am!

I: This, my pet, is your *annus mirabilis*, and is established. You'd like as it were to renegotiate terms. Yes?

A pause in the whole disgusting episode was Snell's insistence that Merle had been sounded out on this, responding with customary equanimity.

July 1. I recorded my second cigarette of the day, while that loose co-ordination of hand, eye, and a mind that floats in cotton wool, levitated over my ledge. Ah, this enveloping perfect peach! Adam I couldn't help notice seized petulantly on an earthy kebab skewer. No one can possibly know (Blandford) how that should find itself in a remote parterre. This is just by those first iridescent enamels in a clump of hydrangeas, pale blooms that are beginning to show. Incidentally I am now reminded that there is, somewhere out there, a shattered wine goblet, which the bibulous Gloria Punch drummed with a table- and dessert-spoon, whose contact resounded, she claimed, in the short-lived rhythm of the *Marseillaise*—oo_oo~aah~~Cant_on_aah. (Just joking.)

July 3. Isabelle again missed her Sunday morning rendezvous. I know that because, having slept fitfully—shall I call Merle, or not?—I swept back my curtains in that Homeric hour of dawn (a flush of early-world orange). She and Michael were loading the Citroën: the boy's five racquets, one set plus one change of whites, tennis shoes, sandwiches, a tartan Thermos. He had made progress in a round-robin tournament, on his preferred all-weather surface, and now faced an older, and a much taller boy, in the first semi-final. 'How I beat him,' he said, 'was with top-spin balls to feet. Made him bend.' That strategy had occurred to him, thinking back on Miss Overmars.

My concluding aside is this. He went on, winning his first final, to come home with a slightly tarnished cup (its wooden pedestal on a square of blue baize). Also he showed me his medallion.
  Michael: bravo!

July 4. To work, and a fine day indeedy, as I smoke out more of that Stateside correspondence. This next collection I found in a cyclist's back pack, scrunched in the bottom drawer—so stiff that I jerked it open, one resisting knob at a time—of a dilapidated chest. This is of lustreless pine, which I don't doubt is antique. Zob admitted that he had never really curbed his appetite since the banquet of his youth, though naturally his metabolism hadn't kept to the same pace. In passing I found an air filtration device (for mouth and nose, with strap), and one of those elliptical helmets, in that utility hue of yellow, which he must have looked attractive in, pedalling the gutters of south west London. But enough. Let us amuse ourselves with that studious corner that the futile Professor Glaze gradually, imperceptibly, painted himself into.

4143 Bay State Rd
Boston MA 02215
27 April 1992

Dear Marsy,
  Safe ground, I assumed (the wonderful, wonderful Updike), and a fitting audience, as I thought (academics, book people, students). Ah but no. Having declared a moratorium on that unimportant 'time' element, which might just as well NOT be a component of my

theory—I might say my GIGANTIC theory (because I know you understand) ... well! Words almost fail. Some fool student of theology asked me if I had invented my solid continuum in the same spirit as St Augustine's deity, i.e. from a co-ordinate outside it. 'Only in the sense,' I said, 'that literature has a beginning—it may or may not correspond with the book of Genesis—and is probably approaching its end, given that other continuum, the TV.' Waffles of dignified laughter. Then at that precise moment the tubular bulb in my lectern light began to blink, then fizz, then went out. 'The way,' I said, 'of all contrivances, which it's as well we all take note of.' I was handed a pocket torch, but of course by now had departed from my papers. Inevitably *Four Quartets* crept in (as it were through a fire exit: a mumbler at the back). 'I might as well tell you now,' I told him, or her, I don't know which, 'I regard that as a complete waste of, yes, time.'

A day or two later I found myself in the university bookshop, and picked up a student magazine (poetry, most of it trash, some promising). You know the sort of thing. Cover, an ink line drawing, whose background is curved, a suggested arch. On close inspection the heady vortices of hair of the five persons seated round a dining table are in fact birds' nests. Hands look like mittens. The carafe they all pour from is bottomless. Well, I didn't expect to find this on a latter page ...

> so, then, time unwinds
> its macadam: right and left
> lanes, past and future

which broke the first rule of haiku, bearing a title: 'Lines for a pioneer, Professor Glaze of Exe'. Touching. I shall keep as a memento.

Keep writing.

Yours ever, Andrew.

[I might further address my lines to the transfigured professor, whose visage I suspect is a radiance of fool's gold, whose cloud is a cloudlet, and who shall pluck the electrified threads of a lyre in everlasting solitude. Is this memento not more of that trickery from the McTaggart tome of pressed flowers? Permit me to ask, on this unwinding macadam (from that vantage you have, far from these temporal intersections), what is the traveller's perception? Of the past as it approaches the future? Or vice versa, the future incessantly tumbling into the past? Also I hazard the view that in our haiku's correlation of 'right' and 'past', what we most probably have is an English author, that is to say a left-lane driver. AW]

Flat 5
147 Trefoil St
SW18
5 May 1992

Dear Andrew,

There are bound to be misapprehensions. God knows I've suffered my own—at the hands, guess, of Gloria Punch. I'm sick of her tyranny, her resounding clarion, that so-called 'cross-write'.

I don't suppose I have to tell you. This means fitting up the script as siren for several audiences together (the word being 'class'). What drives me barking to the morning toaster, is that alacrity she has, detaching gobbets of dialogue, to re-squash under her gauntlet. Still, I think of the money.

By the way I've advertised for an assistant. Am about to process applications.

Don't let them grind you down.

Marsy.

[My own, highly decorative application, was not among that first batch—nor, incidentally, the second. I can't begin to conjecture as to his strategy at that time. It was one that attracted …

… a retired batman, from Leics. A typist from Pinner, 'keen on Agatha Christie'. Numerous school-leavers, still unimpressed by the unsettling discovery of life and the world as NOT a media network. A professional minutes-taker. A great many people who described their work experience as in 'human resources'. My first task on accepting the post was to file this correspondence. AW]

100

c/o Roland Spatz
Long Island University
Greenvale NY 11548
21 May 1992

Dear Marsy,

Now it's getting silly. What do I find, on opening my first bundle of mail ... but that ... I am a man pursued. In this instance by the *Boston Review*, which carries a lethal broadside. I am condemned, for, apparently, my 'cheap Lacanianism', for whose 'symbolic order' I have substituted my own 'pet literatures'. These seem to function as the sole synchronic code into which readers, writers and academics find their pre-ordained role in life. This, I learn, is mighty useful in propping up and dignifying my 'absurd' notions of time. It's news to me.

Thank heaven for your letter, kindly forwarded by Professor Happs. (In my opinion there's plenty of time to choose an assistant.) Needless to say I have made probably my final visit to Fifth Ave, where Sam and her voyeuristic binocs have unthinkingly lit on a mugging (three Hispanics closed on one white American)—Central Park. There was a gum-chewing cop when I got to her apartment ('Just go over that, huh, lady, one more tamm ...'). When, amazingly, I squeezed in five mins (this was with my ex-wife, that sole partner in the moulding of my mattress) she said to me 'For Chrissakes, Andrew ... Nothing *needs* to be done about Jessica.'

I shall tell that cop, I have been in the Museum of Natural History, where I met his contemporaries (display, with label: Ancestors of Man).

Let me know how you get on re assistant.

Yours, Andrew.

[Author's note: the walrus Cornelius engaged me with some aplomb in the news that Jessica is again 'with child' (which was his, biblical way of putting it). He was less animated however in the serious declaration that she was unwilling to participate in a commemoration of her father's life and work.]

Dear Andrew,

Tell them philosophy's like those certain fruitless variants of courtship. A dead end. As certain academics feel safe in a cul-de-sac. Perhaps that'll be my next book. (Though don't fancy the research.)

Just can't imagine how so many unsuitable people have come across my advert. Hundreds of useless applications. However. Have compiled a short-list, currently topped by a very clean girl from Bath. Incidentally she's back from a teaching job in Cadiz. Before that, the 'pleasure'—her words—and the 'untroubled' spires of Exe, where her specialism was Wyndham Lewis (I don't hold that against her). We had a long chat in a pizza house. I'm tempted.

Most recent interview took place in my pool hall (since *Aristotle* I go there a lot—helps me to think, to relax). I couldn't make it—or rather him—out. A native of Manchester, yet talked like colonial Tunbridge Wellian. His name's Alistair (didn't hint at a Scottish connection). He seemed—which is perhaps the operative word—seemed (stress) well informed in matters of art generally, society, politics. He assumes I'm of the Left, because, on the current administration, he had this to say: Its wicked face is precisely that that has lurked behind the decent, genteel exterior of former Tory prime ministers. I didn't say hear hear.

For all this his degree's in computer science, though the man was evasive about his university (a sleight of hand I thought these boffins weren't capable of, having no intelligence outside that realm of the microchip). He could be very useful. As, I wouldn't mind all that hardware paraphernalia (though God knows can make nor head nor tail of the box of tricks I have got). He works, he says, for a theatrical properties company in Mortimer St, for whom he designed, wrote and installed a stock-and-order system. He reads Nabokov, and for that reason thinks he can talk down to me. I showed him a thing or two on the pool table.

I'll see what support I can give through the *Massachusetts Review*, through a contact (though this goes back years). Try and scotch this time thing, which is getting out of hand.

The best, Marsy.

[I shall have my say. First a note about that 'colonial' Mancunian, whose early travels south rendered an alien tongue ('bath' to rhyme with 'hath') unintelligible to his school-fellows. Solution: watch the mouth move, and imitate those 1960s' BBC news broadcasters. Now can y' hear me, mate!

I stumbled on Mr Zob's patient advertisement in a barely current issue of *Writers News*. This was left on my desk by Playwright X— in fact a boy of twenty—who, having been handed the palm in a drama competition, now thought of himself as a theatre mogul. His play—*E for Euripides*—was due for its 'world première' at the Riverside Studios. He wanted, he said, an Attic *ambiance*, which to him inferred square columns on pedestals (capitals supporting only that flimsy void under the stage lights). He insisted—he thumped my desktop—on statues with scoured faces, 'preferably' the odd truncated limb. Did I have a monument of Semele? If so how could we rig up a low flame above it? Let me say now that X's *Bacchae*, though vouched authenticity by virtue of period, was peopled by moderns (dialogue vernacular). Dion (Dionysus), a West Indian with shaven head, was the purveyor of amphetamines. His Meanies (or Maenads) were ecstatic with rap (and danced). A magazine astrologer, the amazing Theresa, supplanted the blind seer Teiresias.

'Why,' I asked, 'truncated limbs?'

'Huh?'

'Wouldn't they be pristine, four, five hundred years BC?'

Look! Had I *read* the script! Thankfully no. All I can find on my database is a Cupid, but that's at the Nottingham Playhouse.

I jotted down Zob's box number. I penned, I sent off my joke application. Did I expect to hear (he's a busy man of letters)? No, and gave him no second thought until I did hear.

The conversation we had in his pool hall was over a best of three games, which did, it is true, go to the final black ball. This, naïvely, he potted. As for the light ... it was tasselled. That was in the fringes

103

of its canopy, whence, discretely, it escaped (in a varied dilution of yellow). Here perfectly was Zob's imperfect illumination, to whose glaze I emphasised the soiled nap of his table. 'Successive smokers,' I said, and chalked my cue. With me he bent to those greenish archipelagos, atonal swipes of ground ash. 'I am interested in music,' I said. (What existed, he had asked, other than the written word?) On the question of 'prostitution'—this, merely, is a term in a series: I apply it to a bankrupt school ... I conceive our so-called 'fiction serious' as, well, an abomination, by, and for those, in the van of literary exploitation (which is curiously English). I shall invoke that abstraction, our glumly glibly *status quo*. Few authors (and let us discount certain Labour politicians) have the courage to challenge. Does this not leave your fellow pool players intellectually *in vacuo*? And to talk of society's imbalance: isn't this 'society's' impregnability? I don't see therefore how your elevated tribes and scribes can claim to be socially moved.

He potted a first yellow, calmly: wasn't he after all 'fiction comic', and so exempt? Then, he imagined, he snookered me.

'Let me show you,' I said, 'how to bend a ball ...' Awkward, of course, to cue, just as our human quarks or men of conscience can't with certainty cast their vote. Nevertheless. My stolid white dragged its heels round an interposing yellow. It struck a cushion, struck my object ball, simultaneously. Result: not the pot he'd expected. I allowed him, O ye dumb angels, bearing the professor's footstool, just one more visit to the table. I took that first game, it has to be said without much effort. The second I gave him, only because he bought lunch (egg, cress, warm mayonnaise—somehow sandwiched ineptly in foam).

Now. As for those levitating letters tailing my surname. I cannot legitimate the embossed sheen of a doctorate, the gold plate of a BSc, nor even the albata filigree of a lowly BA. As a short-trousered first-former (I agree, a touch Romantic), I took Browning—'Vanity, saith the preacher, vanity!'—and that ricochet off the book of Ecclesiastes—'... all is vanity'—somewhat to heart. What after all is 'education', but the remorseless hum of commerce? At seventeen I wrote a one-page constitution, governing the life, aim, and ideals of Wye's pantisocracy. The project was doomed, naturally,

depending for its sovereignty on a deserted—and a disintegrating—
cottage, just outside the village (or rather hamlet) of Capel (where I
was known, and where I was loved). That wider kingdom sent in its
head-shaking representatives, blued in uniform. Arguments 'against'
reduced to that minor matter, ownership (our adopted country, or
cottage, belonged to a Medway vicar). The 'discovery' of marijuana
also helped break up our experiment. This was one smoke-filled,
winter afternoon. The sky was, I recall, a blossom pink (as I looked
out, and up, through our weald of arching elms).

I told Zob my qualification was as a computer scientist (which in
terms of my actual purview isn't entirely untrue). I watched him on
that final black, in its equidistance from two corner pockets, and saw
as inevitable the white as it holed itself too. Lucky we didn't bet, eh,
Marsy? Amazingly he sent me for second interview, with Cornelius.

We shall ride, Professor, this heavenly ether again, I am sure.
Signing off for now. AW]

c/o Crispin J. Tucker
University of Pittsburgh
English Dept
Pittsburgh PA 15260
9 June 1992

Dear Marsy,

At last a clear blue sky! No barracking. No flame-bearing guide to
the catacombs (damp under-culture we're pleased to call 'time').
And NO awkward questions. Fact a civilised reception altogether.
Why? Simply I've changed tack, last week delivered my (very old)
paper on Thomas Wolfe (that one, yes: he of the prolix adolescence.
You remember it). And what about this? In a long spell of applause I
found myself presented with a bouquet of lilies, from such a lovely
bridesmaid—all courtesy and violet bows ...

Am hearing too, from Sam, that Giles is involved in a supermarket
deal, with the Château Le Clairiot. What is more, mark, is this: he's
about to buy property—in St John's Wood. It's shocking! Years of
harassed parenting have done something for the boy ...

Let me know what transpires apropos of your *Massachusetts*

Review. Any issue your contact's willing to dispatch will, eventually, reach me (albeit probably through a cascade of forwarding addresses).

There now follows a storm warning, re this Alistair. Never, trust a Nabokovian. The scholar-clown of St Petersburg has put back the social cause of literature by (I don't know how many) decades. Your Bath candidate sounds a good deal more wholesome. Keep me informed. I shall be here for some time—already I've been a sightseer. The Frick office building has white granite exterior walls, with stained glass in main hall (by John La Farge). This represents Fortune at her wheel, I hope a good omen.

Seriously. Give your Alistair a miss.

Yours, Andrew.

[Adieu, dull sprite! AW (with sword)]

Flat 5
147 Trefoil St
SW18
17 June 1992

Dear Andrew,

I can myself consider a house move, now that that first trickle of real money at last curtails those dreary quarterly bulletins. You know, boundaries of overdraft pushed into unknown territory. Dear Mr Zob, I do not recall etc. This has been my own bank manager imitating any other.

The Alistair question's a good deal more amusing than you realise. This is a man who is highly opinionated, yet whose arguments lack formal precision (typically redbrick, about which he's coy). For him the purpose of 'literature' seems to be light entertainment, but of a kind directed to the brain's higher centres. He offered me his discourse over a gladiatorial game of pool, which, after mainly flukes and one or two quite good trick shots, I hadn't the heart to let him lose. I see him as strictly of the industrial class, being quick with—and not much else—science and technology. This has its uses. Not to say how much fun I'll have observing (I love these human studies). But obviously I take your view. For that reason I think I'll let Cornelius give him the once over.

My man at the *Massachusetts Review* says he will publish my brief appraisal of all your academic work to date, which pro tem is the best I can do. I hope this will go some way to put your present tour in perspective.

In the meanwhile, I have this unctuous estate agent—Hoop and Spaghetti and Co.—phoning me with house details every twenty minutes. He doesn't cease to remind me he is also a chartered surveyor.

All the best, Marsy.

[Let us pass over these injurious asides. The laxity in Wye's pool-hall dialectic won't embrace E for Ethics, not today. Snell's solid slice of England offered itself after a square of green lawn, at whose centre a sunken precinct—a blue stone cankered by sun-bleached cement—checked itself in a symmetry of herbal niches. These were for Merle's thyme and oregano, and more lately sage. Tubs—asymmetrically arranged—promised their gift of watered soil mainly for begonias, and slightly less so petunias. A stone hollow on a stone pedestal cupped a nice collection of pine cones (not in so far as I could tell from anywhere close by). In defiance of secateurs, a cotoneaster climbed the porch, where a hint that the Cornelius escutcheon (a copper blaze in oblong) might be overrun, was a thin finger of green as it scratched at a closing parenthesis. There was, intermittently, the scent of honeysuckle. The mat outside said WIPE FEET. The one inside, WELCOME. Merle, who in the preceding moment had admitted her visitor, tapped on Cornelius's office door. She introduced me. I mean to Delilah Scuff. Whose *Farmhouse Recipes* had been a runaway bestseller. She—a notable—had a withered look framing a misanthropic mouth, which contradicted the smooth contours that, I imagine, the world's wistful cooks examined on her dust jackets. Merle and her client went off into conference (the back room with french doors, doors that would open to that pear tree outside, with its satellitic bench). Cornelius—a man avoiding land mines—stepped into the dark hall (too much polished wood). A superficial grin pinned itself to his broad mug. His giant hand ushered me to his office. What, my cherub, my late professor, is left to relate? Cornelius? in an infraction with his internal phone exchange? wanting Merle to bring coffee? No, because finally he walked to the kitchen himself (his handset buzzing, extension lights aglow). Well then. How he reclined in his executive chair? fingertips together? specifically to tell me How in this grave hour of English social history men of Zob's vision are ignored at huge cost. Would be a privilege to work etc.? Or how later we joined 'the girls'? in Delilah's latest celebration (series of six TV kitchen shows, deal by Merle)? I had the supreme honour, Merle having poured and distributed drinks for all but herself, of stirring her Martini (finding myself by the cocktail tray), and setting within it the cherry I lanced. For hark, Professor, and consider fresh evidence (below). I have stolen in at a quiet hour. Into Zob's study. I have plucked a leaf from his business correspondence file. Meaning that—you may never, never trust a Nabokovian. AW]

Snell Literary Agency
12 New Caxton Grove
London NW8 5HL
19 June 1992

Dear Marsy,

Saw your boy today, quite a personable young man. Hung on my every word when high importance of your work was explained. Am sure you'll have no trouble kneading him to fit your purpose.

As you say, seems pretty clued up technologically. Sorted out my phone—that incredibly complicated new exchange I've got. Some of the things it can do!

It so happens we celebrated one of Merle's recent successes: you know, a little lunch time splash. Alistair proved most accommodating in passing out drinks. I think he'll be okay.

I will as I promised phone Maxwell Hayste.

Best wishes, Cornelius.

[Zob had taken a pink highlight pen to that closing pledge, which one could see had been swept with huge deliberation over that important committee name. AW]

July 5. A coincidence, doubly so, whose significance only the passing of time will unveil.

I was feeling, at 10.30, '11 o'clockish'. That impulse welled, to a careless descent of the front stair. Aim, Zob's coconut cookies—which I knew Mrs St John would partake of—if I dispensed. O that crooked smile of hers. At this plain moment—what perversions, discursions, what kinks in those kitchen curtains—the plain Geraldine Crouch honked at the horn of her soft-top, out on what is supposedly the drive, and therefore demilitarised zone. This got Zob up from his chair—study, blinds drawn, desk light on—while not exactly into his flak jacket, certainly on the defensive (their war of the *cognoscenti* sexes). She was frumpy. She was rosy. She was ever-so ever-so posy. Of course, Zob 'hadn't' forgotten their appointment. And, it wasn't hush-hush (though I got the inside patter from a third party). Anyway …

… Zob cast around for keys. Assuming they would go in *his* car. (They did—*she* drove.) Here Geraldine darkened (outdoor, rubiginous), and entertained me, the only onlooker, with true-life stories of suburbia. (She was frumpy, she was scrumpy, she was ever-so ever-so lumpy.) I don't know where she lived, though I gathered not in a house—I imagined Gothic corbels, ivory turrets, broad pearly apartments among Highgate's moonlit mansions. She told me the buck-toothed girl in the garden flat—snub-nose, freckles, ceaselessly up to her elbows in mud—had recently shown her a squirm of leggy tadpoles, each the size of a thumb nail, in a bucket of orange water (now I misquote), in an orange bucket of … yes, seaside bucket … bucket of muddy water. 'With floating mosses.' This being the nub of her city-dweller's *détente* with Nature, she had witnessed tiny frogs, now the size of a small fingernail, a greenish brown, from that same bucket of water—orange, muddy, with floating mosses. 'What a bright kid can teach you,' she said. I crunched my cookie disrespectfully. Fortunately Zob emerged from his door frame, having chanced on his keys, and off they zoomed (she was driving, she was thriving, she was ever-so ever-so blithe-ing).

I phoned Merle. We had lunch. Our first few words in an amazing sub-plot were spoken. But that's not really the point.

I got home in the full flush of my miraculous afternoon (Merle, you accepted my dinner invitation!)—a half-hour prior to Isabelle. She, 'dead' on her feet, slumped in her two-seater, her shiny black shoulder-bag disrupting its riparian pattern of flowers. Her feet, lethargically still shod, extended over one arm. Her drowsy hot head indented the other. 'Make your landlady tea.' Tea I made her. 'These! Pull!' I tweaked off her buckled shoes. I whipped off her ankle socks. I stroked an exploratory hand up her—SHAME, oh Zob's infection! out, vile fiction! Actually I filled the plastic kitchen bowl with a warm froth, and myself drank tea, the first of two lay witnesses in Isabelle's beatification, or the soaking of corns. Just as Michael thrummed in (tennis racquet, rock guitar).

She had been (oh Michael don't) to a private viewing. To prove that was no hoax, she produced a printed card. Which I read. YOU ARE CORDIALLY INVITED &C. TO AN EXHIBITION OF 'ART OBJECTS' &C. BY THE 'VISUAL BLOCK-BUILDER AND [assorted epithets]' NEWSOME BARRINGER, who was from Phoenix, AZ. This had taken place at premises in Soho. 'Funnily your boss was there,' she said, 'with that, you know, that what's-its-name. Always on TV.'

'Crouch.'

'Uh?'

Relax, my pink-ankled dunkle. 'Geraldine Crouch.'

'Yes. Her.'

'What was it like?'

'How do you mean?'

'The exhibition. What was it like?'

'Oh, that.' Apparently lousy. The centrepiece was an enlarged human skull, got up with zonal streets, pendulous lights, midnight cars—all emblematic of the Western City.

'That sounds a gas,' I said.

July 6. Drove up, not particularly early, through the yawning street where Zob lived. Next door, that liver surgeon, whose life to me was bleary and insubstantial, had got himself in a flap with his wife's dipstick. Buy her these toys, what does she do!

Parked alongside Geraldine's soft-top, where on the sumptuous back seat I saw Volume 2 of her memoirs, whose catchy subtitle is: *I go up to Oxford*. That car, and that car's autobiography section, wasn't there when I stepped out for a walk at noon, though I hadn't heard her go (hadn't heard her at all).

July 7. A note from Zob on the kitchen table. Dear Mrs Clapp— Don't, repeat don't, do my bedroom today—which had that good peon in a puzzle all morning. Bedroom-wise he was generally 'most p'ticular'. I wondered what order of gymnastic apparatus Geraldine, now living out her Volume 3, had left there. (She was spacious, not curvaceous, she was ever-so ever-so voracious.)

July 8. I reproach my Englishness. That, in its aptitude for comedy, is naturally feeble on stilts out on its pier-end, and I see—from my personal book of histories—transforms itself no more successfully when put in the open air. What is a sideshow? (Who asked me that question?) I shall try to be brief (trying to give an answer). Here, look, are my painted clowns—let's call it a trio. Enter, platform left—this is a raised structure, glued together on the paved outskirts of insanity (location douched in a criss-cross of light) ... 1), my trumpeter in big red shoes—to put an occasional leap in that shilly-shally gait. Those are his trousers—baggy, black/white checks, bouncing in a panta-balloon, almost approximately at the waist (his dotty braces). Fanfare, please, as that announces 2), solemn and whey-faced, the bearer of my single snow-petalled rose. Should I, ye that are curious, scent its fragrance now, I would find that yuk, it squirts water. (Ha-ha!) Finally 3)—a pierrot—just look at those pompons! Huge! And what's that, a platter? With a card, and inscription?
Merle O Merle. Regardez. Pierrot's platter. That is, that was, for you.

July 9. I possess—proudly, as a confirmed dupe, lashed to that turning wheel called Capital—an antique address book (I exaggerate. It's twelve years old. Or no more than thirteen. Possibly fourteen). This goes back to my time in King's Langley, or to be perfectly frank, at a backwater there, known—I think this is right—

111

as the K. L. Western Meditation Centre. Hold on to your chair leg. There IS a point to this story. I digress out of courtesy.

I was, personally, an inmate—not, you understand, in any ordinary arrangement. What those sandalled, shiny pated elders—the serenely robed of that institution ... what they wanted (because business was good) was this: a computerised booking system. They could not afford, they said, investment in expensive time-sharing. Nor could they consider the purchase of equipment. This meant selecting, liaising, and finally co-operating with, a suitable bureau. They wanted, specifically, my services. At interview I suppose I came across as neither smirking nor poker-faced (the two kinds of sceptic they knew). Nor were they surprised when I negotiated principally by barter. I would take, week by week, cash for expenses—while at the same time I fancied, I said, a break from routine. Retreat to these wooded knolls, these dewy brakes, these diminished tracts of rural England. Of course, 'so-called' civilisation (as for brief weeks I came to refer to it), was not that far away (the railway nearby, Euston to Milton Keynes, and God-knew-what in the world beyond. There was a golf course. A particularly rancid stretch of the canal. There was, as everywhere, insipid commercial property. There was also my address book). I do, I know, digress.

I had the privilege of induction—this, with a fresh wave of 'students', from as far afield as Smethwick. This was with our shaven guru, quite a youngish man, whose interpretation of Capitalism was from strictly the lotus position. I shall paraphrase. Capitalism—which one may scarcely regard as a 'philosophy'—was a system doomed never to penetrate the surface gloss of our cosmos. It involved immense pains on the part of its ministers (in this sense political), merely in the co-ordination of resources (meaning persons), whose goal was nationhood (which translates to: the uneven distribution of, importantly power, importantly wealth). Individuals were afforded no profounder reality than that. I confess, that for all my attempts, which gained no more than a semi-whole (or a wrestler's half-lotus) ... the fragmenting parts in my 'personal', and as it followed 'more meaningful' reality, could never transcend their great vaulted roof, never mind consider atmospheric views of the railroad. Nevertheless. I pressed on with the bureau (and found one, back of Oxford St). The system—the Capitalistic system—that I finally delivered, involved form-filling, dispatch to the punch centre, daily program runs, weekly plus *ad hoc* reporting (*ad hoc* being in response to a phone call). I did learn in exchange, and I quote, that: 'Life—is a mystery'. Nor did I surrender my worldly address book. Which IS the point (promise).

The manufacturers (of that address book) had kindly inserted an index of restaurants (with cinemas, cinema clubs, music venues). Yesterday—before I knew I'd summoned those clowns (it will, it will be explained)—my animated pointer—one of those ball-nibbed, disposable pens—quivered—in the detection as it were of desert water—finally magnetised itself to these few exotic entries under 'M' ... Ma Cuisine. Mes Amis. Mon Plaisir. Ludicrously—because after twelve, thirteen, fourteen years, did they exist?—these were the names I offered up to Merle, on a comic platter. There now. I think that about wraps it up. Inscrutably—that is to say without irony—the bright Merle or pearl of my life rallied with a counter-suggestion. At the same time insisting (pleasantly) that I did not wear those beige slacks, which after several hours of duty tended to whole oceans of crests and adumbrated creases. (Endless apologies. I think I'm in love.) She lived, Alistair, with unforgettable desires, she was refulgent—while in the gold nimbus of her own recollection, my golden girl described, Alistair, or I should say improvised, Alistair, lyrics. No. I will say she sang me an Oriental house front. [Get thee, tired critic, to a bunnery. I repeat, bunnery. Don't tell me this is all impossible. That is merely your fatigue. Get thee to a bummery, you reviewing newspaper hack—I repeat, bummery. I, am in love.]

Her little Chinese shanty had maroon pilasters enwrapped in painted green dragons. Its chairs were rickety. But the Yam cakes divine. And, Al, her recommended Hung Shao chicken was, well, an experience. And why was it our short smiling waiter lit us a candle? And served us coconut egg rolls, compliments, with that finalising pot of perfumed tea? Exquisitely, in that contention for the bill, our fingers intertwined briefly. My map shows me we were in the aerial ken of Eros, should he fly (no farther north than the south canopies of Carnaby St, through which we later walked). A gaucho in a broad-brimmed hat strode in off the lapis-lacquered street. He

113

pressed me to his roses, singletons in heart-spotted cellophane. Music, please, a violin, something Brahmsian, gypsy! 'I will,' I said, 'have that snow-petalled one.' Then a few streets away, Extasis—a night spot—where we sat on padded bar stools, under a tropical awning. Here in secret we hatched our clever professional plot, which at this point I'm sure you'll understand I can't divulge. We drank a coconut cocktail. Then I unzipped my cardigan. Then, Pulcinella, we danced. The night away.

July 10. Dawn. Some daimon in my club coffee (Turkish, is not the explanation), has had me bowling in a Bacchic mummery, on the grey pavements just off Monmouth St. I recall that the black cab, which resolved itself to a shiny cabbage green—as that thing responded to my dumb show, plodding to the kerb—advertised stranger transport on its passenger door: viz., the mobile sandwich (with an inner city number). The sour, cabbage-soup cabby, wasn't pleased to take us to the suburbs, where over the horizon of his dash (the back of his head, nodding) he complained when I opened my door—'into' the line of traffic (traffic!) … Which, looking, was a solitary jogger, pounding the gully thirty, thirty-five yards in his mirror. Well, there goes his tip! I paid when he'd set us down, but even so did not escort my new business partner, my Merle, to the lattice of her door (the mosaic of a leaded sunset). That's because there was, at a slant from her bathroom window, in the flap of her neighbour's washing line, a dewy triangle of uncut grass, supporting …

… one pair of rubberised swings, a tyre on a chain in a frame, a silver slide, three concrete cylinders (two for base, one for vertex), (in the shape of a bison's antlers) a seesaw …

… where in the glory of her adulthood, I swung, rocked, 'assisted' her through the park. All is, she instructed, play. My tensile grin, when later I shuffled to my own door, passed on that simplified information—to of all people Isabelle, no doubt resuming that Sunday liaison, and whose damned Malkin mewed at me in the hallway. Now I do feel exhausted (hope she puts that rose in water) …

114

July 11. Geraldine's soft-top again, and this time her morning face, when she showed it round the kitchen door. 'Marsy would like coffee taken up,' she said. So. I made another, in that mug whose design is the unstoppable ascent of six red, and only one plum-coloured balloon, all threads dangling. Geraldine left with her briefcase, having deposited certain large wear in Zob's attractive Ali Baba laundry basket.

Zob, bored and argumentative, later replayed Part 5 in his radio masterclass, which the design team shamelessly titled *Art of Fiction*. The whole series having been broadcast after that surprising, and belated success of *Aristotle*. Today's lesson—again, and again, and again—was: Characterisation. Here was Zob's five-hinged framework on to which you stretched the fabric of a dreamed-up or fictive persona. 1) Think of a name (amazing how that simple act is decisive psychologically). 2) Appearance: is your invention dark-, light-haired, a redhead? 3) Dress. Someone always in a business suit is not of course someone always in sloppy strides and a sweatshirt. 4) Gestures/mannerisms. Once established, are pretty reliable, announcing your hero's return to the action. Instance my own Steven Kiff, that swagger from the jeaned hips when he walks the west London streets. 5) Dialogue. Cannot be underestimated. Compare: 'My dear chap'/'Oi! You!'

Here is my own quintuplicate, a five-fold, quintessential opposition, where I disagreed with our 'master', condemning these as only the superficial vestments of personality, what I should later term the obligatory notation in popular forms of story-telling. 'She swept back that wild gypsy hair. He, with his strong arm, held her back from the cliff-edge', belongs, untransplantably, to the filmic deceits of narrative, which you, Zob, have corrupted to a purpose— what your friendly reviewers call 'literary intent'. But this is mechanistic. And belongs to that vacant hour of early evening soap (of which Zob is the middle-brow equivalent). How then, he asked, would I deal for example with a heroine? Well, Marsy, I should not confer anything so trite as a 'gesture', which is after all a motor function replicated *ad nauseam*. She might I think be a ghostly presence, whose streaming dark locks are notional, as I swing her on a child's swing (say). Whose smile is of pearls and rubies, as I try to catch at her wrist, the 'author' giving chase through a triplet of hoops (fumbling for my notebook). Her voice might also be a reed, a sympathetic oboe (one that I insist is seldom given to the rough and tumble the trade terms dialogue). A levitated presence, whose sole vestige (unfashionable now) is her creator's metaphysical goal, and does not belong in that realm of simulating cut-outs, so patiently folded away, as the hack, writer or romancer approaches the closing paragraph of his 'book'.

'Good fiction,' I said, 'once it's been opened, lets out one genie at least. Impossible to re-stopper.'

'Are you telling me, Al, I don't write good fiction?'

'It doesn't float. It doesn't dress its silks—doesn't abstract that place called readerdom, through the hard folds of reality.'

'This is fanciful.'

'Precisely. That is, by definition, fiction.'

'I think I can see, Al, why I'm the writer, why you're not.'

'I think I can too.'

July 12. Mrs St John, untypically succinct as to Zob's shammed world of aesthetics, it transpires has suggested, indirectly, through Adam, an assorted configuration of garden flares. This is for the terrace party—dinner for four—that I now learn Zob has got planned for later this week. Adam, who in general can't be trusted to missions in diplomacy, has, I am astonished to learn, made of this a first representation to the 'marster'. More to the point. As reward he shows off (I say this emblematically) the yellow, beribboned medallion so recently pinned on his overalled chest. That is why, on the kitchen table, there is now a potted coleus, on whose variegated leaves (a ruddy brown, fringed with green) Mrs St John exudes syllables so ineptly. Being, as Adam's gift, the first such coleus she's come to possess (it likes the light, he advised). Zob remarked on it only when she, and it, had gone.Geraldine—grumpy, stumpy, ever so plumpy—dropped in for an hour-long 'minute', the time taken to retrieve a document, that, as it turned out, had slipped behind Zob's goodnight TV (bedroom). Zob, whose created characters were 'substantial', did what he could to transcend this (I think embarrassing) episode.

116

Cornelius, driving back from repairs to an erratic screen-washer—
if it rained, it worked, if dry, it wouldn't—gave us the news and
authenticating obituary that had understandably escaped us. That is
to say, our Emeritus Professor, once of Exe, had dutifully expired—
on the final, and unspluttered phoneme, of a haiku:

> how in the quiver
> of a dragonfly's wing, words,
> ah, here where I—

May I suggest the appropriating 'ping'? Though 'sing', and the
violation of rhyme, are probably what that (at last) daring rule-
breaker had in mind. Snell's broadsheet obituarist, for whom we
may invent a soliloquy,

> how in the quiver
> of a dragonfly's fang, words,
> ah, here where I—

'clang', 'bang', 'harangue' … Or suppose we erase 'fang', and
choose something like 'dragonfly's eye', which leads us plausibly
to: 'here where I lie' … 'Lie', of course, meaning that style of things
common to Master Zob's Circus, to deal in untruths … But don't let
me keep you … Who gave us testament was none other than
Masturbile, naturally in one of those reactionary papers (Snell's
daily).

This was a quaint piece of sophistry, whose attempted artifice had
of course been well rehearsed (cp. any review of any piece by Zob).
Sole ingredient is, one of the world's elect. 'Tissue', as package,
wraps itself up on 'champion of the people'—'people' conforming
to all properties of a colourless vapour. One merely imagines it
enveloping our globe. This, you'll note, is 'high-class' journalism.
(These, that I draw attention to, are watchwords—not mine.)
Therefore. What did Philip say of our dead professor? Or how shall
I get out of this maze? Well. The professor had many distinguished
cronies while up at Oxford. This was that 'difficult' time, the
Forties. This explains why so much, frankly commonplace

'material' (a cubic yard of undergraduate verse), wound its way from that young, and self-esteemed pen—which was prone to discharge, furthermore in unpredictable turquoise—to so many prestigious journals. Here we were quoted something in full, the tedious account of 'Under Cover Glover', dying with his binoculars inconveniently on a remote border. Remember. These were the days of the professor's 'dynamism', when he had not yet metamorphosed to a hobbit (and whose style prompts my *docteur* to pronounce a bad case of Bloomsbury).

Alas. Those 'connections' formed no automatic circuit—electric and eclectical—to celebrity. This, I shall remind you, is Masturbile's terminology, which I decline to take issue with here. Because. 'Irresponsibly'. 'Younger.' And 'lesser' poets. 'Bright', 'deviant', 'working-class' boys. From the shires. Who in golden times pursued professional cricket (as a possible career). Found themselves lauded in print, to the partial eclipse of our middle-earther. Just when the mantle of public acceptance seemed a formality. What could he do? Um, well, two things, according to Masturbile. He could, and did become, an Orientalist. And he might try much of that inferior verse as is touted in school anthologies. You know. Those dreary evocations. The dun granite of a man's mind, possessing, oxymoronically, mesmeric powers to repel. In the terrors of our own times, this is developed in The Rise of Zob—which regrettably doesn't belong to the annals of science fiction. That, I shan't stress, is not Masturbile's opinion. Unlike him I cringe. Unlike, too, I pass over our professor's practically worthless, and parallel career, in the sheltered porch of academe. I force, urge, condition my resumption, where he, Masturbile, could close, with, dishonestly, that touching reference, to the professor's other life—I mean as miniaturist—'perhaps the finest these isles have known'. A claim I greet irresistibly with sceptical hilarity. Our deceased hobbit was found in his hobbit hole, poised, or rather slumped, over a bamboo table-top, by his friend and colleague Fiona Trethowan (finally alarmed that his phone had not been answered in two days). 'Nobly', Professor Bilbo, man of 'great academic integrity', was found, 'even at the last', in the spell of his muse (a freckled girl I envisage with a lollipop). Here, friends, simple genius, a very last, summery exhalation—

> how in the quiver
> of a dragonfly's wing, words,
> ah, here where I—

'zing', was Masturbile's speculation, conferring perhaps a timely harp.

'Here,' said Snell. 'Keep it,' and got up to go. 'I see Al's really interested. Hope you've got your dinner party organised. Merle's really looking forward to it.'

Zob said he had, and avoided my quizzical gaze.

July 13. A first, and last, rehearsal. I am glad it's not Friday (superstitiously speaking). Zob drew up his leathern sofa, which someone, Geraldine, had saddled with a woolly poncho, so that its rest—in every other sense an atrabilious shade of pea—was centred by a knitted chain—those tangentially interlocking ovals—whose pattern of rose and cobalt had been folded in a V. The short-skirted Merle sat at one end, in the style of a teenage brunette. Zob at the other, in the majestic pose, co-ordinator. Typographically, or topographically, or in a more objective analysis, geographically, I, with my open copy, *Gimme the Cash*, stood behind her, clutching— and this time pornographically—a coolly imagined tube (of one of those visceral lubricants). For an Ambrose, I needn't change my voice—which, correction, certainly isn't colonial, and isn't Tunbridge Wells. Cornelius, a less likely Kiff, outside of money-talk had not a lot to say, which inhibited the perfection of his dialect. Then of course the whole thing couldn't proceed without debate, to which my following sketch alludes:

AMBROSE: This, my pet, is your *annus mirabilis*, and is established. You'd like as it were to renegotiate terms. Yes?

WYE: Obviously I understand *annus mirabilis* as a pun (as,

119

incidentally, the kind I, Wye, would make). What 'is established' isn't clear.

ZOB: You'll suspect me, Al, of modelling Ambrose on you.

[Slight murmurs of laughter]

WYE: Nevertheless …

ZOB [to Merle]: Be a sweetie. Run through that last line again.

BRUNETTE: Cor blimey mate wotchya think I am!

ZOB [to Wye]: Now you.

AMBROSE: This, my pet, is your *annus mirabilis*, and is established. You'd like as it were to renegotiate terms. Yes?

CORNELIUS: Al, it's so clear. Anyone can see.

[Wye still not convinced]

ZOB: No?

MERLE [side of head to poncho]: Ah! Got it! What's established is what she is—a whore …

ZOB: Though as she learns, Al, that coition is in fact going to be anal …

MERLE: … she'll want to up terms.

KIFF: Aw for fuck's sake!

ZOB: Not yet, Cornelius.

SNELL: Sorry.

ZOB [to Wye]: You happy with that?

WYE: Ecstatic.

July 14. Mrs Clapp, in the transient role I have had to invent, is to me one of those boundless underlings so courteously summoned to the Holmesian detective agency, with domestic brief. I know, Watson, that that dinner party took place here, last night. Good Lord, Holmes! What leads you to that? Instance these garden flares, charred at the flame end. I calculate these sputtered out in the grey hour of dawn. Then these longish corks, that have escaped the majority fate (the bin) and litter the terrace. I have, too, an inkling as to the guest list. Crouch, as was fairly usual nowadays, we crossed on the threshold, as I walked in to work. Merle (because the walrus let that sacred name slip). But duty, Mrs Clapp. Duty. The dining room crumbles in an effluvial, an accentuated air (time and the world heap our bismotered crockery). There is I observe low tide in the gravy tureen. Why yes. Someone did gather the cutlery. Unfortunately shoved it, handles down, in that fine Florentine piece, so distinctive a wine cooler, such is the style of Italian terracotta. Now what's that you've got on that indignant tray—that's right— there among those smeary glasses? A Rolex, you say. Now who do I know would leave behind his Rolex? Thinks ...

July 15. Thinks, Sherlock Wye ...

July 16. Thinks ... what an itch this is—surreptitiously speaking— now as that testing hour is here (thinks). It has found me, having taxied not only Zob, but the walrus too, in a vibrant South Bank foyer, where in the shallows of pre-performance the unruffled, unruffable Merle, reclines in a low-backed chair, sipping coffee with an attentive Justin Simms. To whom Zob restores the Rolex (no more thinks). Polite smiles. Re-introductions. Cornelius does not suspect a conspiracy, and even I'm sure flatters himself (as I measure that Cheshire grin), that the teenage brunette (I mean of course the short-skirted Merle) may attract the marketable Simms. Not as I fear. But into the protected twilight. Under a darkling wing.

Into the commercial poison of Snell's 'literary' agency.

Forgive me, my people, for this was all my, Wye's, idea. My perception was, over the fidgety heels, the nodding heads, that our performance began in a hollow, and quickly gathered too much pace. Zob, as is his usual inclination publicly, sought the authority of a basso, somewhere in a passing cloud. I, as he, doff to that vain meteorological confection, whose injunction is we supplant the depressions of self-apology, so often, Cornelius assures, the 'burthen' of genius. It didn't matter to me. Though I was bitterly affronted, wanting above all to reach our co-ordinated finis, when a Whitehouse heckler, on the stroke of my *annus*, stood up and interjected. 'Filth!'

'... *annus*,' I continued.

'More damn filth!'

To which, a concerted *shoosh!*

It did not take long to eject him—because he went quietly (so young to be so zealous. I wondered, did that boy even shave?). Zob—having at last learned the dignified stance of greatness—left it to the martyr Cornelius to re-settle our throbbing audience (to me just a Cubist's dissection, of eyes, noses, tufts of hair), and re-start our recital. Afterwards, at the book-signing, I pulled out of boxes and opened for Zob's abeyant pen, in excess of one hundred copies (oh, my! One hundred stooges, gambolling off through the reflected ripple of that wise brown river, the Thames).

There is a footnote, divorced, as you see (a blank horizon, an uncertain space on the page), demarcated from my Saturday 16th. White chasm, above, denotes hindsight. Since strictly this is an appendix, and belongs to a later time. (I have, for a floating fourteen days, lived in the padded glow that comes with a publisher's advance. A sum so thoughtfully negotiated on my behalf by the constant Merle, who is now engaged, and quite rightly proud of her new topaz. This is worn on her maiden finger.) I am in a stone cottage, with my standard lamp on, under a southerly spur of Dartmoor. I am reviewing, revising these pages.

That 'heckler', I have learned (from the all-knowing Merle), was an implant, carefully, and secretly arranged by Snell. He phoned the said agency. This was several days after the press furore, the intended consequence to that publicly enacted show of indignation, though on this occasion indignation was genuine. That fresh-faced youngster didn't much appreciate the elasticated cheque Cornelius had written for his trouble. Merle had to phone him back, having investigated (because of course Snell was out at some book launch or bistro). For some reason his emolument was paid from a suspension account (highly irregular), so that is why the cheque had been stopped. 'I will ensure,' she had said, 'that Herr Snell gets you another cheque off asap.'

Incidentally that topaz is set in a starburst of diamonds. But. However. Meanwhile. Those raggy tabloids, whose shared olfaction is often infallible, had the spices of prurience in its collective nosethirles. A 'story' had 'reluctantly' appeared, several square feet from the photogenic udders of student, model, and playgirl Cindy, whose profile throughout the summer was (delightfully) in silky high heels, and, coolly, a string. This described our four-pronged recital, which, in that handy currency popular with newsmen, ended in 'near riot'. A gaggle of cameramen planted their tripods at the extremes of Zob's drive. Reporters with hand phones rang, knocked at the door, solicited comment. In the end I struck a deal, which, having declared it 'a bargain', these moral folk of Wapping stuck to. That is, I read out a statement (in fact a disclaimer), with the taciturn Zob cemented to the doorstep behind me, his arms folded. I am tickled to report that 'spokesman Wye' was quoted in subsequent issues, with one or two choice, and elaborated sentences, from that driveway manifesto. It provided also, as they say, a photo-opportunity. My own handsome features have brightened a muddy corner of certainly one gossip column, as a complement to that used-car-seller's look, so intrinsically the characteristic in Zob's public image.

Cornelius advised that sales increased significantly at about this time.

July 18. Zob's, a whole life honed to communication—

From his home

A Mr Drone
Has dialled us on his telephone—

a life nonetheless prodigal—

It's lax, very lax,
Zob's ignored another fax—

is as well a life plugged to its ears, over our heads somewhere
among Alpine bells:

Our medium's fibre-optic,
Yet might as well be Coptic

(for all the attention he paid). I disposed of Drone—a salesman—
without those usual lies of etiquette, i.e. v. impolitely, because no, I
could not (understand?) bear to talk 'replacement windows', which
he insisted thermo-efficient households must nowadays acquire. The
fax I was more than happy to intercept, being electronically doused
in Merle's hypnotic fragrance. Cannily she imparted that the rough
beast—not only as it slouched, but bore itself to Bethlehem (all
under solar flares)—was, millennially, the 'investigative' journalist.
She had just 'talked' to one on her office phone, and so was able to
warn of his fraternity, that caravan about to decamp to the oasis of
Zob's caravanserai, or neutral pavement. Click.

Infuriatingly, nor could Zob be bothered with that puerile chime of
his door bell. Eventually I answered it. Ah—a commercial traveller,
I assumed. He on the porch mat—thinnish, twenty-five-ish, wiry
hairish—did not exactly deny this. His grip—broken, I saw, at the
zipper … Though it bulged, this was not to the strain of unsold
gadgetry (nor kitchen, nor garage). What he wanted to sell me, so
unalloyed his faith—in, impossibly, the largesse of the cultured
Hampsteadite—was a collection of thirty 'poems'. This he had gone
to the trouble of printing privately. I must warn, I said, that my
litmus is generally acid, all the same I opened its yellow covers.
'Honest work,' I went on, 'which puts it at a disadvantage.' Mood—
was the central fault, which belonged to the *belle époque*. I gave him

a few pound coins, being some way short of the price he asked. 'Mr Zob,' he said, 'I appreciate your frankness.' There, I pointed out, was his second mistake. To all intents Zob wasn't at home. 'Anyway he'll comment only on the work of immediate rivals.' If he didn't mind, I'd been detained for long enough, though of course I returned to the drudgery, of Glaze's correspondence—with that accustomed lack of zeal.

Remember how I soaked poor Isabelle's tired feet? Well ...

c/o Crispin J. Tucker
University of Pittsburgh
English Dept
Pittsburgh PA 15260
28 June 1992

Dear Marsy,

Dr Tucker has a delightful daughter, which one lustful cynic (a medic) puts down to—now how does he put it?—'her famous silicone implants'. Doubtless the poor girl, under the pressure of smallness—in every sense this is a vast, and overwhelming country—was actually compelled, to amplify her cleavage. (Truly this is a market for your books, Marsy.) It appears she's the star student in a recently revised creative writing course, which at first glance seems better than most. She's about to embark on her dissertation. Not surprisingly, the work of my lecture tour could be of value. I have agreed to make certain extracts—some I believe quite challenging—available to that process, on condition she discuss a fellowship (because, silicone or no, Exe demands the highest calibre, and I need more researchers).

Dr Tucker himself has had both professional and personal contact with the visual block-builder, Newsome Barringer, a deeply tanned native of Arizona, and, I might add, an awesomely confident man. His *Golgotha 2000*—a 'masterpiece' of postmodernism—was at a private showing, here on the plush fifth floor (glass, aluminium, plastic) of a life assurance firm, who as investors (and promoters) in his work, are certainly his major sponsor. The said piece, *Golgotha*, is said to be a 'staggering' achievement, which sadly knows no

125

counterpart in contemporary writing (with the possible exception of certain descriptive interlocks found in your own *Aristotle*). *Golgotha 2000*, a hypertrophied, human cranium, is intended, on close examination, as that familiar, and replicated patchwork, the modern American city. You can see streets, the lights, the cars. The whole is encapsulated in a fluorescent green glow.

Barringer, over a fleeting handshake, assured me that all exhibits would at some point come to, a-hem, 'Lon'on, England'. So, if you have the chance, be sure not to miss it. Because, Marsy, that would be a pity.

Mercifully this 'time' question seems to have subsided. Thanks again for your support. I have had to field several off-the-record queries (the most intelligent from Penny Tucker, naturally), and happily all have been at the core of my theory. Sunny days, I hope.

Signing off, Andrew.

I can, with a hoaxer's privilege, correct one misapprehension—and only one.

The phony Barringer finds me magnanimous. I am (my star shall also rise) prepared to leave his stunted cave work—those rudimentary acts of discourse—with the mindless enthusiasm of our Anglo-Saxon supplements. That's where the *Golgotha* sample caught my eye, over a much more alluring breakfast egg. I am, as I say, magnanimous.

But. My hoaxer's privilege is also the satin of time, whose shimmering skirts, as the wearer strides on, discover our recent yesterdays. Let me propose, as I check out certain items (this via the universal properties department), the action of three discrete clocks, each consistent with theoretical relativity. What cosmic pyrotechnics shall I envisage (or reflect on), when Glaze's dated missives form a symmetry with mine, these entries in my journal? All right. I accept. While *his* June approaches *my* July, our changing day and month name may, just may, correspond. Our year never will. So. Permit, please, my third timepiece, a projection into that floating fourteen days, where I live in the padded glow that comes with a publisher's advance. A sum, you'll recall, so thoughtfully negotiated—cleverly on my behalf—by the constant Merle—engaged, yes, proud of her topaz, and rightly so. I am in a stone cottage, with the winged light of my standard lamp washing a timbered wall. I am under a southerly spur of Dartmoor. I am reviewing, revising these pages. 'Time', or that question of, would not, I can now say from my vantage, allow Professor Glaze off its general hook.

Did Marsy really care? You be the judge.

Flat 5
147 Trefoil St
SW18
8 July 1992

Dear Andrew,

I knew you'd sort it. Really it's down to that way you have of not standing for nonsense. Bravo.

I'm going to upset you. These conflicts with modernity put the decision against the golden girl—Miss Clean from Bath. Yes. I've gone for the technician, Alistair. Because I'm tempted to tackle something sci-fi. You know. One of those turgid, futuristic things. He'd make good material. So I hope he lasts that long. Though I've a feeling the real world of books will be a jolt. A blip in his microchips.

My man from Spaghetti and Hoop keeps driving me up Haverstock Hill, and points to the mansions lived in by rock stars. O what illustrious company. Seen one or two things I like. What chance you getting back for the house-warming?

Onward. Upward. Marsy.

Clocks one, two: all movement suspended. Clock three, a quartz, tockle me a heraldee across my firmament. To re-announce, verbatim, what?

> Time's abundance,
> A maze of intersecting lines.
> Zob, his doorbell's profundance:
> Can any bright note out-ring that author's
>   sultry chimes?

... is not the right sequence. I'm tired, and my mind has strayed (to that wiry poet, with his yellow book it seems). More coffee, I think.

Yes. That is better. Now, 'time', for the duration of—what shall we call it?—editorial interlude?—is as accords with quartzy clock three (but only for this interlude). That puts us in Dartmoor, after the death of Glaze. And after the death of Zob, metaphorically. It was he, actually—my unwitting master—who suggested this stone cottage. Its little square panes, set off wonderfully in its solid casements, offer so uncluttered a view of the constellated plough, those studs of varying brilliance in the clear canopy of night ... Forsooth! I detect that yellow poet, back with his wiry book ... A third cup of coffee ... Must try to stay awake ...

Now. Let's run that again. It was Geraldine's idea, whose peremptory exclamation—'Wouldn't it be lovely! Property! I mean round here!—betrayed the timbre of slight premeditation. We later discovered, over a patio table (my notebook records the White Hart, Dartington, Devon) that a firm called Stags had furnished her with printed details of several isolated dwellings. She drank, I recall, a glass of iced rum. Zob, having bought, but showing no thirst for his continental lager, shuffled those stag-emblazoned photographs (predictable logo) under the deep, cigar-shaped shadow of our parasol. Again, the feminist Crouch fingered, mulled it over, longed, she said, while the sun caressed her sandalled foot, for a look at this one (here where I pen my editor's notes), on the peripheral slopes of Dartmoor (south). A handwritten addendum, or rather vortex in ballpoint, confirmed that while the vendor sought a buyer, short lets 'might' be considered. I drove them over—not in the silver Mercedes, but while they canoodled—a riot of limbs in my resisting rearview—in Geraldine's open soft-top (white hood, grey flashing). We found the garden overgrown, yet having potential (as, execrably, I paraphrase the blurb). Sole heating was a multi-fuel burner, a black monstrosity monopolising the irregularly shaped sitting-room (rectangle, one corner sliced by a diagonal, on whose far side 'downstairs facilities' had been added). Zob could smell damp, Geraldine only honeysuckle. He said—or did he ruminate?—that as brilliant London writer, now wasn't the time for country retreats. Though ... although ... it was very quiet here ... 'perfect' for

128

revision work.

I could go on, about the money—no problem there. The beaches, so near, yet to Zob anathema! He, our pale metropolitan, fried in the sun. Then there were the walks brrrng! I said the walks brrrng!

Time tells me clocks pressing one and two will supersede. Away, quartz three!

c/o Maura Grimm
Dept of English
Bowling Green State
University
Bowling Green OH 43403
17 July 1992

Dear Marsy,

Regrets re Miss Clean, not that I remember her—though I do recall, on numerous occasions, the question have I been to Cadiz. I haven't.

Make sure this Alistair doesn't overstep his brief. It's fine if you want a techno-sphere, complete to its man with screwdriver. Electronic self-promotion—if that's what you have an eye to—is perhaps only an adjunct for those already in print, and anyway that should be left to your publisher, who is (I understand) clued up to these things.

I worry about the Nabokov element (must be by definition subversive). That *blagueur*, who got lucky with his nymphet, was never in the sense that we understand a professional. It makes him so appealing to outsiders, who so easily accuse us, at the cutting edge, of lacking any principle—expediency that gets books into bookshops. I ask, how else do unacknowledged legislators, legislate?

I'm not sure too—I have NO wish to sermonise—that a foray into the swamps of sci-fi is, for you, advisable. Your genius is pure, is so much—and without apparent effort—the crystal analysis of England in the here and now. You would need, I think, to understand madmen like Hawking, whose chapter, 'The Arrow of Time' (because that whole question has re-surfaced), was brought to my attention. (In no way was this done combatively. The student endowed, who attended my lecture, approached me after the event,

129

and asked if I saw parallels between 'the cosmologist's view' and my own.) My conclusion is this. The futuristic novel is dead. That is because: to the layman, contemporary science is, in all important aspects—inaccessible.

By the way. Penelope Tucker, who could not help pressing her implants to my elbow, asked me to do a piece for her quarterly review (she is joint editor). The essay I have just mailed her is entitled: 'Marshall Zob, First Man of English Letters'. Hope this helps to raise your profile Stateside. The market here's enormous, if you can tap in.

The best for a red-hot house-warming. Shall be there in all but the flesh. Andrew.

No comment—despite the insistent alarum, which, on the flimsiest strand of midnight, my quartz clock three interjected with. It was later, while I watched its thin fingers jointly overshadow a long Roman I, that I abandoned my MS, tossing it into the hollows of my rented sofa, thence clattered up the wooden stair to bed. This morning it is grey. My copper-green ashtrays, full from the night before, I see have discovered new and incredible niches. All my north windows, whose complex is multiple—variant angles on to a single vista, the moor—open to its distant verd-antique, still tonsured by the dawning mist. Those tufted blades of grass, in the fringes of my garden—of what prophecy a wilderness?—arc to the pendent glue in the ensnared, yet inexorably earthbound droplets of dew. Shall I beat an egg for breakfast, or simply break bread? Then there is one other, and important point to debate: shall I renew my depleted pack of cigarettes right now (that means a drive), or sharpen the red crayon of my trade—(where did I leave that MS)? Where?

An hour's work. Then the drive.

Flat 5
147 Trefoil St
SW18
28 July 1992

Dear Andrew,
Tucker. I know that name. Did Crispin J. once do a piece for

Blandford? Or was that Tusker? (Maybe not.)

Don't worry about Alistair. My technician doesn't in any case start till I move—and on that, there's delay. That's because, I've landed the first couple in London whose conveyancer—ought to sign himself 'Pedant', from Edmonton—is determined NOT to exchange. Question: Can I provide evidence of damp-proofing? Answer: No. This is a first-floor flat. Question: Well, if not rising, penetrating. Counter-Q: Have you read your clients' surveyor's report? Answer (intransigent): Evidence of all precautions taken against a propensity to penetrating damp must be supplied. Answer to answer: My own surveyor, on *my* purchase of property, did not draw attention to that problem.

I'm sure we'll fathom similar pleasantries re timber infestation.

Can't agree, Andrew, with your assessment apropos of sci-fi genre. If (big if) I went that way, I couldn't be bothered with Hawking. I think I would—in fact I've started to do this—absorb the 'culture'. You know. Take my cue from others in that field. Books. Movies. A glance at the fanzines.

Method. That's the real science.

All the best. Marsy.

It is to do with my three clocks that I denounce, categorically, that commercialised decade—my recollection is of assassinations and a moon-landing—whose easy, terrestrial trade was in the moulded goods of psychedelia. It makes it hard to admit an unexpected visitor—an invasion of my page—whose name shall be Max, and who as genie of disruption wears his hair long. He has stitched, and without much care, the smoothness of Paisley to the unholy knees of his denims. Thereby hangs a cold spectrum in autumnal duns. Scrolling, superposed on shiny ultramarine.

He has parked his station wagon under the greened filigree of a roadside hawthorn. Said vehicle, incipiently a muggy brown, I see at once has been augmented with gold pentacles, the peppered cargo shed by an all-enfolding cloud (unreasonably this is in tangerine). A ram, its coarse pelage a muddy cream, has poked its black muzzle through the dilapidated pales of my picket fence, and is munching weeds. Max—a man without a business card—I note with fatigued alarm is encrusted at one nostril, either paste or gem (I shall not inquire) whose coruscation is ruby and indigo. He has a portfolio. He wants to sell me 'art work'. I am obliged to look, therefore hum … and hum …

'Well?' 'Well what?' 'Like it?' Guffaw (beg pardon). Isn't—isn't that dusky Pegasus, afloat in the radial spokes of sunset—just a bit *passé!* 'Oh. Well something classical.' Ah now what's this? The pelagic, tragic, Triton. Now really! I would have to explain a long and recent history with my landlady's cat. 'Landlady's cat?' Yes. It's rendered me phobic. Even at the sight of, what shall we call these … represented scales. Incidentally. Those translucent waves. That phantasised element your mythologised merman seems to command. It was all done with briny lips to a twisted seashell, not as you have it here a cream horn. Sorry.

I closed the door. I heard phuts of exhaust, then the souped-up tune of his engine. My reading-lamp, its pyramid of thinning light, eerily diminished the rose amendments and emendations encrypting this present leaf. Time, as I hold to the square panes a triplicated glass of falling sands, had fused—because of Max—the sovereign anatomies of three distinctive clocks. I tossed my crushed cigarette pack, whose inflorescence is red and white, over a chair—it rises and spins—over a rug (its parabola falls), into the shade of my bin. For a moment I caught its flight in a sky of perfect peach. So that I recalled (now), that I do not mention this (once when I had written this journal), certain cold articles junked in the Wandsworth room (excuse. An unavoidable collision of tenses). Here, row upon row of science fantasy tales, from the house of Gollancz. Here, in Zob's old video library, technicolored, outlandishly creatured yarns, all of galactic warfare. Must get back to my MS.

c/o Finnegan Rich
Cleveland State University
RT1216
Cleveland OH 44115
9 August 1992

Dear Marsy,
  Rabbit is, Finnegan isn't (rich). My host's a man obsessed with his

failures (notably Broadway, mid-70s). If not for his critics (he says)—'Foul sons of Art'—New York's big box office would long have showered him with largesse. He doesn't hide disaffection with his job. He tells me he's discomfited—wouldn't anyone?—in threadbare socks—though there's no need for this. Still. It takes all sorts.

I got Sam on the phone today, increasingly girlish. The bull-neck, whose virility's platinum—that's the concertina tint of his credit cards—well, he wows her nightly, it goes without saying bow-tied, in an endless chain of hotels/restaurants—some his own. All dinner dates. You know. With dreadful commercial types. We, Marsy, may smile. Last week she met the mayor. Also a billionaire attorney. And seems to think it significant human experience! Tosh!

Grave interjection (because there's worse). She's got herself light-headed and grandmotherly, because of this mulatto boy, due, I'm told, about a week from now. The bull-neck's going to put her on Concorde, and will arrange for a limousine from Heathrow to Cambridge (where I've told her to investigate care options—get the thing off our hands).

Not such a blue sky. Take care.

Andrew.

Hasty PS. I committed the hideous error of allowing poor Finnegan Rich a preview of my lecture notes, who perused, then passed them on to an assistant. I really don't deserve this. That person accords my notion of 'literary time' the full dignity of philosophical discourse. I find myself with St Thomas, opposing Duns Scotus (terrible fate), replete of my own 'fascinating' slant on the 'principle of individuation'. What does this mean, Marsy? As far as I understand it, this. Take two individuals, that belong to the same species, and ask: are they different in essence, or are they essentially the same? St Thomas—and so, it seems, do I—takes the latter view, in respect of material substances. Duns Scotus (c. 1270-1308!) does not. St Thomas can justify it so: that matter consists of undifferentiated parts, to be distinguished only by a difference of position in space. Of course, fool that I am, what I posit, a metaphoric unravelling of time, I have described—yes, spatially.

PPS. A relief. No one brought up this mumbo-jumbo in the lecture, which went well and precisely to my pocket-watch.

Andrew (b. 1935!) ...

... round all of which the moor-ish Alistair Wye has inscribed a crayon rectangle, in stop-light red. That's specifically for Merle, for her particular attention ... on those dampish green evenings ... when she will join me here ... and under the prowling tock of my quartz clock, will read my MS. (I note, in its titanic force of anti-climax, that a temporal clash of heads has been avoided, which is perhaps why our shared universe still squeaks along undisturbed. I refer, of course, to my July 18th—cp. Glaze's 17th, also see above, his hasty PS.)

Flat 5
147 Trefoil St
SW18
20 August 1992

Dear Andrew,

I get the picture. Being repetitive. How we've discussed this. Don't you remember you told me? What is challenging is on one hand. On the other's that mothy attraction, those academic odd-balls. I'd avoid them (I seem to recall that was your advice to me).

Well. You can see my address hasn't changed. It's exactly as predicted. That is, having never treated the timbers—because there has been no necessity—Pedant of Edmonton wants guarantees against dry-, wet-rot, insect infestation—from specialist firm(s). I'm about to withdraw from the market and relaunch the sale. I think that's my quickest option.

Blandford wanted me to do a quirky piece on the Nostradamus you see sometimes at the intersection of Oxford and Regent St. You've heard him. His sandwich board. Sins of the flesh. End of the world is nigh. All that spittle on his beard gave me reservations—would give anyone reservations—re an interview. Ergo I talked to passers-by, shop and insurance people, for impressions. Yes, I thought, an 'impressions' piece. Blandford will like.

Now. Who should happen along, but Giles. On his way from Hamleys, with a mobile, a cuddly chick, a string of brightly coloured plastic balls (for the cot). I assume you've heard the news, and that I don't have to explain this. Giles was even joyful. And thinks you should be. I think you should be. Easy. Marsy.

I have smoked almost the whole new pack, and am reminded (as I flick at a warm crust of fallen ash) that Glaze—itinerant without Commedic mask—set certain cold limits to all probable eventualities, after so much life as airsmudge. [Merle, you will have to believe. That untimely volcanic deposit, unwitting censor of I promise only one costly syllable, being 'mail', renders one of many infelicitous phrases I am sure to brush up on, come evening—over a glass perhaps of local beer. As for example in framing this, the following comes to mind: ... so much life as hot air. Anyway enough of that.] Glaze's response was quick, laconic, and sour, and was penned in large schoolboy letters on a postcard, whose scene was an ink line drawing of the Old State Capitol at Springfield:

Evanston IL, August 28. Marsy. There are things you don't understand. You're a bachelor. The family's 'joy'—not even a boy, as, if I'm right, they're going to call it Amanda—is precisely the tribal infiltration to dilute first local then national culture. It doesn't have my blessing. You, I thought, knew better. What's worse this week is I have felt I do want to come home, but not for that reason. The weather here's subject to extremes as well. Yours. Andrew.

So too here, in the wet verdant future on the fringes of Dartmoor, which privileged perspective I shall shortly cast back into its proper chronology. An all-day deluge, a constant, moving film on my window panes, forms its pattern of widening lakes in that rustic wilderness my garden. Shall I, booted, caped, sou'westered, splosh to the pub on that Ariel stroke of nine, or stay home with a vin de Bourgogne? Whatever. I must get back.

July 19. Zob, cocooned in his study—glass cone of coffee courtesy Mrs St John—intercepted the day's first call, before I could reach my extension. I returned to the window sill, whose pattern of accidental burns my morning cigarette had added to. Incidentally the campanula had gone over.

I looked at this morning's mail (bum phodder). I struggled on with it gamely, to the point of an nth loan offer—'competitive' apr—and noted Zob's extension light, as the thing went out, then immediately re-lit (its little amber oblong). Zob had dialled out (I learned) to Cornelius, who was not at his office, and who called back at around midday, by which time Zob had gone out. Ergo:

'Merle's given me an angle,' Snell said, defiling her name, 'on this new scheme of Philip's …' I grunted knowledgeably, with the result that a whole lit roadway unwound itself, with following milestones:

1) Raptorial Masturbile had wheedled his way into commercial radio.

2) His brand new show, slanted, and—so he claimed—intentionally unoriginal, committed itself publicly under a much thought about and, finally insipid title.

3) After much deliberation, that was *Talking Music*.

4) Marsy, proposed first guest, would talk conversationally about his 'interesting' life, eight chosen discs interspersed, extracts of which would be played.

5) The show would go out to coincide with the nation's Sunday lunch.

'Marvellous opportunity, don't you think?'
Yes, Cornelius.

July 20. Adam has broken his hoe.

July 21. Meeting—10 o'clock start—was not convened yesterday, because there would have been no one but me (I, of course, must take minutes) to keep Snell copiously topped with coffee. 'Fresh. And I mean fresh.' Poor Mrs Clapp.

Adam has broken his toe.

July 22. (Thank heaven it's Friday.)

136

Subject: Talking Music
Item #: 58
Date: 7-22, 11:41:36
Reply to: Box #2, Ext. #2, Wye

By: Alistair
Chain to: %null%
Comments: copy to Snell
  routed by fax

Text: Marsy—This, insofar as my minutes record, was the course of yesterday's discussion—

1) Snell very alive to this as further publicity opportunity. Urged that you 'know' what 'public' you want to reach. His preference, as usual, as broad a 'church' as possible—all ages, all walks of life.
  Point was agreed.

2) Important you present very human side. Talk about family life as you grew up. Reflect on: parental influence (wholesome), schooling (irksome), school friends (harmlessly pranksome), holidays (never exotic). Crucial to claim ignorance of father as establishment academic (the masses, which means mostly life's losers, are always so touchy on nepotism).
  Point was agreed.

3) Student life. Play down élitist nature of Exe's ancient institution. Point up camaraderie with working-class contemporaries. Abiding image is: receptive young man taking first tentative steps across threshold of twentieth-century literature (as opposed to Oxford classics).
  Point was agreed.

4) Professional life. Can make much here of initial commercial failure (*Aristotle's Atom*). Implication being, society's usual

tendency to value its gifts belatedly.
   Point was agreed.

5) Current activities. Short break after immense labours over *Gimme the Cash*, a chance to reiterate that this is currently on sale, and, you believe, short-listed for Best-novel-to-be-published (this decade).
   Point was agreed.

6) Plans for immediate future. Keenness to participate in commemorative process re Andrew Glaze—'friend, mentor, brilliant academic'—who died so tragically only last year.
   Point was agreed.

7) The long term. Your most ambitious undertaking, a millennial novel, whose panoramic survey is a broad sweep across the whole Christian era. A tapestry of social history embossed with futuristic speculation.
   Point was agreed.

8) In summary. A kind of conclusion, to put those eight chosen discs in chronological perspective—i.e., what each piece of music has meant at the corresponding stage of life. We have to be careful here, given that all eight selections must in totality have that same broad appeal your comments are tailored to. [This being in Snell's view so critical, it forms separate bullet points, at 9) (below)].

9) Discs.

i. From 60s/childhood Snell recommends cherubic Beatles as opposed to YOUR preference, 'rebellious' Rolling Stones. We want to keep it clean (so perhaps something to sentimentalise the pathetic

138

John Lennon).

ii. The emotional pyrotechnics of youth (and something apposite). Snell advises avoid at all costs the grotesquerie of a Mahler (say). Keep it simple, effective. Suggested candidates were: *1812 Overture*, Beethoven's *Fifth*, Brahms' *Piano Concerto #1*. Slight hints here at the avant-garde could be along the lines of, for example, *The Rite of Spring*—but nothing that is now controversial. We don't want a Boulez creeping in.

iii. Solace. Everyone needs it when things don't go well. So, early professional life could be accompanied by: that Albinoni *Adagio*, or the Pachelbel *Canon*, even a *Brandenburg*. Or what about some jazz?

iv. An all-time favourite. We all have one. That piece we never tire of listening to. There are some obvious choices. The Elgar *Cello Concerto*, perhaps with du Pré (who in herself elicits sighs). Or that Rodrigo guitar piece, which is still v. popular. Or some good old Haydn rum-te-tum.

v. Opera has a surprisingly large following, even among those without much money. This is an easy one. Domingo or Pavarotti, with a Verdi or Puccini highlight. Something that really grabs. Italia '90 springs to mind.

vi. Contemporary awareness. Suppose we'll have to acknowledge those wretched minimalists. Just to show interest in progress in other disciplines. But DON'T choose any rhythmic drumming, handclaps, or syncopated vocals!

vii. Personal horizons. By this is meant a composer you say you know little of now but would like to explore. That doesn't mean someone obscure. It's something you've never quite got round to. You could try Wagner.

viii. No intellectual it seems can overlook Mozart (bit like

Shakespeare). Understand *The Magic Flute* is highly thought of.

Points, Marsy, agreed.

July 23. Isabelle, who has bought a jade bikini, refuses to put it on. We talked about this in the bathroom, where we met accidentally, and where I mentioned Adam's toe. She pressed my hand to her midriff, though the seduction ended there—with litany and variations on her 'accumulated pounds'.
Isabelle! You look, you feel, just fine ...

July 25. (Oh what a yawn, being Monday.)

BULLETIN BOARD

Subject: Talking Music (minutes)	By: Marsy
Item #: 59	Chain to: #58
Date: 7-25, 10:11:41	Comments: see
Reply to: Box #1, Ext. #1, Zob	postscript

Text: Al—That's fine, that looks about right. Any chance, by the way, that you know WHY *The Magic Flute* is so regarded?

PS. How do I direct a copy of this via fax to Cornelius?

Well ... It's why you always need a man with a brown lab coat and a screwdriver. So ... bringing my massive intellect to bear ...
... I shall, Marsy, take these queries in reverse order.

Item. On that simple technical question, really all you need to do is export the bulletin to the outgoing fax queue, led by the prompts up to and including a request for the target fax number. 'Export' can be done in one of two ways, either by source filename (which in this case will be C:\B_BOARD\SEND\T$0059), or by item number, which is of course 59. EXPORT appears on your foreground list of options.

Item. This too is a technical question, though at the bourn of metaphysics. Perhaps I can put it so:

SYNOPSIS, The Magic (Hampstead) Flute

Cast: Queen of the Night

Pamina (her daughter)—played by Wye

Veiled ladies, boys—of the Queen's retinue

Papageno, a rustic—played by Snell

Sarastro

Monostatos, a lustful Moor—played by Zob

Papagena, a wrinkled hag—played by Crouch

Tamino, a handsome youth—played by Merle

Attendants, priests, mechanicals &c.

Scene: Rocky terrain, dotted with twisted trees. Distant hills. A temple. The sky, azure graded to scarlet.

Enter TAMINO (Merle). Enter serpent, scales a lurid green, eyes a reddish yellow, fangs. TAMINO (Merle) overcome by reptile. Three veiled LADIES, each armed with Olympic javelin, appear, and together rescue TAMINO, who is now unconscious. With reluctance, they abandon him, bound to report the event to their mistress, who is of course QUEEN OF THE NIGHT. Enter PAPAGENO (Snell), royal birdcatcher, who stumbles on waking TAMINO. Cannot help but claim, in usual, good-natured mendacity, that he (Snell) has fought off the serpent. Merle, TAMINO, grateful, although returning LADIES berate PAPAGENO on learning of his,

141

or Snell's, dishonesty. QUEEN OF THE NIGHT has dispatched three LADIES with portrait of her daughter—PAMINA, played by Wye—with which TAMINO becomes enchanted. As you can see, this was a bad mistake by Zob, and allows me to put on my four-cornered lecture hat.

Aria: *This portrait so enchanting* &c.

Scene: Resplendent chamber. Sumptuous drapes, gilded chairs, refulgent candelabra.

QUEEN, TAMINO. QUEEN insists that if TAMINO (Merle) rescues her daughter—PAMINA, quietly played by Wye—she (the QUEEN) will offer Merle Alistair's hand. PAMINA is held captive by SARASTRO.

Recitative and aria: *O tremble not, dear son,* &c.

Scene: Rocky terrain (again). Sky, a steely blue.

To keep him from danger, TAMINO receives from LADIES, first, a magic flute, additionally, a copy of *Strong Opinions* (this is a book of wisdom, by the incredible Sirin). PAPAGENO is given a miraculous chime of bells. QUEEN summons her BOYS to guide them to Sarastro's palace.

Scene: Egyptian chamber. Sculpted sphinx. A casket, inlaid with hieroglyphs. Faience cup in form of lotus flower. A wall painting, depicting slaves with tribute (ebony, ivory, pelts, a leopard, a monkey). Attached to wall, a throwstick. Above it, a mounted scarab. MONOSTATOS, who as Moor is played by Zob, has foiled PAMINA'S attempted escape (therefore Wye must suffer his captor's bookish halitosis till he is rescued). MONOSTATOS is intent on making her, PAMINA, servile, but is distracted, to the point of running off, when PAPAGENO (a strange and bucolic-looking Snell), tumbles into the action. PAPAGENO has arrived ahead of TAMINO, and of that comely youth he informs PAMINA.

142

He, he, he—he loves me then?

Scene: A leafy grove, with blossoms. To rear, temple colonnaded to two others flanking. A lintel, temple centre, bears the engraving TEMPLE OF WISDOM. Those flanking are, TEMPLE OF REASON, TEMPLE OF NATURE.

TAMINO has reached the temple, which is ruled by SARASTRO. PAMINA (the bewildered Wye), escaping with PAPAGENO (the cheery Snell), is again checked by the evil MONOSTATOS (envious Zob). Zob is prevented from inflicting permanent harm only by that magic chime of bells. Enter SARASTRO, with entourage, also with triumphal car (this is drawn by six lions). The two lovers (i.e. Al and Merle) meet for the first time. [Starburst, in enriched purple.] SARASTRO deems that Zob be punished, and that TAMINO and PAPAGENO be brought to the temple for trial. He escorts PAMINA to his sanctum. I'm sorry if this goes on.

Chorus: *Ah, divine wisdom—long live Sarastro!*
         His rewards and his punishments are one manifesto.

Scene: A palm grove. Silvered bark, gilded leaves. Eighteen thrones are arranged on a sylvan floor. Each throne accompanies a decorative pyramid and inlaid cornucopia, the largest of which are set at the centre.

SARASTRO explains to gathering of priests how he abducted, from the tyrannical QUEEN OF THE NIGHT, her daughter PAMINA (who is played by Wye, and who will win out in the end). He states that PAMINA (Wye) is destined by the gods (in an Olympian heaven) for TAMINO (Merle). PAMINA he is about to admit to the 'Consecrated Band'. TAMINO (dearest Merle) must now prove himself in a pre-ordained trial of (to Zob these are alien concepts): Steadfastness, Constancy, Courage. To the QUEEN OF THE NIGHT also, these matters are alien, who now tries to persuade her daughter to murder SARASTRO (as if I would!). Zob, that lustful MONOSTATOS, in creeping up slyly on PAMINA, gets wind of the

143

QUEEN'S intent, and hopes to inspire an enraged SARASTRO to revenge (but SARASTRO isn't enraged, and instead banishes MONOSTATOS). Now. This is getting all too saturnine. Therefore we need a comic aside. We should I think induce PAPAGENO (that perimeter man called Snell), a gourmand never likely to be consecrated, into a ribald exchange with the hag PAPAGENA (enter, stage left, our own Geraldine Crouch). Presto! Crouch suddenly seems attractive, and will satisfy his bed springs.

Ja, mein Engel!

Scene: Small garden. Perhaps a well. Perhaps a little pond. Trees certainly.

Three BOYS prevent a disconsolate PAMINA from committing suicide (not that I would ever consider this option), and lead her to TAMINO. Allow me just to scratch my head as I tilt my four-cornered hat.

Tutti: *Two intertwining and destined souls*
        Can't be constrained in commercialised roles,
        When publicity men in a media den
        Engineer for them purely accountancy goals.

Scene: Two mountains, one with the loud, subterranean, diamond torrent of a waterfall, the other erupting fire. Cavities in the mountain walls make these visible.

To the sounds of magic flute, and clutching book of wisdom, TAMINO and PAMINA traverse these caverns (i.e. fire and water), and survive their ordeal. This is a moment of genuine celebration, because of course ART as well as LIFE are affirmed. The works of MONOSTATOS (or the 'novels' of Zob) may be banished to the flames. The night will consume its QUEEN.

Chorus: *Triumph and victory! The destined pair*
         Overcome the whole affair,

144

This is their consecration,
Their cele-very-bration!

Scene: Garden (again).

PAPAGENO/PAPAGENA, symbiotic embrace. They plan for several children. Plus, final onslaught from QUEEN OF THE NIGHT, who, in alliance with Zob, I mean the Moor, is thwarted.

Scene: Radiant sun.

SARASTRO brings lovers together, O happy dénouement. TAMINO and PAMINA attired in priestly garb. So fortitude has triumphed, even in our Zobbish (and, I insist, ephemeral) era of media cynicism, with 'Beauty', 'Wisdom', finally, and everlastingly crowned. There are few who believe this still to be possible.

Chorus: *Heil sei euch Geweihten!* &c.

Here. You. Hang up my hat. It might just be better to show Zob an open page of Kobbé.

July 26. One of those miracles, a slightly muffled suburbia, has left me to the zing of warm blood, or now, as it mounts to a torrent, the physiological roar of selfdom in both my ears. The milkman did not clatter his duellist's bottles at dawn. You, my seconds, can believe—that I woke other-worldish, in a woolly cocoon, in the womb of my duvet. My drawn curtain simulated twilight. Then the mild thud of my radio alarm—as this, itself in a dream, ushered in the tender beams of a *Moonlight* ... (first movement, Brendel.)

The house was deserted. No Isabelle, Michael, Malkin. Nor did I find Zob, nor Mrs St John (who was on the trail of vacuum bags) on arriving, quietly, at work. Zob's business diary, open to today's page, placed him with 'Philip', for rehearsal, 'without engineers'. Adam, somewhere hopping for his breakfast, remained absent too (away, curl of his lip). So. I smoked my cigarette on the squares of the patio—slabs, a chalky white, with lacquered, alternating charcoal blue, a design which Zob called 'Renaissance'. A demotic cabbage white opened, closed, re-opened its wings, considered, then abandoned the mauve tips of a buddleia. A first pale flicker danced on the dewy crystal, that overspanning arc, whose brown vault is London's north-west sky. A nice day coming.

July 27. Isabelle has car trouble (suspension), and has left her Citroën at Dollis Hill—in the hands, she says, of a meticulously oafish mechanic. That 'nice married man' across the road (it's irksome I have never noticed him) helped her to shuttle to and fro. Zob was equally perplexed, checking his inside pocket, thinking he'd seized on, then knowing he'd mislaid his small red pocket book—in fact a diary. 'You haven't seen it, eh, Al?'
Um. No.

July 28. I find, because Merle faxed me her minutes, that this morning's meeting—not here, but at New Caxton Grove—encircled (on the page, as it were) the further enterprise of Philip Masturbile (that airy hack). Why? Well. It is very much to do with the bookish groupie Jacqueline Keys—a new name, so far as my memoir goes, but someone I instantly remember I have met. Let me call your attention to that happy occasion—
She was and remains a tea-drinker, and is, as Philip suggests, 'quite big' administratively, in the Free City Festival—in fact she's the co-ordinating director. However. That's jumping ahead. I must go back to Zob, at about this time last year (that is, in late July), who had got himself in a lather over something (I don't know what, don't care). His repeated failure to hire a dispatch rider—being early on a Saturday—meant muggins here eventually drove, foot flat on the gas, to the brakes of Great Magner, with a package. I recall I had just acquired that battered Ford. Miss Jacqueline Keys, a remote sheen in her bob cut, I had been briefed to identify.
'Look out too for a tartan Thermos.'
I parked with confidence, under the eddy of maple leaves, in the thin morning shadow of a tower (which was Gothic Revival). I opened my door to the sound of crows. Atmospherically I crunched across the gravel …

146

I had arrived for the last edifying moments of her summer school, her class of '93. Her many students, majestically hungry, and rumbling, had all been bewitched by Scandinavian culture, and under present auspices termed themselves 'Hamsunite'—even during a tea break. They weren't particularly young, though lounged, in the typical pose of youth, in twos, or threes, or singly, where there were benches, in the protection of arbours, or plainly on the lawns. Zob's package, and latterly the escutcheon, had borne the same name ('Great Magner School of English'), but 'is that too,' I asked, pointing, 'a part of it?' I had my distant gaze to a circular folly, to the reflective moss in the cone of its slate roof. 'All you can see,' she said. Such Attic tranquillity our Hamsunites reposed in. A sigh, please, for erudition's gentle clime ...

Miss Keys had the seat of her jodhpurs firmly to a woodcutter's log, whose remnant of bark was mottled with fungus. Scars of damp sunshine criss-crossed in auburn in the light chestnut of her bob, but dissolved abruptly—a cloud, a wash of blue-black distemper, cancelling that English moment of sun. Her flask was horizontal in the short grass and decapitated daisies, though its plastic cup of mud-coloured tea sent up its missive in a column of steam, which my proximity agitated. 'Miss Keys,' I said, and motioned the package, a padded manila. That passing cloud, now in the fast, rotating shape, of a wildebeest perhaps—it parted at head and torso, allowing one liquid fragment of sunshine. 'Now please call me Jacqui.' She removed from her knees (and brushed down her jodhpurs) a Scotch egg, with crumbs, in a paper serviette. 'Urgent dispatch. From Mr Marshall Zob.' She quizzed, in the pucker of her lips (which continued, however, to smile). Then having thought, questions were resolved (in the bright arch of those pencilled eyebrows). 'Ah yes,' she said, 'I know ...' She stood up, and put her cup of tea on the log. She took, and ignored the parcel—because, 'Nice place,' I had said. She told me about her summer school. Why do I encumber you with this?

Well. I drove away, while one crow flapped around that ornamental tower. I pulled up for sheep in lanes. Was rounded by a collie. I emerged, in a dream of country spires, with a fan of red mud to my offside wing. I forgot, with my wet tyres to the motorway, all

147

about Miss Keys. Until, that was, today. Careers, of course, move on. Her borrowed venues for capital from books (now no sign of Hamsun) had given ground to the trade exhibition, whose dignified epithet is 'literary festival'. She had been wooed. Masturbile had bought her, intellectually, an after-dinner drink. Something he said over a calvados had secured him an event on the programme, the real *coup* being 'on the opening day', for that Free City jamboree. Naturally he had thought of 'friend' and 'top writer' Marsy, who when sounded was found to be in agreement, to a proposed pre-lunch session ... 'Format' (to be finalised) was the usual interview (audience to pay from twelve to £35 per ticket). Well of course Cornelius had to thrash out the details ('No word by the way from Flude'), and ergo this fax from my enchanted Tamino.

Here was the scam. It is assumed (it is assumed by Cornelius) that any paying audience, and here I quote Merle's fax, 'will be composed largely of would-be writers ...' Joint abettors are Philip and Snell. Glazed bust with laurel is that of Marshall Zob. The belief—and I am afraid this is inveterate—is that no one within that shaky circle, blue on road maps, and indeed London's blue orbital—and certainly no one outside it—is capable of approaching the impossibly high standard set by a text by Marshall Zob. (Allow me to snigger into my flight bag.) Let me say in passing that for Cornelius it was never worth his while to open the mail, except of course to clip to its contents that standard, and by now well rehearsed Dear X, Regrettably our client list is currently full. X being a Tolstoy or a Bloggs. These are the parameters I want you to understand, since, as I now float free of my worldly obligations (such sweet joy in a publisher's advance), I am able to paraphrase that deliciously practical ethic our world-led trio beat out with Hephaestos's irons—

MZ: Okay. We'll be seated, on a raised platform, with microphones. You will ask questions.

PM: Absolutely.

CS: Moreover, Marsy—questions on how to get published.

PM: Got it in one, Cornelius. Propaganda line is this. You try and try and try. Eventually you write a good book. This is the only way.

CS: Good books always find a publisher. Caution: don't analyse 'good' and 'bad'. And DON'T discuss the net book agreement.

PM/MZ: Okay.

But enough. A filter on this tragic scene. (I, Wye, have been huffing all day, and must I think buy myself an expectorant.) Contain your contumely, you fellow-scribes in vain. Pay out, I say, good money for verse (not festivals). Look at what I find, still unwashed by a bookseller's tide:

> Let those who are in favour with their stars
> Of public honour and proud titles boast,
> Whilst I, whom fortune of such triumph bars,
> Unlook'd for joy in that I honour most.

[Sonnet XXV]

Away, sons of Art!

July 29. I should have known, I suppose (I mean from what occurred before breakfast). My planar dreamscape, transparent cupola of ministerial conversation (it seemed, in the visions of my night, I held the high ground in a Wonderland cabinet room) collapsed (is a half-remembered echo). This, under a ferocious assault of decibels, or really quite quiet voices active on the street. It is Friday. I twitched my curtains. I can now say with certainty that 'that nice married man' across the street is from the italicised *Number Nine*, whose anachronistic door (imitated Georgian) is flanked by hollyhocks. Their flower's a deep, luxurious red. To him it seems clear, that having got her suspension right, Isabelle's starter motor has given up the ghost. Tacky French (he did not say, himself having a cherry Peugeot). I hope it's not the start of something—in that receding grind of his gears—because, nervously, he's giving her a lift.

Later that day. Zob, I find, is in levitating shoes. I discover this routinely (Here, my lord, is the morning mail, such of it I designate 'personal'). I am completely unable, with that flutter of charismatic wings, to tie him to the floor. He's on air, sidestepping his author's chair. Floats to his desk's west bank. Passes a green hand under the green shade of his reading-lamp. We are, I am not too delighted to hear, 'getting away for a few days'. This is because the unbeautiful Crouch, loud on the phone just now, has got us an invitation. This is *en masse*, to the ancestral home of—not my infelicity—'esteemed family Simms'. I try and cobble together a large, plausible lie protesting my commitment to the Glaze project, and for once this is not technically beyond him (though like Snell he is troubled by the terminology). 'Take the laptop,' he says. 'Put what you need on flaccid disc.'

At midday I packed my canvas bag. I wrote Isabelle a cheque (yes. She was home. Here was my July rent). A man on the drive rattled spanners, having lifted her bonnet. He, superfluously, I have remembered. Hair, sandy, a green gob of grease above the right temple. Fell boots (!). Filthy overalls, to protect a radiant tee shirt. Even at six I could not extinguish him, by which mellow hour the Mercedes' dusky rearview gave me a dozing Zob, in the plush of his upholstery (chauffeur Wye turned the radio off). The car turned. The haze-capped Quantocks shrank over my right shoulder. Soon that golden disc, the western sun, in its descent to the squared fields ahead, to the bluish ridge beyond, would blush crimson, would halve itself, would abandon to its darkened roof space its last loose threads of scarlet.

I am looking for somewhere whose address is—now what is this hasty scrawl?—'near Ashburton'.

Darkness. In it, the emerald luminosity of the dash, with its flicker of orange needles. The swish of passing headlights—an effervescence over the ceiling, across that thundercloud so soon to be Zob's brow, out through a rear quarterpane—unfortunately woke him. 'You know, Al,' he said (or rather these words rumbled from his core, his mind still swaddled to the motion of sleep). 'That diary did turn up.' It was all too terrible. 'Yes,' I said. 'In this morning's mail.' He told me—because he was infuriated—that having left

Philip, who had ordered a tuna and peanut salad (an early, 11.30 lunch, Tuesday), he, the deep-breathing Zob, hiked across Covent Garden, to one of those antiquarian bookshops off the Charing Cross Rd. Why? (Al, don't interrupt, but to get an illustrated Le Fanu, a present for Merle.—Oh. It's her birthday ...—Yes. But as I was saying.) He checked pockets for cash—this, an expensive Le Fanu— and pulled out, and put on the counter, in precisely this order, his claret-coloured pocket diary, his cheque book (its plastic enclosure an Adriatic blue), his concertina of bank and credit cards. Of all things a Nabokov caught his eye (*Ada*, first edition), though on handling it he passed it up. 'Condition didn't match its price,' he said. Mere slip of a girl at the cash desk, standing in, as would soon transpire, for her monocled grandaddy (who frequently needed to rest his hip), received Zob's signature with a capacious, a stupendous yawn, and even held his cheque to the light. No fame for him here. He marched out, to the Dickensian tinkle of an overhead bell, leaving his pocket book on the counter. It returned in the post this morning, which restored his faith in shop people. Not such fun were the quirky witticisms, penned in a violent red in an alien hand.

'I want you to write, Al, first thing tomorrow. Demand an apology.' 'Ah,' I said. 'Now here's the Newton Abbot turn. I'd say we're getting near ...'

I remember: Isabelle's mechanic. I recall: a sudden pool of yellow light, a slow truck groaning round a wooded bend. A green gob of grease above the right temple. Tired, very tired ...

July 30. There are, my fellow-subjects, things I cannot quite believe. I say this, inclined to recollect the high-browed Justin Simms, who last night perched on his balustraded steps, smoking a cigar. We shared the same moon—I, who glanced up through a tinted windscreen—he, who lost the intersecting shadows of his sycamores, every time the night's domes, peaks, or purplish cloud wrapped themselves round that waning orb. I had got us, Zob and me (that babble from the back), recurrently lost. In honesty what did I care for his diary?

Crouch, impossibly animated, had parked—oh, hours ago—on the yardage of gravel half-circling the house. That was mid-Georgian

151

(c.1758). The conducted tour was this morning, naturally, though I remain stung by the night before—when, having had a longish life—of fairly useless toil—any last thoughts I had, on the politicisation—the non-literariness of the *putsch* I had jointly planned—seemed not out of the question. Simms, whose father was just now buying companies abroad, and whose mother sunned herself in Tuscany, directed me to the attic (i.e. the servants' quarters), but told me which suite of rooms to drop off Zob's baggage in. Guffaws from Zob. Here, ye put-upon, is one of those vagaries of work-place bureaucracy—with which I reproach the quacks of industry (of whom Simms is a legatee)—that's to say an epitomised 'structure' for the labour force. At a few minutes after ten (Saturday, a.m.), time which records the four of us, crunching that driveway gravel, I rejected (being a bit touchy) the various symmetries in Simms's seven-bay façade. Its stone quoins. The plain ledges, each offset above by a winged lintel. The three, centralised bays, being doubly pedimented (porch and roof). Then those balustraded steps ascending to the door, to each side of which is a Palladian pillar. I do not allow the randomness of hierarchies—exemplified here in our social quartet—ever to smudge the dappled complexion, the robust good health of my mind. I told him I didn't care for his stucco, whose caramel was not the right shade. Nor have I been driven to the arms of a trades union. Simms had a look, a sneer, but had no answer. Had I made my point? Perhaps so, as my blood rebels, though my watchword's militant.

I declined coffee on the terrace, which would have meant their insufferable chat (O how pleased they all were). After all I'd got work (of a spectacularly laboured kind), wherefore, in the moving shade of my garret, I prepared that penultimate chapter in the epistolary life of Glaze. Notes, all flat. A celestial twang. A lead angel, tone-deaf, reverberant via Zob's laptop. All that coaxing with abysmal harp. Understandably I needed my breaks (what sane man can bear professorial nonsense!), and so contented myself that Simms too paid an Adam to remain prosaic. A world from my sill, precluding that sixth-formish murmur, as that intertwined with the warm scent of coffee beans, was a hotchpotch of palm trees and pines (the cut lawns and dusty tracts littered with cones). There was—and I shall write this down—a tamarisk tree, helplessly out of place, shading our threesome clattering their cups. Distant gunnera dotted an ornamental lakeside. Beyond that, a square of sunshine caught on the cedar shingles slating a boathouse roof ('nicely weathered'—as I would hear Zob say). An extended roar from Simms, whom I imagined hirsute, stripped to the waist, combined itself with effects from Crouch, who imitated steam through a whistle. That did not indicate he'd squeezed her in a bear hug (not yet), rather that Zob had told a joke.

I went down. A nylon coated flunkey, oldish, brown-haired, a villager, alas creased at the sacks of flesh that enthroned each eye—had come from the terrace. She bore her master's tray, with a world of moulded ceilings whirling in the plated dome of the *cafetière*. That, and three china mugs, were bound for the scullery. I went to the dining-room, where the rectangular window sashes reflected themselves in the lacquer of the table. I reached out a hand, for the russet and green of an apple, which until that moment topped an assortment, the yellow, peach, and orange flame, a fire of fruits in a stencilled glass bowl. Simms came in too, just as my newly capacious jaw closed on that innocent English apple. He had changed—miraculous click of fingers—into cricket whites, and had since angled a croquet mallet jauntily on one shoulder. 'Marsy's looked high and low,' he said. 'You're here I see ...' Why of course. Far away as possible ...

He directed me past the boathouse, 'to the croquet lawn.' Here I found Zob, whooping, with Crouch (incessant giggle), whose all-live sculpture (note, Barringer) I could invoke, then garbage, pretentious critique in the description of. 'Sinewy strains of immobility'—is a perfidy that common sense alone won't let me unleash, though the couplet

> Zob, pathetic,
> So unathletic ...

was one I later penned, though never found time to develop or recapitulate. But. I should put this to rest—with our two children of destiny instantaneously locked, in shoulder-to-shoulder combat, over the linear course of Geraldine's ball—unerring through a croquet hoop. After that Marsy, elbow to vertical mallet, ankles crossed, exhorted me to all-day sobriety, since he wanted me to drive the three of them—'just before nine'—to the venue of Simms's birthday celebration. He was twenty-five (a boy, with sycophantic publisher), and was gathering his legion for an all-night bash. This was on a pleasure boat (up, down, then a mooring on the River Dart).

'And I hope, Al, you've got that letter for me to sign.' Geraldine had already detected blankness: 'Oh Alistair really!' Zob, in that incipient flab of his forty pointless years, swelled up from the waist. He had I think noticed his counterpart, loping past the boathouse. For him this was no fun, and had exchanged his mallet for a lemonade bottle. 'Al, I'm frankly surprised.' What had I been doing? 'I'm trying to close off the Glaze project—at least my part.' 'A whore!' said Crouch. She had had her ear to reliable gossip, an odour so far seeping no farther than a fluorescent web of corridors, and of course the odd cocktail lounge. Officially his death had been 'comic'. For commercial reasons only, there could be—in ten to twenty years' time—a reappraisal. Zob smacked his heel with his mallet head uncomfortably. 'Okay,' I said. 'I'll do the letter. You'll need to give me the name, address.' Simms interrupted—'Anyone for lemonade'—then I left them, deeply conversational on the condition of those shingles.

July 31. It has been an irritating night (it is now 5 a.m.!). Sleep, impossible sprite, has goaded but failed to seal my drooping lids. Therefore in the gloam of a strange, and creaking house, I have sat before the metallic glow of the laptop, waiting for Simms, or Crouch, or Zob, or someone's inebriate phone call (which I received just after three). Also I've been thinking. Most persistently about last night—when in all but cap and livery (such is Simms's way) I opened all the car doors: three fizzy party-goers ensconced in Zob's saloon, having been delivered to the quayside. You may imagine, what social equality the three merry hacks put their pens, and their bankers' cards to.

Merle, with pearls, and a high neck—to what I shall always dream of, a gorgeously fitting evening dress, in coruscating henna—had already boarded (and this is not my joke) the Penelope. That simple craft, awash gently in a first ladle of punch, compulsory for each new arrival, had the kingfisher flutter of buntings to its mast. Friends—for Simms unbelievably had these—had inflated twenty-five party balloons, not with human gas, but with helium. These bobbed on the rails, whose painted ironwork was leaned on at the stern by Merle's naked forearms. Odysseus, by whom I mean of course the chauffeur, at last smiled. Merle waved vociferously. Simms, who at that moment sidestepped a capstan, waved back importantly. Here heads turned to the fitful explosion of music and laughter, which melted into balm. Cornelius, in a white summer suit (and a carnation for buttonhole), stepped meaningfully from below decks, where a portal swung to. He had brought them the punch, but shouted ahoy (to Zob, at the gangplank). You can see how this plays on my mind (yesterday, today, and tomorrow it's August).

I returned, with instructions to wait by the phone, for 'whatever' eventuality. I admit I have dozed, here at the laptop. Have reviewed, groggy sentry as I am, the imitated throb of gaslight, a splutter of yellow condensation, in the tide-bouncing sway of the Penelope's portholes. Ah me those windows! Convivial, and trivial—rondures dabbed-in on the foam-crested wash, all under, Merle, a canopy of stars.

I dashed off that letter (Dear Mr Mansard, I must protest &c.), though Zob later dismissed it as old-world gallantry, and made me re-write. I stumbled about on Simms's oaken landings, or sniffed at his chambers. I tried hard to avoid, when I shambled in to his studio (its golden south aspect), the diluted prose of what was certain to be a 'new' fastseller. I found its casual folios loose on a secretaire table, and discovered later that this was 'material' Cornelius was keen to see. (We may anticipate Zob intone 'Judas'.)

One guest room had bolection mouldings to the fireplace, and a mahogany tester bed. At the window, whole histories of south-westerlies had lined the transoms with black pencil, where well into the morning the two woven drapes, which I shook for dust, would continue to be drawn (lights to the bedside). It turned out that the walrus Snell would snore here until just before lunch (of baguettes and insipid bel paese), while for a brief visit only the rampant

155

Crouch—who scarcely drew a veil in the composition of memoirs—settled her feet first to the foot, then the pillows, then again to the foot of his bed. Yes. I did say a tester—with doubtless its frieze and cornice forming our birdcatcher's wooden firmament of thunderclaps.

My own room, Justin, had a night commode, which I took to be a birthday joke. Your rapacious elders cluttered their boudoir—into which I glanced: out of which I marched—with a mahogany linen press. Also a sofa with serpentine back (this, too, mahogany). Now that I've come to confess, I recall, over the fire, a giltwood pier-glass—under the centre window, a Queen Anne chair. Outside, a longcase clock had stopped at a quarter to two. Here the landing generally, cloaked in historic shadows, rendered tasteless the celebration of a name—Simms, the name Simms—with its depicted lineage, or projection of falsified 'light'—which sanguine persons ought to find depressing. Not, I make clear, for the catalogue of antecedents. Here was a house whose self-made progenitor (that's to talk of wealth) could not be deferred to the clammy mists prior to the halcyon years of Justin's paternal grandfather—a man spotlessly bald. That glossed portrait offered background clues as to the primal source of all those Simms' doubloons (beaten silver in a Moorish arch; the fringe of an olive branch; a distant hacienda). Evidently Spanish trade, and not a picture I liked. Another showed a woman with chihuahua.

I am exceedingly bored. All I have for these sleepless hours is the Glob/Zaze correspondence, which is still in a jumble (and is sizeable as refuse).

At three-ish—or on that landing still at a quarter to two—I received my 'final' directive, via the slurred imbroglio of Simms's telephone voice. I got in the car and turned on the radio—a mistake. Its sultry waves brought all-night news from a therapeutic counsellor, whose vocal incisions deepened, before she could cauterise, a life's psychic wounds—some such (presumptuous) technique. My car lights ballooned over the hedgerows. My engine purred on the riverside streets, with its velvet echo: the stone elevations, all those timbered gables, crowded shop fronts, some with painted gargoyles. On the pleasure craft the Penelope, over the

156

starboard side, Crouch threw up, and was cured, 'feel marv'lous!' Cornelius, on the white bonnet of his Jaguar, bellowed that he never got drunk, and would drive (critically with Merle, who was flushed). 'Just lead on, eh, Al ...' Simms dozed in the back. Snell's neon headlights cascaded over my rear bumper and re-silvered the mirrors. Marsy had the window down, his blurred eyes lolling over the squared red fields. Crouch, whose hand touched my knee, my thigh, then casually stroked my loins, got distracted when I swerved (and re-tuned the radio). Nevertheless. Not half an hour ago a night-capped Cornelius (brandy) checked into his guest room—'Wow! A four-poster!' Simms disappeared—to bed, half-undressed, with a last suspiration for his party blower. Marsy said 'Night' (but made mountaineer's work of the stairs). I myself saw Merle to her room, while—I am more or less certain—Geraldine retouched her rouge (insatiable). Ten minutes ago I watched, from the open door of my attic (because I can't sleep. Because I want to shake off this purgatory called Glaze). Geraldine lumped from her *en suite*, and from the deluge of a toilet flush, whose cataract I have learned to sing:

> She was bra-less,
> She's not harmless,
> She was ever so, ever so
> Parlous.

Zob it seemed couldn't be roused, so she abandoned his and tried Cornelius's room (remaining there for some time). So to those thunderclaps. (Should I, with candelabra, tap on Merle's door?) Well ...

... perhaps not tonight.

Footnote. I am inclined, in the first orange streaks of dawn, to entrap the erase key (though I resist). Try, please, to understand, that I have spent an exhausting night (notwithstanding aged teenagers) with the fatuous observations of the late Professor Glaze. Is it enough that my horoscope assures me, there shall be one bright day? Mr Patric Walker, I shall hold you to this.

August 1. I poached myself an egg for breakfast, and left enough devastation in Simms's country kitchen that I hope will weary his hangover. The bright Atlanta of his quarry tile floor I have spotted with toast crumbs. On his sunny worktops I imprinted circular tea stains. Latterly I have found (and connected the laptop to) his laser printer, which action results in something quasi-baroque as typeface—substance as follows ...

c/o William Spiegelman
2001 Benson Ave
Northwestern University
Evanston IL 60201
31 August 1992

Dear Marsy,

I am sure the power of foresight is seated in the prostate, since the *bonhomie* with which I was received, driven about, and made to feel at home, was responded to by a long bout of jitters in approximately that region. Spiegelman is scatty, and really quite charming. On the first night we had a candlelit dinner, accompanied by aeolian harp. This was through an aged gramophone, whose sound, although spiky, was quiet and not intrusive. He told me all about his healthy daughters. One is a dental technician. The elder's an Egyptologist. This was over a nut-roast with green salad, which he had prepared, and to my taste had over-peppered. Spiegelman's a pale vegetarian.

He told me he'd lost his wife, a vegan, ten years ago in a boating accident. The poor man kept certain of her artefacts exactly as she'd left them (for example her full shoe rack).

Apart from those two lovely daughters (nubile photos were proffered) we discussed my forthcoming lecture—not, I regret, in any great detail. We so easily drifted into asides on the latest Kennedy biogs, which is an industry he's morbidly keen on.

So to my prostate, whose soundings I shall learn in future to take note of. What I have found—and this was accidentally, several days later—was an entry in the notices, which listed my contribution (a rumour hard to quash) as Professor Glaze's Theory of Literary

Time. Of course, these misapprehensions have to be corrected, which on this occasion, in the half-light of the lecture theatre, it was impossible to do. My disclaimer, which I assumed was clear, was met with chair scrapes. Someone stood up—her appearance recalled one of the Spiegelman girls. She articulated a single word— 'Nevertheless ...'—with what a world of subterfuge lurking in those innocent four syllables ... Soon she had me having to justify myself.

Let me remind you of where it is said I stand. It's with St Thomas, on whose opposite bank Duns Scotus proclaims difference—i.e. of essence, between individual things. My own metaphors are strictly to do with the action of writers writing books, for which articles my commentators substitute 'matter'. To St Thomas, this 'matter' is, or suggests, undifferentiated parts. Distinction is merely a difference of spatial position, a co-ordinate tantamount to time (they say) in the Glaze system. Here unfortunately it doesn't end, because Scotus and Aquinas need to be dismissed before this rationale can be viewed in 'modern' terms. Enter Leibniz, who rejected the distinction of essential from accidental properties. So, now, for 'essence', read 'all the propositions that are true of the thing in question'. It is not possible, for Leibniz, for two things in this sense to be exactly alike. This, I'm told, is a principle he has termed the 'identity of indiscernibles'. It didn't go down well with physicists, who declared that two particles of matter may differ solely in terms of temporal and spatial position. That view has since been rendered problematic by relativity, which disposes of space and time as relations.

The problem is further modernised by challenging the conception of 'substance', or to make of a 'thing' a package of qualities, its having no longer a core of 'thinghood'. This is to circularise the whole argument (which in my view is what the entire canon of philosophy does), since, in not acknowledging 'substance', we arrive at a position more reminiscent of Scotus than Aquinas. This incidentally highlights 'faults' in the 'Glaze theory', and leaves us once more with the 'problem' of space and time. I am sustained, Marsy, in the calming resolution that there is no reason why I shouldn't cut this tour short. Please let me hear of the real world, for example more about your house move.

Take care, Andrew.

Dear Andrew,

Glad to see you've risen above these pointless researches. Must say the minutiae of everyday metaphysical life hold no clues as to how to pay the bills. I'm slightly put out because Blandford rejected—yes, rejected!—my Nostradamus piece. This is while my book's a top-ten bestseller ... Should have thought the name alone was worth something. In the end he commissioned a gloomy poet from Huddersfield, whose approach was predictably anti-Thatcherite. Provocative, of course, but by now cliché'd.

Mixed fortunes on the house front. There is a crotchety octogenarian in the adjacent flat (a part of the next door house). The outflow from her and my gutters is carried by a downpipe on her side, and unfortunately this has become overgrown with moss. As a consequence a recent, and quite prolonged downpour caused seepage under the eaves and into her dining-room. Because she can remember paying ten pounds several years ago to have her gutters cleaned, she assumes a lack of maintenance to *my* gutters, and holds me responsible. I pointed out that even at ground level one could see where the moss grew, but at this she waved her walking stick and claimed I was 'bandying' with words. I would be hearing from her solicitor. I say all this because it is such good newspaper material. You know. The human territory thing, as is contrasted with indifference to the real plight of humanity.

Comically the story doesn't end there. Next day a man resembling a sumo wrestler arrived with a ladder, not exactly to remove the moss, but to transfer it into my gutter. He did not flinch from this action even though I watched from an open window.

Better news with the new agent. He's found a buyer who wants to move quickly, and whose conveyancer is sane, rational, business-like. I'm satisfied the whole thing will now go through quite quickly.

But I'm tired, Andrew.

All the best. Marsy.

c/o Dr George Stanford
963 EPB
University of Iowa
Iowa City IA 52242
19 September 1992

Dear Marsy,

Things don't pick up. My contact here, Kathryn Fitzgerald, having carefully denied improper relations with one of her students, could not finally refute evidence of a parking lot surveillance camera. This has reputedly shown, in ankle-to-thigh close-up, how, after a late night party, she so to speak 'arranged' herself on the 'hood' of someone's convertible. This was while her young buck, whose penile tip was also the subject of close-ups, pulsated in anticipation. How true this is I don't know. Though she has certainly gone, and has left no forwarding address.

Dr Stanford is her successor. Though a mild-mannered man, he is just that kind to get my back up, whatever he says or does. A *bête noire*. He knows nothing about my visit, has received no handover notes, and anyway would rather accommodate me as guest at an extramural workshop group. He would like me to talk about the sestine (as a man profoundly in the grip of extinct poetic forms). I am afraid I snapped at him—and have been doing so since—though in the end did agree to the workshop.

Phoned Jessica, really to see what arrangements Sam had managed to make. She has made none. Worse. I have been given a Christening date, and am expected to come. Worse still. The godfather's some kind of activist (and has links with Amnesty International, which I told Jessica doesn't make it easier). To cap it all, I have committed an abysmal *faux pas* with the workshop group, calling one student's work a hangover of 1960s' psychedelia. It turns out she is synaesthetic, and her 'sights of sounds' and 'tasted shapes' are an attempt to encapsulate her 'natural' sensory experience.

I keep getting a rash, and in scratching abrade the skin, around my ankles. Need a holiday, perhaps.

Andrew.

161

Flat 5
147 Trefoil St
SW18
30 September 1992

Dear Andrew,

I've followed up these time/space propositions in a book by Bryan Magee, whose gift is the gift of elucidation. It tells me you are right—perfectly right—to remain airborne above that particularly murky water. It's so obvious too that the corridors of fiction open doors to far richer vistas than the circumlocutions of—what are they called!—'thinkers'.

I'm sorry to say Blandford's gone overboard on this Huddersfield poet—a tacky versifier, who's big, I'm told, on the performance circuit. That's amazing in itself, since (to me) he is virtually inarticulate. I say this not without having gathered empirical data. I was at the Blew Nose Café—working, not by choice, and with my assistant—where he recently topped the bill. His rendition was a first-person dirge, called 'Elaine'. Elaine was a childhood girlfriend, a year above him at the secondary mod (a co-ed). Wordsmith from Huddersfield first had the hots for Elaine during a school holiday, in Dunoon—or so the dirge ran. What was he getting at? Well, the relationship—which had always been coy—spilled over into school life well after the holiday, though never developed beyond walking home from the bus together. These walks—and this is the point—were never accompanied by conversation, except to say 'See you tomorrow' at the point where they went their separate ways. His summarising stanzas were a 'focus'—critical term—for the thing as a whole, which point of light is the current media debate. To what extent do TV and video condition the minds and behaviour of the young? Disgruntled from Huddersfield thinks he has an answer, having shown that as recently as the early 1970s, innocence was possible.

I had been commissioned, Andrew, to produce a 'vibrant' critique, while as you know, I am not the best person to talk 'poetry'. I got this Alistair to do it for me, as a test piece, and at least on this topic have found our views similar.

162

See a doctor about that rash. The best. Marsy.

Zob, we shall see, whose life is a sequence of pragmatical illusions, shall come to consider that an act of plagiarism has been perpetrated against him. That is my point of issue number one (on which more later). Point of issue number two concerns the foregoing lines, these you see addressed to the late Professor Glaze (which, yes, Zob intends to publish). Especially now as I don't have the immediacy— of not one, but two foggy London nights. Step this way, please— into this vaporised ring of light, a lemony halo, in the hollows of which my wounded capacity to reflect has meant I embalm that fateful September (deep sigh for a thriller-writer's hand) of 1992. (O what is that noise?)

It is not that difficult, on the streets of north London, to identify the slop-shirted poet, this being its habitat. It is a species well known for its violet proboscis. Its fraternity is such that whole groups get together on alternating Tuesdays, for the purpose of: (a) performance, (b) workshop therapy. Zob, through an understandable blunder on the part of Blandford's administration people, chose the wrong Tuesday, therefore we unwound our thread—among those brown brick terraces—to the café door on workshop night. We sat down not suspecting this, and were asked, by a sour-faced cocoa-drinker (mug, female, recently jilted), if one of us would read first. Zob shook his head, and I passed (but 'composed' something on my lap). Meanwhile a thin Jewish girl read her delightful piece on the pogrom. (I am not being facetious. As merely the framework or substructure, that grim subject was inescapable. The poem's moist jewel was its cluster of personal lives, in prismatic detail, as found extensions in minor properties—like a button, or a photograph—and so rendered domestically pointless that evil ranged against it.) The team guru, a paunchy, middle-aged man, clad entirely in denim, dismissed this kind of thing as okay when it came off. Only one jaw dropped. Then, we moved on—to a thing in nursery couplets, whose jangle related the commonplace of Christmas shopping in a glass arcade. Blue denim critique pronounced it 'definitely' competition material. That made its author flutter her eyelids.

Then I said I had got a piece, and would like to read. So, to the thud and shoreline slop of that descending cocoa mug, I was offered the table. Ready? It goes like this (a one, a two, a one-two-three):

> Who will believe my verse in time to come,
> Should I adorn it with your just deserts!
> Heaven knows, the 'scene' is a living tomb—
> It stifles, or allows our dying parts.
>
> If I describe that vacancy, your eyes,
> Or enumerate all your disgraces,
> I'll hear you critics say, 'This poet lies.
> It's the world, reflected in our faces.'
>
> So these lines, empurpled in their rage,
> You'll scorn (as persons less of truth than tongue).
> Say life's so (this, an un-poetic age),
> And repeat one grey, ubiquitous song.
>
> Were there a spark, no matter the dark time,
> So I should tinsel my ragbag of rhymes.

Electric mind in blue thought that this was, then it wasn't after Shakespeare. 'Bacon,' I corrected. 'Seventeenth slice.' Zob said nothing, though out on the street confirmed that I had got the job. (O what is that noise?)

That fog was no less pendulous when, on the following Tuesday—and this time alone—I strode through the brown mizzle under the street lamps, or later, in an onrush of blue smoke, wiped my shoes on the stunted bristles of the café door mat. I now regard it as a tragic mistake that I took my seat to the rear of the audience. That action's memorable result was prolonged embarrassment, when—a hacking cough, you know—I walked out (during Sullen from Huddersfield's encore).

Here, briefly, is, or was, my evening's entertainment. As preamble, two straw-hatted yokels, who called themselves word-painters, and from whom I felt entitled to anticipate polychrome ... Alas, words,

164

paint combined to that usual diatribe—subject, that unalloyed social evil, the supermarket. Other artistes bemoaned the lot of the minke whale. One commended an onanist's angular variations in the sheen of an adjustable cheval-glass. Another offered the 'phraseological' truth (*sic*) of war (how much wiser I now am, politically). Finally we got that theory of innocence (everyone said aw!) from that short-trousered adventurer via Dunoon, my paraphrase of which it is irritating to see—as it were in paste-up—in Zob's letter to Glaze (September 30, 1992). He does not even take the trouble not to sound like me. (The piece, originally for Blandford's quarterly, was turned down by that editor. The truth of the nation's 'vibrant' poetry scene is not sufficiently mythic to our purveyors of culture.) O what is that noise?

That noise is—is Merle, who was in the kitchen, the twisted bomb site of which I would have preferred Simms, or Crouch, to encounter first. Ah me. The others have proposed 'snacks', I am told, and so here she is, afloat on that mosaic in the hallway, as she turns and turns a plastic handle (amber device for wringing out lettuce leaves). 'You hungry, Al—like some lunch?' 'Why yes. Just let me gather these papers.' 'We're all in the garden.' Snell was sockless, on a stripy lounger. Crouch touched his knee, in passing the cutlery (light that you see, in his eye that you see, is mingled with overnight ecstasy). Begone, impish muse ... Let me just sit here on these moss-encrusted flagstones, on the patio, and examine my papers. Ah, now what's this! A history lesson, plus cant from Kant et al. ...

c/o J. Anthony Spatz Jr
Andrews Hall
University of Nebraska
Lincoln NE 68588
14 October 1992

Dear Marsy,

My host has salted a wound, which I suppose his intervention ought to have warned me of. My arrival—I shall go further, and say my optimistic arrival—was crowned by a lecture he took me to (to tell me all about the place). Here, Marsy, is revealed truth (refer to enclosures)—

In 1838, a commissioner sent by the US government, whose brief was to settle 'certain' Indian disputes, reported on the salt basins of Lancaster County. These amounted to smooth floors of hard clay, covered with a layer of crystallised salt, which glistened. In 1856, these were brought to public notice by government surveyors—which attracted the first permanent settlers to the region. A number of smallish salt operations thrived in the early 1860s, though were seen off by the railroads. The railroads, of course, facilitated competition from eastern manufacturers, whose production methods were cheaper. In 1886, the State sank a test-well, which was deep, but was disappointing in its result. No serious efforts were subsequently made in the use of deposits for salt production. One of the larger basins was converted into a salt lake, and developed as a pleasure resort. I am trying very hard to remain rational. A hamlet called Lancaster, serving as the county seat, survived these experiments.

Now, Marsy, it's important to know, that the State of Nebraska's first legislature, empowered, in 1867, a commission—whose remit was site-selection. This was for the new capital city. A city to be named Lincoln. On July 29, 1867, the commission chose Lancaster, which was no more than ten or so houses—of stone and of timber—situated on the bald prairie. This was a hundred miles from the nearest railroad. But progress was swift. The city was incorporated, and declared the county seat, in 1869. In July 1870, the first railroad—the Burlington and Missouri River—reached Lincoln. This was followed by several others.

Why am I telling you this (see enclosures)? It's because Spatz is pseudo-Betjemanesque re the buildings here. The State Capitol (he tells me with relish), completed in 1932, has been one of America's 'best architectural achievements'. For him it's a sense of all that preceding history. From its massive, two-storey base, emerges a central tower, to a height of 400ft. This is surmounted by the figure of a sower. I am now talking guidebooks. The architect was B. G. Goodhue. The sculptor was Lee Lawrie. The interior mural décor was by Augustus Vincent Tack and Hildreth Miere. The inscriptions and symbols were chosen by Hartley B. Alexander. A statue of

166

Abraham Lincoln, by Daniel Chester French, is at the western approach to the Capitol grounds.

To my horror, the genial Spatz thinks I can view the insane philosophers of Europe in the same pioneering light, and has even assumed my life and career owe them a debt. It is becoming, Marsy, intolerable. I sat for an hour, for the commencement of my own lecture (this a few evenings ago), while one of his trained monkeys primed my audience with quite irrelevant gibberish (I have since read up on it, and still say it's gibberish). Take Kant. He says the external world causes only the matter of sensation, while it is mentally that we arrange this matter in space and time (which is how *I* am dragged in). 'Things'—like railroads and towers—i.e. the causes of our sensations, are inherently unknowable, and are not in space or time (because space and time are subjective, are merely a part of the way we perceive). Therefore what we experience is only ever fitted to our perceptual pattern of geometry and time. Spatially, temporally, we 'experience' grains of salt, but do not 'know' them. This makes geometry 'true' only to the point of our experience of things, but not of those things in themselves. Kant tells us space and time aren't concepts. They're forms of intuition. You might as well say a book isn't a book, but so far as we're concerned, it's a book.

Hegel is even more confused. For him, the process of time is to the more from the less perfect, in both an ethical and logical sense. He needn't really bother with what is 'ethical' and what is 'logical', because his theory treats these as exactly alike. Their perfection is the same, i.e. a closed whole, a complex of interdependent parts all working to a single end. That end, which is the fulfilment of history, concerns the progress of 'spirit'—I think he means human spirit—whose object is to be free. Spiritual freedom comes about, Marsy (surprisingly), through the mundane system of monarchy. People spend whole lives in the study of these propositions.

Schopenhauer abolishes time and space, and subjugates everything to 'will'. Will, he says, is the source of human suffering, made endless because it has no goal. It has no goal because we pursue what can't be achieved—happiness. What we mean in referring to any happiness that has been attained, is no more than satiety. Conversely an unsatisfied wish results in pain. It's with this reasoning that Schopenhauer turns to the doctrine of Nirvana, which prescribes that the less we exercise will, the less we shall suffer. His pilgrim of human will sees through the veil of maya (illusion), which shows him that all things are one. All things being one, he cannot differentiate himself from another (or for that matter from any given object). This is his knowledge of the whole, which quells volition. In this state, our will is repelled from life in a denial of our own nature. Time and space being the 'universal forms' of will, these are also denied. What then the cosmos is, is nothingness.

Spatz cheerfully intervened at precisely this point, on the understanding that I would now deliver myself of an extension, and as he put it 'further illumination', to all this gobbledegook. I did consider a way in through Schopenhauer. Interest etc. in Eastern thought etc. that has underpinned etc. some of the work of Modernism. Etc. I recalled my earlier study of Scanziani, and might have rattled on about this. Instead I retired with a 'migraine'.

I'm not putting up with much more of this. Plus that rash has spread to my underarms.

Andrew.

Glaze's enclosures, which I do vaguely remember—having come across them in the Wandsworth room—were undoubtedly photographs of the State Capitol—not that I ever paid them much attention.

12 Hampstead Hill Drive
NW3
9 November 1992

Dear Andrew,

Made it at last! And in the end with hardly a hitch re sale of flat.

Must say the garden's a mess (I mean by that it's not to my taste)—so, shall have to get a man in to sort it all out. Alistair likes his two-room garret, whose sloping ceilings are a permanent reminder of his position. Here he'll co-ordinate much of the administration. For the rest of the place I shall need domestic help. The neighbour, who's a liver surgeon, has lent me his directory (his 'list of mops', as he terms it).

So, Andrew—how has all this come about! Yours is no small part in it, and nor is Snell's (you may be surprised to hear). He has only to get the scent of money in his nostrils and suddenly he's motivated! Film has given him negotiating room—a two-book deal, in fact—from which my accountant extrapolates a first million.

Andrew, I feel fantastic! You must see a doctor about that rash.

Marsy.

I could, at first demurely, contemplate a spring onion, though before I had poured salt on to the raised circumference of my plate, I rejected that idea. I left my lunch as a reluctantly chewed circle of baguette, with a cream cheese I had failed to taste. 'Why Al you're not hungry after all!' Merle, on the thick uppers of her flip-flops, flip-flopped into a cane arch, a trellis festooned with the flaming girandoles of a passion flower. She had I recall tennis shorts, in wash-day white. And a transparent blouse, checked in a shade of marmalade with apple-green—a cheesecloth whose exquisite tail she had bunched, and softly knotted at that perfect, ivory navel. The long-lashed Simms, now on the connecting path (red-brick zigzags), in part filled the opposing and matching arch (this one with honeysuckle, its red berries and many withered blooms). I overheard their conversation. Merle, in the kitchen, had come across lemon grass and tamarind pods, with which, she said, 'I can cook up something exotic, this evening if there's time …' Simms's smooth brow in a garland of fading honeysuckle, his whole upper body swimming under those wild scents: 'That would be charming and delightful!'

Crouch took the point of a pair of manicure scissors to the quick of her toenails, so exhibiting the dark fringes of Forest Pubis under the cocked leg of her khaki shorts (these had turnups). Snell, flourishing a blue hanky, said he was hot and, loudly, that he would take another shower—though she did not follow him ('Insatiable!' she muttered). Simms, I noticed, now had his hand to the small of Merle's back, flesh on flesh, and steered with good-natured precision over the green sward, I felt sure toward the boathouse. Crouch asked would I like a shower (Not tonight, Geraldine). 'Or a bath.' Well—thanks all

169

the same. I shall I think take a stroll around all that mare's-tail, to the far side of the lake—which I did. Casually.

Geraldine finally cut her nails, shovelling what clippings confronted her lunch plate (O her brittle rhino claw) into a Chinese bell pot—whose design was dragons, willows, pools. This she used also as a spittoon, getting up to go somewhere—for the sake of theatre, to a potting shed. Here, under the larded luminosity of her cold feminine buttocks—the flab of those stellar revolutions—a startled garden boy limped from his climax—or so, according to certain purple passages singled out by the Sunday reviewers, her most recent memoir has since that occasion revealed.

I examined a dovecot (peripherally), a dark chalet printed to the deep blue backdrop of an unhurried, and uninterrupted sky. Simms, his legs wide to the stern of a painted green boat (risibly the Venus), I don't think suspected my easy-going scrutiny (as a man with hands deeply pocketed, who liked to be alone). He helped Merle aboard and seated her aft, then himself wobbled to the bow, where, in the reedy lakeside—perhaps to Crouch's same slow rhythm—he first dipped oars. It was so romantic. I imagine it stirred the rainbow trout. Or that Merle, with a lazy hand in the gathering foam, caught at her knot, watching the lash and the golden slither of carp.

I was, eventually, satisfied that they talked only, and began to walk back, but was not so satisfied that at one point, centre lake, they seemed to confer. That was just too intimate. Sympathetic groans, please, for little boy lost ...

It was approaching the cocktail hour when Zob presented a gift-wrapped Le Fanu. Happy birthday, Merle (a capable thirty-three).

August 2. Snell, who'd got through the night without the intervention of his succubus, made a dawn resolve—at ablutions decided to push on back to the office. 'Wonderful, Justin, to see you,' I remember was the valediction (gigantic right hand proffered). 'Tremendous bash!' Merle, who handled the maps, pointed out— pointed out by a back route—that it wasn't out of their way (much) to drop in on a client in Lyme Regis—an old, filmic 'trouvère' (or so that crone often described himself). This I hear resulted in fruitless gestures. In his novelettish way, that grandee plied them, in the weave of his drawing room, with tea from a silver service, and endless, refusable rock buns. Recently he'd acquired a parrot (the companionship), which aside from stocks in piracy, had since achieved only—imitating—the revolving whine of a neighbour's auto alarm. Merle pursed lips and tried to teach it pretty things. Really-must-be-going Snell couldn't see how to utter it (the verb 'to go'), until a wall clock tinkled. It was as well it did. Our two got back to New Caxton Grove a little before 5 o'clock, in whose back office Merle's answer machine winked its green spot of light fairly furiously. Poor tired Merle! I don't need to imagine, in that next hour or so, that she returned calls, having no time to change, and so suffered the dampness of her Sistine chapel tee shirt (extract, ceiling, Adam's electrification). The vague scent of pear to her perfumed wrists was past a certain ripeness. Then to top it Cornelius came in with urgent, days-old mail to reply to, while he ran a foam bath.

My own day-long cast me in the role of chauffeur (again), this time dropping off those three colossi in a shady interstice, that Simms, as far back as boy with fishing rod, had discovered in a coastal corniche. That opened to a rutted path, which under its wooded canopy—a padded oak and pine quilt, peppered with silver birch— cut a conical section to the rock and silicon arc of a bay (secluded, to all intents 'private'). Zob, unsteadily sandalled (those dry, lumpy clods), carried the cold box (beers, pasta and potato salads, spare ribs in a marinade). Simms took the towels, which were bagged, and the barbecue. Geraldine the tongs and charcoals. Driver Wye had the lap-top and was told to kill time (till either rain or sundown), and so drove to the next touristy town, where I parked the Mercedes and wandered.

Not much to report. Bric-à-brac shoppe, with large etched windows, for the display of miniature brass boots, a collection of toby jugs, pewter lamps with frosty glass globes. There was, in the doorway, a basket full of plastic footballs. Nothing here for me—so, in a low-beamed tea room, all stone walls and horse brasses, I amused myself (not very successfully) with a glass of frothed-up coffee, plus Danish pastry. Not that I was hungry: bored, you understand. Soon the next table gave up its starched cloth and napkins to a self-appointed guide (sturdy new boots, flecked grey ankle socks, cotton trousers, lumberjack shirt), and two distant females (day trip under duress). I say this because I met this party again, not long after in the tourist information office, where I found myself innocently scrutinising a series of stratified models. These were of the local coastline, with its steep slopes, and 'hog's back' cliffs, now a rare nesting site for the peregrine falcon (he said). He also told me the Exmoor path story, which was to do with the colour-coding of interesting walks. Here one of his companions touched his elbow sourly. Nevertheless he rattled on. So that I have come away with a dream of wild brown trout in the cellophane glitter of all this man's rivers. Might soon have to visit the barrows of Hangley Cleave. Shall tramp one day among the purple moor grass, or the more reddish bell heather, listening for a curlew, or a snipe, or a plain mountain blackbird. Could find myself in pursuit of a fritillary, or an emperor moth. 'One other thing,' he said, though he found himself dragged to the car park ... 'uplands', I heard, 'bog asphodel', 'heath spotted orchid', something about wild cranberry. We crossed paths again, this time as he reversed his orange camper truck, and acknowledged the nose of my Mercedes with a wave. Has he hired a boat, I wonder, and is a man out at sea, casting his line for heavier fish ... No matter. For all I knew now, for all I intended to tell Zob—whose car at dusk I left with hazard lights on—for what he had learned that day of the great outdoors, was that the naked sun, slanting over those narcissistic rock pools, left a nasty pink stamp across his shoulders. I carried the cold box. Geraldine squirted him with a cool white lotion—and rubbed. Simms had a contented, and not altogether a friendly smile.

August 3. Was the day we left Simms in peace, at the discretion of his street-corner muse, who, as dreary scion of antiquity, never made the least suggestion as to the use of waste bins. Perhaps she was timid. Geraldine on the other hand wasn't (timid), and in no matter what public place (I recall a mini-market, a town square with fountain, a very crowded post office) lifted Zob's shirt and palmed in yet more of that summer salve.

Yes (as I refer to notes). It was after all the day we stopped for drinks. This was at the White Hart, in that quaint and pretentious place called Dartington, Crouch having already scoured the Totnes and Newton Abbot estate agents, and come away with a portfolio of 'character' properties. Very wearying. Nor, as driver, could I, as driver, do justice to the Blackawton brewery, whose beer was on tap.

'Blackawton,' said Geraldine. 'That's where they worm charm.'

We are—as I must just adjust this parasol (wobbly table)—in many ways privileged to know that.

I have the benefit of Crouch's most recent memoir, published with fanfares. Her vulgarity is southern in its lighting, and has a lot to do—in that political stance she adopts—with coaxing out the machismo in her men friends (to demonstrate I know not what obscure point). She dragged us to the edge of Dartmoor, to look at this cottage, in whose cool stone shadows I complete my own memoir, a place then as now peaceably set in a wilderness. Zob looked at the roof slates, some of which hung by a corner. Inspected with a wilful eye the angular inclination of much of the pre-war guttering (a subject he'd involuntarily researched, back in Wandsworth). He prodded—rather sullen, I thought—with the toothy blade of his house key, an infested lintel, followed by a wormy post. Finally he sniffed at the damp air inside and announced remotely that this was not a place he could get on with (anyway he had long thought of France and a *gîte*). Geraldine laughed this off— 'Marsy, you're not looking at this in the right way'—and wanted him right now to get down to the agent's office and write out a cheque (for the deposit). 'I mean the place has SO much potential.' Zob's only comment was huh. I scraped back the kitchen door, where we had managed to gain entry, and quietly pocketed the agent's blurb.

August 4. Was the day we left Simms altogether, Geraldine with pyrotechnics, the two of us awkwardly. This was at a breakfast of cereals and orange segments, whose tonic of bitter-sweetness was one I still recall light-headedly (not to say with a touch of nausea). A second pot of coffee arrived stage left, which is to say a double oak door under precarious antlers. Geraldine roared at the house maid (with laughter, that is, and at her servility, or her quaintness, certainly the impression of a curtsey). Simms pressed the enfolded corner of his napkin to the enfolding corner of his mouth. Zob looked on with terrified eyes. I myself cast about the room: would a paunchy Belgian detective, with waxed moustaches, enter stage right (patio doors), to dissect the monstrousness of our crimes (and incidentally dismiss the maid with all that Gallic civility)? Not regrettably this time. Geraldine left slops in her saucer and mentioned that her bag was packed. So soon as Simms got one of his flunkeys to stow it in her boot, she was off—'... it's been such a pleasant break.' This left Zob with difficult diplomacy, his relation to Simms never quite exceeding its present concordat, which was respectful only. 'Perhaps in the circumstances ...' he said, meaning I don't know what. 'Huh, eh, Al?' 'Why yes of course,' I said. 'Geraldine's so right. We can't keep Justin from his work.' I have recorded in my notes that, our humming tyres to the motorway, we overtook her just this side of Bristol, though Zob, browsing through the Glaze letters, failed to notice this. It has to be said that Geraldine was drumming her dash, to the frenetic rhythms of her radio. This, I believe, is a measure of her inanity—'brilliant' though she undoubtedly is.

August 5. A curious reply, from not Mr—but Dr Mansard—whose gum-chewing grandchild you'll recall returned Zob's diary. Mansard quotes his granddaughter's transgression as 'spontaneous', a note in the lined rectangle called Tue 26 (of July). Silly me, she writes, left my diary behind. Mansard, though apologetic, puts this down to youthful high spirits, and points out there can have been no ill intent, in that she has gone to the trouble of returning Zob's property. It is a fact that the bin was never far away, under the counter. Zob, whom I have never seen with white knuckles, and who is generally mild mannered (but repressed, as our resurgent Freudians would have it), upsets a lot of negligible objects, bringing fists down on his desk— for example an ivory paper knife, which has inanimate surprise in its leap. There are obscenities, he states, under the early dates of autumn (is this prescience, I ask?). 'You can't say that's not ill intent.' I am to draft another letter to Mansard, making all this clear, and asking (rhetorically) should Zob seek legal advice—an area of professional life he does in fact venture into—in my view incautiously—though in another connection.

August 7. Malkin strayed in, during Isabelle's Sunday rendezvous, with an ear half-chewed, the remaining velvet caked in dry blood. The Citroën's on the drive, so the mistress is out in a borrowed car (not, as I view from the window, that cherry Peugeot).
  What am I going to do about Malkin?

August 8. Zob, as tetchy as I've seen him, now cracks the whip on the Glaze project. 'Why, Al, is it taking so long!' (Lucky I've worked on this!) I tell him I'm there or there abouts, and will do my best to close it off. Therefore ...
  ... day one, end game—

c/o Ludo Marcinkiewicz
University of Denver
Denver CO 80208
20 November 1992

Dear Marsy,
  Glad the move went well. Mine, into host's after host's, is getting me down. Not least of it was the quack I saw about that rash, who prescribed a powder spray (for of all things athlete's foot). He suggested—which is why he's a quack—that I might be diabetic. After all these years. Still. After a few days, the spray did work.
  It's almost certain now I'll wind this tour up, with Denver the last straw. Because, you see, I have had my own brush with doomsday— on which yours, or I should say Blandford's, isn't a patch. Some hoaxer thought it might be a wheeze to jet in from Europe the globe's leading scholar (to boot a cross-disciplinary scholar), on that fraud of our temporal corridors, Nostradamus. I can't seem to shake off this reputation of time-watching. Add to which all my lectures are now preceded by another speaker (to whom I am usually expected to reply). How could I answer this authority, one Dr Xavier Rée (almost certainly a *nom de guerre*)? His theory, I imagine

appropriated from that dubious world of sci-fi, is as follows.

First (disputed) premiss is that Nostradamus 'knew' of events occurring since his death—which was in 1556. This does not imply a deterministic universe, for with what cosmic tricks we may banish all our teleology! This, in favour of our faculty of choice! (Yes. I did say choice.) We come to the notion of parallel realities, and the depiction of time not as a flow ('river' is the popular allegory), but as branch work (behold the time tree). The inception of time is the base of a trunk. We see boughs, branches, twigs (there is no mention of foliage, or the fruits and flowers of time). Our world and our cosy reality, which most assume to have no parallel, is (it is posited) merely a twig among many, its past being unique only from the point of its first sprouting. Other twigs represent times, worlds, cosmological culs-de-sac similar, but not identical, to our own. Not quite the funniest part is this (the real joke is contemporary physics): that it all comes about through sentient beings exercising their prerogative of choice. Choosing to do one thing rather than another results in a new twiglet, so that you, or a replicate you, when you didn't get up with the alarm, spawned an alternative you (complete with universe) who did. Where, Marsy, does all this end (for one can't begin to consider the multiplicities)? With not only human choice but animal? Or with the consciousness of plants, responsive or not responsive to whatever tropism? With intelligent machines perhaps?

Can you believe this is serious science? I can't—paraphrasing Rée, who mentions Hoyle, and himself paraphrases a Dr Clutton-Brock (I understand, mathematical physicist). He asks us to envisage our universe sliding into a plurality of worlds, of which we experience only one. This myriad is a mixture: 'closed' worlds, 'open' worlds; worlds that are uniform, worlds that aren't; worlds of high entropy, conversely of low. Mostly life never evolves in these worlds. In some, life is scarce. Just in a few, life is abundant.

How does this relate to Nostradamus? Rée says this, that we are to regard Nostradamus as an adept in tree-climbing, as a man who's tested the branches and glimpsed the many boughs. Why most of his predictions are plainly wrong (those that seem right are gnomic) is that he has looked into the parallel worlds of which only our clones have experience.

I should have chosen a career teaching infants. Hope to see you soon. Andrew.

Zob, who glanced over my shoulder—up there in my heaven of perfect peach—picked out that penultimate paragraph as I proof-read (while, incidentally, I tested fonts, today a kind of castellated italic) on its printed page. 'Don't,' he said, 'saw the branch you're sitting on. Try to predict why I can't get hold of Cornelius. He doesn't return my calls ...' Well, Marsy—I had special agent Merle, and knew (in what I'd describe as time's unruly undergrowth) what Snell was up to (he was wooing Simms). What prescience the forces of parallelism attributed to me (in the sense of prophetic success as is synchronised to that human tide of what is self-fulfilling) suggested it was time to resurrect my three-act soap (do you remember? *The Guilt That is Hampstead's*), and finally pen its finally disintegrating scene. Finally. Perhaps I will (some day).

12 Hampstead Hill Drive
NW3
4 December 1992

Dear Andrew,

Just about getting straight (so now life begins!). All that junk from my Wandsworth days—those horribly middle-class accoutrements—I have consigned and locked up in a single room. Edith was here with catalogues [Edith Zob, née Parkes, the writer's mother, by then a divorcée], so I have been on a spree in the department stores. Will my credit card stand it? Michael has been too [Michael Zob, MBE, a curmudgeon rather than philanderer, the writer's father], and gave his seal of approval.

I shouldn't if I were you, Andrew, persist with this tour, which I see is taking its toll. At bottom you're dealing with a gun culture, so it's no surprise to me if these shallow academics want to make a fight of what you say. Stuff 'em!

And, hey, what about this! Yesterday Blandford tried to present me with a dog (actually a bitch, actually a pup), a lively brindle boxer—

called Gemma—which he thought I'd be just right with, strolling on the Heath. Sounds too much like hard work. But a nice-looking animal. I allowed him to exercise the thing on the front acreage of concrete (which I must have dug up and properly landscaped). This was a definite put-off: the bright ordures Blandford took a makeshift glove to (supermarket carrier bag), and the long hunt he had for my dustbins (as I laughed).

So, Andrew, when shall we see you? There's going to be lots to catch up on. Take care. Marsy.

This was Zob's last letter to Glaze, bar some final scrawl daubed on a picture postcard.

August 9. End game day two—

c/o Antony Lester
Box 9131
Berkeley CA 94709
23 December 1992

Dear Marsy,

Feeling much better, having spent a few days in San Francisco. That was with my old friend Maria (I've mentioned her), whose bastard offspring—a little before your time—did astounding work at Exe, and who now runs one of the biggest agencies here ('here' being New York). Maria's made herself quite an authority on the streets and boulevards, and has walked me round. She tells me the street system commenced in 1835, with Calle de la Fundación, or Foundation Street, when it was first laid out. In 1839 came the first survey (oh to be so young!), which covered what is now the retail and financial centres. Avenues and other streets were added—then in 1845 someone called Jasper O'Farrell made a second survey. This has resulted in the checker-board layout, Market Street being the main artery. Streets north of this run north, east, south, west. Streets south run parallel to Market Street, and at right angles. Of the scenic boulevards, I have seen the Marina, Twin Peaks, Lincoln, Embarcadero and Great Highway paralleling the ocean. It is nice to

178

have been able to take all this in calmly.

On my last night we had chow in Chinatown. I've got some snaps, which I'll show you.

Maria kindly gave up her study during the daytime, where I have worked on a final, I hope epoch-making lecture—to be delivered here at Berkeley, some time in the new year—which I intend will finally set the record straight. Squash all this clock nonsense once and for all.

She—Maria—keeps on her shelves back volumes and numbers of *The Five Dollar Review*. I found in one, from the fall of '67, a quite wonderful collage constructed by someone your daddy tutored briefly at Exe. It's a poem, a paean, with everything in place. Proprietors and employees. It's got soaps, printers' inks, serums. Gasoline engines. Coconut oil and pumps. Margarines, mayonnaise. Ketchup and fertiliser (in one breath, yes). Tanned leather and tabloids in print. Title? Well, Marsy (cf. Bishop Berkeley): 'Verse on the Prospect of Planted Arts and Learning in America'. The kind of thing your daddy sat up half the night attempting to do himself (though of course England's over-ripe for that). Still. His protégé learned something.

Will see you some time in the new year, when I'm heading back. Happy Christmas meantime. Andrew.

Curious how Glaze, in his moments of deepest uncertainty, resorts to that professorial fallback, the catalogue (cp. his missive from Nebraska, dated 14 October, which bears an identical stamp).

Marsy's reply is via picture postcard from Rome. It's one of those with a quartered laminate, whose scenes I review, from top left-hand corner clockwise, under a lamp, being myself at one remove, in the gloom of an English rainy day. The Colosseum is statutory, with pedestrians, cars, coaches. A detail next, of St Mary Major—its sumptuous interior. For the Fountain of Rivers there's a night shot, made a luminescent green with artificial light. Then St Peter's Square. An oval, superposed at the centre, is there to demonstrate the young Michelangelo's chisel, in the Pieta.

What's indented on the reverse side, in deeply felt ballpoint, is not so high-flown—as a matter of fact, Zob is frankly vague as to the importance of Rome come the frosts of London's January. I, Wye, do have some recollection. It's to do with an American beauty, robust and a strawberry blonde, who said Aw! in proteiform ways (winks, wrinkled nose, etc.), and had allowed herself to be cornered. This, I feel sure, was in the platinum foyer of one of Zob's smart new London friends, where he had lingered on a transparent cocktail, as a conversational prelude to dinner (for in excess of a hundred guests). She was heiress to a perfumery, and had business in Rome after the yuletide festival (an exclusively Italian promotion). Zob of course hitched up his trousers and chased after (unsuccessfully), though there is no clue to this in what follows, dated January 11:

Greetings from Rome, where I am spending a few days (research). Small world, isn't it! Shared a taxi from the airport with Anthony Burgage (I don't think he knew who I was), and yesterday, at a *bureau de change*, on the Via Palestro, which is near my hotel, caught sight distantly of Geraldine Crouch—who doesn't seem quite the lioness one recalls from TV, when she's tearing strips off complacent men. Glad this tour of yours is at last near an end. See you soon. Marsy.

Zob's pursuit, I suppose ineptly of American collateral—which was futile—of course pre-dated Geraldine's election to the committee (Best-novel-to-be-published [this decade]). I go further and express my personal view that Zob had not previously met her. I say also, and with absolute certainty, that we had not yet entered that vigorous media vortex, one of whose sickly green symptoms, latterly a shade of jaundice, was Crouch herself—as regular visitor to Hampstead Hill Drive (in her cabriolet). From here on it becomes a circus, in sight of which you are privileged to share my *loge*. Zob adopted his *faux bonhomme*, in which at least one person saw salesy possibilities—I mean Masturbile, who could not, as parasite, raise his own profile without fatuous men like Zob. That happy rapporteur, whose links to the committee were not merely professional—he had a good line in after-dinner patter, exhaustively round the dining rooms of Hampstead—he would I know ensure a *succès fou* for whatever the marketable Zob might turn his hand to (*Gimme the Cash*, as it happened). It is, I'm aware, anserine—yet so typically Philip. (Now then. It seems some obscure communication from the worshipful company of turners has got itself mixed up with these last letters from Glaze. More research, I assume, which Zob has since dropped. But this is beside the point.) Where was I? Ah yes, these letters from the hapless Glaze. There are—I was very pleased to inform my master—only two others we might bother to consider, which strictly speaking didn't belong with all that previous correspondence. These I refer to as the 'Rosewood' letters, as a kind of dramatic epithet the world of Anglistics likes to adorn itself with (this is also very anserine). These two received no written reply from the 'giant' Zob, all of whose intelligent gossamer had at this time borne itself up in a much airier calling (or evacuant).

The evangel according to St Andrew (that late competitor with harp, St Andrew Glaze), drove him in the last months of his life into his favourite south-eastern corner of England, that garden paradise he has somehow made all his own (fondly in our memories, or so I exercise, prefatory in style, our literary propaganda). 'Rosewood' was that nursing home, among tall pines and clipped Elysian lawns, over which, from his upper window, he might chance his gaze on the surrounding hops and freshly painted oast houses. Corn fields and chestnut woods are more distant, through which I have driven Zob several times, up and down those hilly Kentish lanes. This was over the course of three distinct seasons, so that—as it were recently photographic—I may pass, in a single page of my album, over the feathered trees with photosynthetic shafts of light (and at intervals a woodland floor of bluebells), to the ghostly fields and brush strokes of snow on the farmers' five-bar gates.

Zob—as mere entity one is entitled to think of, squashed to the shape of a sigh (or perhaps sluggish ampersand—I remember his hands, profoundly pocketed)—recalled a more voluminous exchange of letters than was in fact the case. I don't think he faced this position with quite the commercial realism he had so far demonstrated as purveyor of fictive trash. His first thought was to exclude the 'Rosewood' letters (as not suitable to the commemoration of Glaze's life and work). Later he performed an

181

about-turn (acknowledging the need for padding), and wanted to see them appended—as the 'Rosewood testament'. For the time being, I was instructed not to print.

August 10. Unable this morning to park my car, whose offside wing—I note with no immediate prospect of remedy—has broken out in a nasty rubiginous rash. The obstruction amounts to two beefy shot-putters, in shorts and perspiring vests—one with pneumatic drill, and wearing headphones, who bores at the concrete once Zob's drive, the other with a pick, lifting flagstones. Zob, who will surely find a distant lunch appointment (and travel to it now), is also in headphones, and is hunched in his study, it only appears with neuralgia.

I had just about dealt with the mail, a half-dozen letters I have marked 'attention' (as formed no part of that paper mountain my foot compressed in the bin), when I was asked to move my car: To make way guv (for the rubbish skip). That pneumatic drill was replaced by a ballpoint, for what was now an enamel tea break. Remarkably its sausage-fisted owner made short work of his *Times* crossword—which I mentioned to Zob, eliciting a well, didn't I know? there are all sorts of people out there. Why thanks, Marsy, for that insight.

Could not help but notice, shunting my Ford through an adjacent parallax, and stepping on to the paved vista abutting the liver surgeon's, an uncertain shrimp of a girl (mid-twenties, about), who with the point of her Victorian shoe tested, then considered, the disrupted purlieu of Master Zob's castle. Her jeans were a faded blue—studded, not zipped.

I locked up my car. The tea-drinkers caterwauled. One of them cat-called. Would see, would they, a *danse du ventre* (as somehow figured in that crossword)? The diamond mesh of her knitted summer top, ending in elastic, versts above the navel, part revealed in apricot cross-hatch a firmness of young fruit. A hand many times to a strand of loose hair, she skirted the rubble to our door. Zob, who at this time discerned the flagitious in all human motives, softened to this 'completely' unexpected case. After five minutes or so they went out together.

182

August 11. I am apprised of 'certain' explanations. This is because Zob, whose husbandry is again open to the charge of incompetence, launched first one, then a second official communiqué. This took place casually over the kitchen table. Politely he had called Mrs Clapp Mrs St John, having framed, as counter to that worker's union-ish demonstrations, the following question: 'Well? What's wrong with these brushes?' (I am incredibly bored by now.) Mrs Clapp I am afraid did not control the verbal extreme of her (tutting) indignation, and scurried off (with brushes). Zob, as an admission having no logical connection, told me he was having the front landscaped. The workmen, I dared not confirm, had abandoned the rubble and had overturned their barrows, and had not so far come back. Also 'that girl' I might have seen yesterday was Dr Mansard's granddaughter—Arabella—whose plea of innocence he had 'totally' accepted. Tonight she would leave her toothbrush behind.

August 12. Last night she left her toothbrush behind (in bathroom one). I noticed this because its bi-directional handle, so styled in an ebullience of market waffle, was a translucent saffron. Its bristles were fierce and mauve. One other clue was the toothpaste tube. This had two pristine indentations to the mint of its broad shoulders— cool signal of contempt for the neat folds Zob had gathered over the weeks to the reverse end, to the wedge foot.

August 14. Somehow one of Isabelle's house-and-garden magazines, quite a tonnage in my hand, had found its way to my bedside table. This, as company for a Sunday morning, I can say was more inspiriting than the gaucherie I put down, a Poetry Society 'leading' practitioner, whose 'recommended' paperbacks Zob insists I read from time to time. I would not, other than 'professionally', soil my palm. On a late page—of Isabelle's bourgeois glossy—I confirmed my glowing horoscope, diminished not at all by its femininity (nor by the variant good fortune shored in our circles of heaven, for my eleven counterparts). A voluptuous double-fold pictured perfect people in a perfect conservatory, the full course of their lives completely untouched by the greater, and fuscous dome that belongs to the natural architecture, our permanent English mizzle. Instead we see burnished marble, as a floor. Potted palms. Lots of wicker chairs and glass table tops. A housewife in radiant charmeuse. A happy husband in a light knitted cardigan (has lost, has he, his pipe?). There are, and this is obligatory, prone children with construction-kit towers. And smiles.

Unusually, for a Sunday, Isabelle got home in time to make us all lunch—her leek and macaroni, in a red cheese sauce. I could not bear her Lambrusco, so myself furnished the table with a modest Chardonnay (its hint of herbs, honey and guavas). Michael—quite rightly, in my opinion—vacated the table, not with the appearance of dessert, which was a Neapolitan swirl of ice cream, besieged under a glistening chocolate sauce—but when Isabelle tuned in her all-booming radio. Such waves gave way briefly to a soprano— 'Now, *Talking Music!*'—then, on a background dream of Delian poppy fields, the baritone belonging to Masturbile. Perhaps I should not have to reiterate the accustomed lie—'… my guest today the writer Marshall Zob, whom many regard as England's finest …' I have by now adopted the saneness of detachment.

I listened …

Some short audible mummery placed Zob as the innocent in public affairs, a man who cannot impose the rules of society, nor do anything but submit to its market place. He therefore pens comedy (a grim sort of comedy) for the delight of his audience everywhere. Zob is a 'universal'.

Philip: 'Was it always so, Marsy, or did you have to work at this?'Work, of course.

'Your first record, then …'

Well, as someone who grew up in the 60s, something (touching) from the dead John Lennon (there were places he, the dead man, remembered). Lovely (but it surprised widow Lavante). Moving on, then (here Masturbile attempted plummy tones), what about family life? Answer: very caring. Emphasis as you'd .expect on communication. Though Zob was left alone a lot, which naturally explains the 'unusual', even 'extraordinary' development, of his imagination.

Another record. Zob recalls a very first trip (alone) to the Festival Hall, for a performance of Stravinsky's *Rite of Spring*—

exhilarating!

Student life.

That of course was hard-working at Exe.

'You got a first.'

Philip. Zob wasn't about to boast. Here, you're supposed to point up camaraderie with working-class contemporaries. Abiding image is: receptive young man taking first tentative steps across threshold of twentieth-century literature (as opposed to Oxford classics).

Never mind that. Let's have some more music.

Well, things didn't exactly go swimmingly after Exe (it took a long time to get hack work). Even now, in irksome moments, 'I still have recourse to that wonderful Pachelbel *Canon*'—which to me (Wye) is news.

'Success did eventually come ...' We are referring here to *Aristotle's Atom* ('staggering' first novel), which was remaindered, and would have been left to an unmarked grave. This but for the tireless Glaze, who nudged it, without the tiniest blush, into the lucrative world of low-grade movie-making. That, with concomitant advertising, launched a reprint, which reportedly sold in excess of half a million copies, paperback.

'These things are sometimes slow to take off—but let's have some more music.'

Zob professed an old favourite, in Elgar—the *Cello Concerto*— which I'm certain does not have a place in his CD library. Cynically du Pré as soloist (we imagine much head-shaking, we hear the word 'tragic').

'So, Marsy, what's going on in your life NOW?' A chance to promote *Gimme the Cash*—on sale 'in all good bookshops', and incidentally short-listed (Best-novel-to-be-published [this decade]). Accompaniment, Italia '90.

'Now. What of the future, Marsy? What does that hold?' Plans, stupid, for the Andrew Glaze memorial (a lot of inconsequential nonsense here interspersed: 'friend, mentor, brilliant academic'). Music that followed, was: *I'd stake my Cremona to a Jew's trump.*

'So to the long term.' Don't, Philip, encourage it—that whirl of saccharine, that 'ambitious' air, that placenta Zob terms 'millennial' (meaning we're in for a novel, dodo size).

Conductor taps lectern, wields baton, launches, elastically, from podium. A leather-clad demiurge clashes cymbals in the cloaked halls of Valhalla, and we're away, riding with the Valkyries.

Can't, I'm afraid, stay for *The Magic Flute*: 'I don't think, Isabelle, I can finish this Chardonnay. I shall I think just put it in the fridge.'

Be gone, salesman Zob.

August 15. Adam—more nimble on his feet—in a nightmare of infantile handwriting, left a recipe for Mrs St John. This was in turquoise ink (with spots and spider's threads) on crumpled notepaper, which he has pinned down under the weight of her steam iron, prominently in the laundry room. I had wandered in there while the kettle boiled. The recipe was for pumpkin chutney, which nicety I later connected with just such a plant, whose fruit—the size of my fist—and loud orange trumpets shaded themselves to the rear of the chalet.

Zob complained that he was still not getting through to Snell.

August 16. Mrs St John held that recipe amply to her bosom, sighing deeply. Zob said, 'For God's sake, what's happened to Cornelius!'

August 17. Zob said the same thing again. I said, that it so happens Merle is having problems with her new file-transfer software, *$$TransPlant$$*. On the pretext of helping out with that, 'shall I get over to New Caxton Grove, see what's going on?'

'That's the first sensible thing, Al, you've said. What does she want with file-transfer software?'

'She'd like to work from home more.'

'Oh.'

August 18. Merle, I gather, was tied up for most of yesterday with one of her TV gardeners, who had 'come up' with another book. This was a man whose Impressionist's polychrome brush strokes, plus haze of mosaic paths, had enlivened the rectangular plots of new housing developments everywhere—which trade he had made his own. This being so, she agreed to meet me 'first thing' this morning, which I have assumed to be around ten-ish.

186

Cornelius, I ascertained, was 'in'. His contented purr, punctuated less and less often by a second, and boyish voice, emanated through his closed door. Eventually he and Justin Simms exploded in good-days and handshakes into the thickly carpeted hall, where the non-feminist Snell passed his prospective client to the 'very good care' of his 'right-hand man' (meaning Merle)—who I fancied left her chair, which turned a half-revolution on its stalk, with an impish smile. Snell then closed his door and picked up the phone.

Merle's 'very good care' was of course too good, for now, while I checked her protocol tables, she and Simms talked unguardedly of the rival agency she was about to open up for business (and run from home). She was sure, she· said, of Delilah Scuff. Simms confirmed she could also count him in. Yesterday she had worked on her TV gardener, who as loyal, earthy type, was unlikely to desert Snell. 'Even our technician has certain ideas for a book—isn't that so, Al?' You know it's more than that, Merle, though naturally I equivocated, passing to that other field of communications. The PC, which she intended for home use, and had here parked temporarily on the floor, and under the desk, she had connected to the phone network, but not to the closed world of Snell's office system—which all sounded to her 'grimspeak' as I explained this. 'Never mind,' I said. 'We can run tests between here and Zob's.'

I told Zob, having picked my way across the rubble of his drive, that Cornelius must have been out on business.

'This file transfer,' he said ... 'Is it something we should be using?'

He would, I told him, have an opportunity to assess.

August 19. Zob—and I confess I've never seen him puce—is today furious. The steel-tipped toe he aimed at the hall skirting board, till then an attractive soft wood (beautifully, perfectly mitred, and with so many intricate knots)—that size nine boot left its petulant indentation. Zob also danced on his hat—a flat chequered one, which he had bought for but never wore on country walks. In current mood we are all here to witness (regard, O you hundreds of thousands, who have tuned into *Talking Music*) some lively resurrection of the sullen boy Marsy—gifted child, &c. This is owing to the cruelest trinity, which I present in reverse order (having myself vegetated before too many television gameshows lately): 3) there has been no sign of his garden landscapers since that opening destruction; 2) Simms's much vaunted book has been put on the short-list, Best-novel-to-be-published (this decade); 1) Zob's own—of which I have spoken many times—called *Gimme the Cash*—has been removed (from the short-list, that is). I was instructed to get Snell immediately on the telephone, and succeeded only in his recorded voice. 'Then for God's sake send a fax!' which I did, though not to the precise wording Zob favoured, this being his electrified moment of rending spars, of shipwreck. The reply, which arrived at close of business, was from Merle, and said only: 'Cornelius out. Will call you Monday morning. Pleasant weekend.'

August 20. A profoundly mottled Volkswagen, a bright yellow where it hasn't disintegrated—at some point in its long life deprived of its front bumper—has been parked on Isabelle's drive most of the morning. Lent to her, she explained. Someone from her arts class.

August 21. Similarly, a Saab, of around the same vintage—colour, a charnel-house ash. Though this was absent for the usual duration of her secret Sunday liaison. She was not home in time for *Talking Music*—Masturbile's guest this week a pustular Tory (once of its cabinet). Atrabilious swirl of dance music, mainly.

August 22. The political Cornelius Snell, in an extraordinary meeting—which I had the misfortune to chair—reveals only now that he has long suspected moves to have *Gimme* rescinded—a 'tragedy' of postmodern myopia. The reasoning he gives for his own last days apparently incommunicado—which condition Zob was rash enough to couch as an inculpation—is that he has moved, behind the scenes, 'heaven and earth'—to get that 'important' piece of work re-instated. 'Y'know,' he said, 'I detect Geraldine Crouch behind this. Never trusted that woman ...' Snell's large hand on the arm of his chair, perilously near my own (of a more modest, and artistically chiselled design), thrums nervously throughout, and seems likely to slap my wrist, should I casually mention that not

188

only is Simms in town, but was witnessed at his office. Zob wanted to know what to do about Simms, whose precious throne of literaturedom he seems to have usurped.

Cornelius: 'Well you know Marsy in the press only this weekend I see Marvell'—the fistic Algernon Marvell—'has challenged Moorland Frames'—Oxbridge (yawn) Professor (yawn) of Poetry (yawn)—'to a public poetry bout'—a challenge whose bait the latter won't rise to. 'Here's your precedent. I mean, why not be as dismissive of Simms!' Simms, the young pretender to Zob's crown.

'Now what is all this debris?' is what Snell said, in departing, as I waved him from the threshold.

August 23. Not the easiest day to get through. Hourly, it seems, Zob is metamorphosing—is the enraged parody of that drama in which I have cast him so well, as my adapted Monostatos. He breathed fire, sulphur and garlic, in some slight reprimand for Mrs St John, who scuttled home at noon dabbing the corner of an embroidered handkerchief, almost mechanically, to the runlets of salt tears stinging her inflamed cheeks.

I kept more or less to my peach domain (décor having lost, as I turn my head, none of its silk). I am blessed with the charmed whispers of delicious anticipation, and cannot usher in this evening (of all evenings) at the same accelerated rate as the thump of my heart, which is inditing. Eventually my hour came, and I drove—not home—but to the cambered crescent abutting the green railings, the park and its paths, overlooked by Merle's. Here I left my car. I did not climb her stairs, or tap at her door immediately, but enjoyed the first of two evening strolls (this one alone) along the shaded walks, over the greens, in an arc round the cricket pavilion. I plucked pink anemones in a rocky garden among its ornamental pools, and interlaced my bouquet with ferns. These wrinkled the freckles of her nose (when presented), and were scissored over her drainer, where (for now) the inviolable Merle arranged them in a vase.

Her simple suppers were blue ribbon—tonight, pink salmon, with potatoes, lightly buttered. Over a delightful pot of tea, we talked business. Which meant that Simms's revamped *All That Glory*—coming on the back of recent publicity—as a youthful tale of erotic self-realisation, would head her list (respectability-wise). The stalwart Scuff, whose down-to-earth cuisine was likely to engender a thousand more titles, could be relied on for core income. My own piece, this diarial insight into the life of a deposed populist, should (by the trend of events) find its market niche (as a matter of fact she knew just the publisher).

'I'll arrange an advance.'

Merle—this was all too fast!

At sunset, I needed reassurance, therefore in an orange glow through a silhouette of hawthorn trees—that second, and accompanied stroll through the park—she enwrapped my waist in her naked arm, as we walked. (As we walked.) I cannot describe this twilit sorcery, with its first dim stars over the distant roofs of her suburb. Cannot describe its narcotic pulse in my veins, nor her majestic head on my shoulder. 'I shall need time,' I said, for even under the dead weight of commerce, there are poets and perfectionists who think it still worthwhile to sweat and to labour over mountainous re-drafts. 'Also I shall have to change all names. We would not want a succession of law suits.' Was there, she asked, somewhere I could get away to—to complete my work?

'Yes. There's a place on the fringes of Dartmoor.'

August 24. Zob, whose acuteness is the test of Snell's loyalty (which he would see nudged to the margins of adulation) fired a salvo in that direction over the fax network. His next great masterpiece is to be on the subject of literary rivalry (it said), with a working title *The Super Super Highway*. For this he demands a million pound advance. Incidentally my own needs are modest in this respect. The advance that even now Merle is negotiating—is for a sum to see me through, as I begin to look for a new job.

August 25. Snell said a million was 'steep'. Zob said he'd 'throw in' his Glaze memoir (material he over-estimates).

August 26. Free City Festival, day one. Can't help thinking, here where I sit among the ghostly, eviscerated echoes of that triumphal venue, the Royal Albert Hall, that this is in truth the resounding theatre of—I finger an example only—Handelian joy, hearty hymns launched up to that brightly enamelled cupola overspanning the whole incredible creation of life. A handful of people off the streets, having flapped sodden umbrellas in the foyer, sat through a handful of poets down there on the stage. Subject matter ranged from infantile- to adult-masturbation ('these things have to be confronted,' we are told). One bearded man, a northerner—not professionally so—plumped part way through for the sheets of rain darkening the pavements outside. For those one or two whose attention was still intent, he declared prurience in literary art its utter and absolute failure, with which sentiment unfashionably I concur. Unlike him, I did not have an umbrella—for which reason I learned minutely how I must 'rethink' my genitalia. O for the want of shelter …

August 27. Day two. Had the pleasure of Isabelle's company, who held my arm across Waterloo Bridge, where, in one of Zob's cosy back rooms in the South Bank complex, his interviewer—the prickly Philip Masturbile—seemed ill at ease, persistently adjusting his lapel—which interfered with his microphone.

The structure underpinning this well patronised event, was approximately so:

PM: A welcome, with slimy residues of some fool frog that had croaked in his throat (which into a Kleenex was never fully evacuated). Such an 'encouraging' audience.

MZ: Okay (in answer to appeals). Will sign books later.

PM: Am proud to present, etc. … (AHEM!) who will talk today about the whole business of publishing a book—a business more 'open' [now—that is a scream] than ever before.

MZ: Yes I will field questions …

PM: … time permitting (cough!), excuse! For most people (writing) it's a question of try, try, try splutter!

191

MZ: Why absolutely Philip I couldn't have put that better.

PM: Eventually you write a good book. This is the only way.

MZ: The ONLY way!

[A raised hand, a question from the floor]: Does that mean good books always find a publisher?

PM: Caution: who's to analyse 'good' and 'bad'?

[Another question]: (stifled).

PM: No. I don't think we want to get into the net book agreement. Spit.

MZ: No absolutely not there isn't the scope not with the ground we're intending to cover.

PM: Absolutely …

… and so on to the book signing, at which Isabelle got her *Gimme*— I detected a twinkle—bombastically monogrammed.

In contrast Bloge and Simms had a wonderfully nostalgic time, in open discussion of the latter's woodland unbuttonings—usually with barmaids—material that constituted the kernel of his forthcoming book, *All That Glory*. Good audience response, genuine belly laughs, &c.

Isabelle told me, going home—an arm through the vent of my jacket, her hand flat in my rump pocket—that the Citroën would one day return. At the moment it was garaged somewhere in Kilburn.

August 28. Day three. Some quite tedious lectures at the ICA— biographers waxing unashamed on yet more truck-loads, glossy plethora of shop-window books—on Shaw (yet again), on Wilde (yet again), on … snore, turn out the light … is there an author in the house!

192

August 29. Day four. Flude's operetta, a matinée performance, in the rough and tumble of the Coliseum. Not only did I see Snell, queuing for a programme (incidentally in a quite ludicrous lounge suit, shade a shiny anthracite), but he saw, and avoided, me (off with some florid housewife, to the cloakroom). I bought a programme myself, and on that first superficial glance at its cover plate (artwork by Julietta Simms—someone's coz), thought nothing of it. Welkin was a pastel blue, under which a green hill, upon which a grand Georgian house—stucco a sickly caramel—though this had been rendered fragmented, as it were tears in the ménage. In the grounds of which a buskined tenor (actually a half buskined tenor, having had a terrific accident involving one foot). It began to be familiar.

I took my seat (that tingle of excitement, with a bassoon, a piano, a mellifluous horn warming up). I turned to, and read, the synopsis—a few straggly paragraphs penned by one of our leading ladies, in the best pugilistic prose of whatever movement she belonged to, but which I roughly translate (or re-translate), as follows:

Genevieve Purefoy, sole issue of Sir Walter Purefoy, wealthy industrialist and sometime government adviser. Mother, deceased. Enjoys sweeping views of South Downs from family home near Hailsham. Sir Walter has long been generous contributor to Tory coffers, and has mapped out career for Genevieve as party worker. But. Genevieve falls madly for Daddy's driver and protector, Lobridge, who is blond, tanned, virile (and nocturnally a student—of chemistry). Won't on that secret ground move to Ealing, where Sir Walter has given her the keys to a house (in Montpelier Rd). Sir Walter blunders in on their night of love. This is in the stable, where the buck, in a ripple of moonlit buttocks, is up on his toes. Miss Purefoy, whose knees are spread, is perched on a sill. Later, in daylight, and fully attired, Lobridge refuses to be bought off. Sir Walter's hand is forced. Decides that he *will* risk a scandal. Fires his man. Only now does Lobridge reveal a political identity, which is nondescript, but vaguely Liberal. He campaigns for electoral reform, but at a rally has his foot crushed under the wheels of a pantechnicon. The foot is amputated. Lobridge, convalescing, completes his degree (I don't need to stress with distinction). He acquires work and limps in to the office each day. This is with a petroleum firm, from which platform he invents, patents and markets a miraculous new plastic. Now a millionaire, Lobridge hobbles back to the South Downs, where, high on a green hill, and with the wind in her hair, Genevieve has all this time been waiting. Lobridge goes down on the knee of his bad leg, weeping. *She* proposes to *him*. Tears escalate, to a deluge of joy. There's a no-fuss wedding, which Sir Walter, who is aptly heartbroken, misses, not having survived surgery. A last word goes to Sir Walter's obituarist, who is certain an elevation to the Lords had been likely. The house is shut up and sold, while the dream couple move south to Antibes, where Lobridge is determined to overcome his handicap.

Lobridge is a tenor. Genevieve, a soprano. The problem of Sir Walter, Flude, the composer, had overcome. Sir Walter is a baritone. Justin Simms—that rising star in the world of popular fiction—had 'written' the libretto.

I may note in passing some peculiarities in staging, rendered difficult, not to say problematic, with our man Royston Flude—not so much a minimalist, as a bare minimalist. For example Genevieve's split loyalties were almost always illustrated in the zenith of that poor soprano's register—parturient shrieks, and the wave of what looked like an order paper. Accompaniment (incredibly) one hundred kazoos (blown by the children of—it says here—the Moonshine Choir). Or take that steamy love scene. This had Genevieve encouched on a hay bale, in a pool of red light, unrolling—from her thigh, round her knee, over an arched foot, with toe-points to the gantries—a silky black stocking. Flude's writing here is for raucous trumpet, muted. The choreographer—by coincidence another Flude, Ingrid—places Lobridge (Lobridge in a pool of purple light) at some distance stage left—his pelvic thrusts of course exaggerated. For this we had piano thunder, somewhere way down for left hand. Sir Walter, as always, and on this occasion too, enters to the querulous meander of an oboe. Alas the reviews, particularly in the Tuesday *Guardian*, were gushing. 'Precisely what,' its hack rounded off, 'does make a city free.'

August 30. No sign of Mrs St John.

August 31. Zob, who only last night found time for (a whole week of) reviews, is furious—erroneously tells me he has been plagiarised. Unfortunately he can't get Snell on the phone, but can get that pleased recording. What about Merle? 'It appears,' I say, 'this is one of her days working from home. I don't know where she lives.' Towards sundown, in reply to his of the forenoon, he hands me a fax, a smooth, reflective script that Zob has earlier crumpled in his palm—and has re-opened as a rose. It's from Cornelius, who advises that: 'plagiarism's sometimes tricky.' Circumspect Snell suggests a polite note to Simms. Which advice Zob—whose complexion I later jotted as a downy nectarine—goes along with, but only to a certain point. His note's a tirade, tramped all over by the foot-stomping threat of lawyers.

September 1. No sign either of Mrs Clapp.

September 2. Stayed off work for the whole day—with 'a headache'. A reptilian succession of old jalopies, all camouflaged according to provenance—baked potato skins from a hard southern plain—rolled on and off Isabelle's drive, all day long. Some she drove, in others she was passenger.

September 5. Am asked to scrutinise Simms's reply, and, for the record, key it to disc. Here goes:

> Justin Simms
> c/o Erlem Management
> 97d Cromwell Heights
> London N6
> 2nd September 1994

Dear Marsy,
    So nice to hear from you. Confess to bemusement, am certainly the innocent in all this. Flude gave me synopsis—*his* property, I assumed—from which I worked libretto. Hope this clears things up.
    Festival an unqualified success, I hear. All the best. Justin.

The only point I can raise, but didn't, is that Erlem is an anagram of Merle. But. And as far as I know. She hasn't yet resigned from Snell's.

(Okay. I'll own up on the address too. It is undeniably my pearl's.)

September 6. Don't really know what Marsy now intends. A letter he wrote to Flude, as his *aubade*, after a sleepless night, he thought better of. Come those first spiralling motes of dusk, he binned it.

September 7. Adam, who has not so far mutinied, I saw this morning bent double—concerned, as he reported to 'Marster', at the continents of moss, more correctly their multiplied land mass, as engulfed the rear lawns. Then, only this afternoon, after a very light lunch, I partook of my second smoke, having slung myself low in a cane chair, outside, on the patio. A still air. All my blue rings softly melting. This was while, with the voluminous crash of kitchen utensils, Zob—yes, I did say Zob—repeat Zob made us both coffee. 'What, Al,' he asked, 'do you make of it all?' I saucered my spoon, reflectively. 'Well, Marsy …'

September 8. Joint manifesto delivered by Mesdames St John and Clapp—in a black-bordered envelope, gummed, I can only guess, with snake venom. As stark-eyed camp leader, naturally, it is St John the Shroud—it's she wants Wye 'personally' to pass this on— to (she hopes) an ill-fated Zob. It has to be said, he's got his share of trouble.

September 9. An encouraging sign. That's to say a builder—a third face—arrived and strode grim-necked amongst that rocky Armageddon, once where I parked my car. Zob too is fed up of leaving his Mercedes on the road. They exchanged unpleasant pleasantries—this new contractor predicting, that not even the golden seams, deeply at the heart of Zob's bank vaults, could ever be enough to put things right. He would, he said, prepare a 'quote'.

I saw the two letters of dismissal, awaiting signature on Zob's desk. I have not since seen St John and Clapp. In passing, he asked if I knew what a Hoover was for. Obviously I said no.

September 11. Strangely Isabelle asked me the very same question, shortly after she had parked up (a dilapidated 2CV, whose folding window plates were rather as washing hanging out). At this I smiled, and later checked her broom cupboard. Bourgeois preference here, I saw, was an Electrolux.

September 12. The Zob household—which the great man himself intuits—takes a different brand of weekend propaganda from that of widow Lavante (a point I shall explain). I found him in presidential mood, Arkansas heels planted firmly on his desk. He was on the telephone (simian line of repose curved where butt engaged tilt of chair). He was on the telephone to Snell (a man now prepared to talk at length). I shall go further: he was on the telephone (loud) to an outraged Snell (long and loud)—a man more capacious now that Simms had signed up with whatsitsname?—Erlem Management. (A firm no one appeared to know much about.)

I trudged to my peach empyrean. Here Zob had kindly left open for me one of the weekend supplements. Its scoop (or so I regurgitate)—and I am just too refined to quote this in full—it said was its 'vibrant' excerpts from Geraldine Crouch's 'forthcoming' memoir, here produced with *haut monde* photos. Succession of flashes. Crouch shakes hands with Mrs Thatcher. Reads proclamation to Lord Longford. Is gowned at Bristol Hon D Litt ceremony. Is shown with ageing novelist—or is that a toad shaking triplicate chin? Hard to see in this light, etc.

Crouch invents names, for example Queensly Armistice. Or Arthur Pole. Or this one, slightly obscure, Marjorie Drab. Larkin, however (deceased) remains Larkin. Her premiss, she says, in wanting to publish her memoir, is described as a series of reversals—her own, formulated, social corrective, which she inflicts on males. She has been wrongly accused, she says, of what she calls nights of Hellenist love. This is graphically gone into, and involves what her accusers have termed 'brief' procedures in 'strapping up' (they attribute her electrified dildo). Consequence being that now, among many, this is thought to be the means by which she 'entertains' young college girls. Yet (and here is another name). Martlesham Sob, whom she treats as 'any male' treats his cuddly female plaything—she insists is 'not' a 'good lay'. The same can be said of Clerihew Snail, whose seed is explosive, and has a slight flavour of vanilla. Some men, she finds, are priggish, unyielding, even as she lets loose her matchbox cockroach (sickly puerile pun her punctuation sniggers at). A certain Elasticare Wile is a case in point, whom she describes as 'boorish', as 'literary groupie'.

I can't say that I'm shocked. Certainly not to the point of Martlesham and Clerihew, who I see from the exchange lights are still gassing on the phone. (By the way, beg pardon, all this filth.)

September 13. A clean yellow sunlight, at certain times each morning, pours in at the miry windows. This in odd movements is apt to transmute that clinging fur—I mean where cornices meet in corners, or where the line of a straight staircase intersects the horizontal of an upper floor—into ripples of quicksilver. All goes unchallenged by the duster.

The hall carpet begins to suffer, because so far the frontal eradication, wreaked by that two-headed whirlwind, has not been put to order. Despite all this, Zob is cheered.

September 14. Apparently there has been a letter, from Glaze's executors in Exe—a tired trio of academics—who only at this time are able to release papers that are intended specifically for Zob. Zob, clearly, has the breeze of publicity ruffling his shirt cuffs, and says that he is now interested in the 'Rosewood' letters (which I have foolishly mislaid).

September 15. The drive to Exe contemplated. Certain memories revived. Foremost, of course, on a leaden day in February (of last year), was the news of Professor Glaze—as 'convalescent' (no more the peripatetic). This did not come from him directly, but from Giles, who phoned to tell Zob, who in turn told me (while, I recall, I had my two blue hands wrapped round the warm glaze of my coffee mug). I said something like 'Oh', the whole scene amounting to one of historical unimportance, which nonetheless repeated itself, with the much later news of his death.

We did not fly to him immediately (I mean during that fated

February). Zob was at this time toasted in every West End restaurant, and kept a punishing round of social engagements—not to say Dianas warming his bedtime quilt. It was I think early March, with the sunny wag of daffodils—these to the circular beds of soil, as footstool to the saplings in the various stages of new leaf—that we passed through Rosewood's massive pillars, and first snaked up the loose gravel drive. Zob and I stood momentarily at the great studded door of the sanatorium.

Glaze, I considered, liked his many affectations, no more so than now, which in the plight of his exhaustion—that dull electric of mental enervation—plunged him irreversibly into the slough of a Bath chair, complete, quirkily, with equipage—the red and navy blue check of a rug (for his knees). 'Good to see you, Marsy,' he croaked. 'You must be Alistair Wye.' And of course, I was, with the job of wheeling that defunct ante-postmodern to the vast glass canopies affording—as a photograph reminds—all wide views of the surrounding pines, with his Kentish rhododendrons. Glaze had the pale auburn stubble of a man who now only occasionally shaved, and wore the soft tieless collars of a man whose wardrobe was limp.

His room was sparse, but was furnished with a table, at which, in his moments of diminished inspiration, he pursued his transatlantic muse, or in a squeak of schoolboyish handwriting still attempted, 'once and for all', to set the record straight. He imagined a late flashlight, beyond it a night of furious scribing—his prize that of salvage, those first rising bubbles off his personal Titanic. Could still believe, unverifiably, in man's recorded life, thought, experience, as the immense unknowable—as that inexorable passage of time. Yet there was, he knew, no convenient detour, no theatrical sleight of hand—however conscientiously he palmed his prospector's pan. This was what he had posited.

Our next trip (in the days before I kept a diary) I am nevertheless sure came at the end of that March. Then our concern was the recurrence of Glaze's rash, which had imprinted his cheeks with the large angry ink of a butterfly, or its tattoo. A visiting GP prescribed ointments, which with persistent use held the patient's fires in check, although 'stress', the diagnosis, was an issue our invalid argued with. He insisted his health generally was in decline. This was his often enraged sentiment, to which Jessica—who had arrived from Cambridge earlier that day—remained indifferent (though she tutted). She had got her gurgling Amanda (with wobbly head) awkwardly sitting up in her car carry. Blessed Amanda—into whose elastic mouth I have seen spooned a canned pulp of sweetened apple (happy syrup, green paste that bespattered her bib.) Needless to say, this, for Glaze, was overly visceral, and so—and not solely to the preference of his sanity—I wheeled him through the sun and polish of Rosewood's reflective system of corridors, to the glassy cavern of the 'reading room'. (A journey not without incident. He insisted on transporting, though I never saw him walk, an aluminium stick, which was calibrated, sporting a fearsome ferrule. This he brandished poetically—his rage the rage of genius—at almost all passing staff, none of whom was in the slightest perturbed at his insults.) Jessica burped the baby (I am told). She mentioned to Zob that Andrew's bad temper was in truth down to the bullneck, who was footing the Rosewood bill. 'I can see,' said Zob (later, to me, in the car), 'how that must hurt.'

Other trips, should I try to remember them chronologically, have left—in the thin red trace on Andrew's temperature chart—no recognisable pattern of decline. Sometimes he was up. At other times down. There is one 'upwave' I have come to establish particularly well. Glaze watched us to the gate—after only one pot of tea—which gave us time to test variants on our route. I plunged us, I recall, into the dappled shade of a wooded declivity, with Zob, in his cosy corner, tossed about on his back seat—this, at each new twist in the road. There were bluebells, an interrupted sun. A greenness of leaves on the odd silver birch. Zob—as is characteristic—responded only to interiors. In the dampish brakes of that man's internalised bucolics, one shady thought turned its all-bright flower to the rays of the woodland roof, wanting to be caressed—which was, that certain quiet critics hadn't ·'yet' been won over. To me it was clear why, though I made a show of checking our road map. The man's infantile pursuit of popularity, not much surpassing an addictive demand for the ethers of respectability, were not both in his scope to satisfy—though naturally, those persons he had called to duty round him, accepted that they were (or themselves fell silent).

Glaze was at his gravest when, it seemed, attempts to shave (I subsequently noticed the tremble of his hand) had rendered his face a quite colourful patchwork—v-shaped nicks, with interconnecting clumps of stubble (unsuccessfully mown). Our journeys there were—perhaps unnecessarily—at high speed, which means my vistas of memory make not much sense in a whirl of village greens, or the haze of newly flowering orchards. Glaze on one occasion was very acerbic, even with Zob. Jessica, I suspected, had preceded us by a couple of days (and, had she, left him things to reflect on?). A tooth mug on his table had been part filled with water for an arrangement of campions, with a slight swish of spurge. There was an empty tin of something yummy for baby, in his bin. Zob was talking about film, radio, TV tie-ups—media in general. Glaze, with an issue of *The Five Dollar Review*—which was in the hollowed rug of his lap—kept telling us 'Now—now I'll read you that poem'— something he had long threatened (it was a metropolitan 'idyll'). He in fact broke down in a tremulous fit of sobbing, not having reached a turgid second stanza. He waved his stick, and us away: just one in a catalogue of scenes for which there has been no explanation. Others were …

… a broken bed head. Post he returned to the mail unopened. Two bedding sheets tied together (Glaze's room was ground floor). A letter to the bullneck pleading for Jessica's (yes, Jessica's) release. A refusal to eat breakfast, unless under the watchful gaze of one of two women who cleaned his room (who was too busy to do so). Zob, I have to say, never noticed much wrong, or as policy failed to react.

He was better in June. Deteriorated slightly in July. In August the GP pronounced him in the rudest health, at which a relieved Zob bought his old mentor a psychedelic tie (apparently a joke. Zob inscribed the gift tag so: Andrew, remembering the 60s!). Then, in September, Giles had to sit for long hours in the dome of Rosewood's reading room, of all things ploughing through Ginsberg. Only this, it seemed, could smooth his daddy's crumpled brow, and shut his eyes peaceably. Then one Wednesday Giles got suddenly called away (business), and did not thereafter see his father alive. Samantha I don't think ever visited, but kept in touch by phone. She even phoned Zob, notably one mid-October morning, having got herself in a silly panic over something Andrew had said. Was Andrew at this point raving? Did she believe in Zob as the only being on earth capable of pulling him through? I am, I hardly need say, the disinterested Wye, and just don't know, though of course was compelled to drive, through a child's wonderland—clustered dew drops on a thousand ghostly webs, a bright distant sun, we in our dusky Mercedes cruising east, plain quadrant of the compass I beheld, as a single morning ray transfused those swirls of English mist. Unexpectedly we found Glaze rosy and jovial, to discover that the bullneck had arranged for him membership of a country club. We repaired here buoyantly, where Zob plied him with dry sherry. That obeisance performed, we returned him to Rosewood, gushing and flushed. A crisis, Zob assumed, averted, though it was there, for the last time, that we left him.

Jessica, the rebel Jessica, was the last of his circle to converse, to touch his warm flesh, though like us knew nothing of the monsters invading the dark pool of Andrew Glaze's final November night. He managed to noose himself, in a psychedelic tie, and was found— jowls a deep royal purple—his socked feet dangling lifelessly in a circle, somewhere over that overturned Bath chair.

September 16. No. 28a, Scriveners Mews—Glaze's modern three-room flat, behind a stone façade—though it belonged with the worldly estate of Exe University, in deference to its other-worldly resident had been left uninhabited, since his passing. The three academics who conducted us to the professor's roll-top, were, well, academic (by which I mean archetypal, and dull). One had a shiny dome. One was thinning (detached hairs clinging to shoulders). The other was wrinkled. What they gave us, or rather gave Zob, was a bright yellow folder, which contained not that many loose papers. There was also a bundle of business correspondence, tied with string. This included Zob's postcard from Rome.

Glad to leave that sepulchre.

September 20. A fourth builder, truck compressed under the encouraging cargo of a cement mixer—plus orange sacks of sand—

arrived to survey the ruin of Zob's rutted front. He traversed, in a fidget with extensible rule, the graded circles of that particular purgatory, but breathed in sharply. He left a card (not his, a colleague's), and drove off forever westward into the mildness of the morning.

September 21. Zob, having left that yellow folder on my desk, now asks me to add to it one more paper—programme for the thanksgiving service, which he has kept in a drawer since November '93. Its cover layout is worth reproducing:

THANKSGIVING SERVICE

FOR

JOHN ANDREW GLAZE

PROFESSOR OF ANTE-POSTMODERNISM

EXE UNIVERSITY

on

Tuesday 23rd November at 1.00 pm

in

Sir Galahad Hall, Exe University

Zob is keen that I 'study' what have become known as the 'yellow' papers, should they cast light on that extinct theory of 'literary time'. In Zob's mind this has a bearing on the 'Rosewood' letters— shall determine whether I am to resurrect them. Let us, however, take a closer look at this programme—a service I did not attend, and which Zob has not till now spoken of ...

Page 1, wrongly the verso, headed by service commencement, the playing of Music for 'Cello Bows, by S. Collerant, a rhythmic, percussive piece for an ensemble of bows (no accompanying cellos). Welcome and introduction by the Revd Jonathan Dyke, followed by presentation of 'emblems and diplomas'. This consisted of Glaze's many degrees (most of course honorary) preceded by Giles with Daddy's ancient camera, Samantha with Inveraray toasting fork (acquired on their honeymoon), and a J. Hunter with brass rubbings (whose significance is lost on me). Then a reading, from *Rabbit Redux*, by M. Pritchett.

Page 2, the recto, from top to bottom: reading—'News of the World III', a poem by George Barker, by M. Zob; organ transcription, *Fanfare for the Common Man*, played by Mrs F. Deboyes; tributes (various names); readings, from a selection of Glaze's own works; prayers; silence; hymn, *Jerusalem*; final blessing.

God grant him peace.

September 23. The harpy Crouch (Zob's own touching epithet), whose branch of humanity exempts itself from all tones of reconciliation, has accented herself in the booms of theological bravado—or so I read it—in her invitation to Zob, apropos of forthcoming festivities: public/private celebrations of her fiftieth. Zob is even vain enough to accept.

September 27. Have now had a chance to study the 'yellow' papers. These range from notes, references, embryonic essays in Glaze's immature hand, to press cuttings and torn pages from a number of American journals. Between them they shed no light at all on the absurd theorising of an English academic, who it is clear spent much of his sabbatical attempting to demolish—without success—those points and counter arguments posed in print and in the lecture hall. I am sure he cannot have seen justification for that intellectual slip of the wrist, and in my view sought ways of establishing either of two things. 1) That his 'literary time' was 'in fact' metaphorical, not to be taken literally. 2) Some further complexity, some twist, to render the whole sorry hodgepodge deeply impenetrable, and in the short-term—i.e. the duration of Andrew's American jamboree—

unanswerable. Glaze was not above this latter option. Let me direct you to one of his Stateside critics, some of whose published comments Glaze himself draws attention to, via highlight pen. I quote from mid-sentence, from an editorial found in the journal *Hesperides*, in its depiction of Glaze at work, as follows ... '... one of those campus hangers-on, whose Bronze Age was the 1970s, when no nonsense went unrewarded. In those days, our English professor was applauded, having coined phrases such as these: "coercive reducibles", conversely "reductive coercives", then there was that famous one, "synergic bilaterals". All relate to technical issues in the construction of blank verse. You shouldn't doubt, that no one ever really knew what Glaze and his confederates were getting at, though they collected many academic prizes ...'

It is amusing too that far from consign the many objections (previously touched on) to the sci-fi bin, Glaze actually toyed with some. I see that 'time tree' notion at least made him think, for he has worked through—as it were on the back of an envelope—some highly deleterious future for his beloved Samantha—all based on the decision to blow his nose.

September 29. Glaze, Glaze, Glaze ... Everything Zob says is Glaze ...

October 3. I have, Marsy, as requested, considered the commemoration project. Some trick of literary time means you 'remember' a great deal more correspondence than is actual. So—let me furnish statistics. In an exchange that began on December 13th, 1991, and ended, with the second 'Rosewood' letter (both of which I am now instructed to drop), dated April 21st, 1993, approximately 11,000 words were penned or keyed. There are in total forty letters and cards (a thirty-five/five split). Nineteen of the letters were written by Glaze, and only sixteen by Zob. To Glaze's four postcards, there is one, Marsy, by you (remember that trip to Rome?).

'Eleven thousand words, eh, Al? That's going to take some padding! Got any ideas?'

(Well, Marsy—just a couple ...)

October 4. National Poetry Day, and the spectacle of Annie Cryles (the redhead), who has somehow scooped a string of awards-with-bursaries, reciting her catatonic dirge on early evening TV. I am in favour of promoting all high-ranking Arts Council persons to the first manned exploration of Mars, after a ministerial van.

O that studded crystal, our modest little solar system ...

October 7. Zob Snr, acting for Zob Jnr, has been talking to one of his learned friends of the Temple. This morning we received a high-quality vellum, with medieval illuminations, whose unpunctuated blocks of type culminate in an indecipherable signature (balloon, dissected by slanting pen stroke). This confined gas of a man has agreed to take up the young Zob's allegations of plagiarism, now directed at Royston Flude.

Beg pardon, your Honour, but ...

'What was that, Al?'

'Why nothing. Except to say Merle wants me to test that file-transfer software, tomorrow ... Saturday ...'

October 8. Merle, I find, is in a state of euphoria. That is because her paperwork has progressed with unexpected celerity. The point is, that on Wednesday, she anticipates clearing her desk (at Snell's), and on Thursday officially opening Erlem's for business. I cannot prevent her floating to the various ceilings. Nor will an innocent smile depart for any clockable duration—not that I, the amused Alistair Wye, ever wear a watch. That slightly pinked satin, that happy, that gorgeously animated face! I am asked subsequently shall I propel her on those park swings near her house, where the breeze gets in her hair, and the points of her toes score two ecstatic arcs in the light bright air of her new heaven.

She insists on buying me a seafood lunch, somewhere on the brink of Ealing, and drinks rather too much vintage champagne (Lanson, 1979). It's the kind of celebration that goes on, and on, and I therefore postpone our file-transfer tests until tomorrow.

October 9. I arrived at Snell's (Snell in his white bath robe, with a clutch of Sunday papers), on whose doorstep I intoned much mysterious gibberish concerning *$$TransPlant$$*—which Snell assumes refers to something called—or he calls—'electro-surgery'. 'Why of course come in, dear boy!' he said, and ushered me to, and left me with, the dotted lights, and the humming fans, of his computers and modem. I constructed a block of ASCII text for transmission, but this was not a success. Zob's receiving equipment did not, for some reason, respond.

I drove over (I had, it was certain, installed the software). I parked up behind a Renault (beige, ancient, peppered with burgundy rust). I picked my way over the rubble (reflecting that yes, I had set Zob's FT server running). What—as I slipped in my door key ... yes what (all, so, irritating!) ... what, I couldn't guess—was wrong?

I blundered in to the study, where Isabelle, in only a lemon bow-tie, plus matching ankle socks, was prostrate on the desk, though supported ably at the udders in the squeeze of Marsy's palms. Zob—the hirsute Zob—throbbed, and I suppose shrivelled in her loins (in his exertions had toed and unplugged the modem). I said something like 'Oh', as did Isabelle (though her monosyllable acted as gate in a fence of exclamations). Zob, not unreasonably, said only 'Get out, Al!'

October 10. Not surprisingly Isabelle, who has 'gone away' for a week, expects me to 'find other lodgings' before she returns. Zob, for whom these things are merely a recreational hazard, did not expect me to fill my briefcase with computer discs, and resign.

October 12. Merle also resigns ...

October 13. ... and so 'Erlem' is born. That firm's senior partner is shrewd enough to set aside sufficient start-up capital for three-months' rent re that delightful damp retreat on the fringes of Dartmoor. Here my first task is to write a synopsis, which she expects to discuss over morning coffee with one of her publishers (CentreHouse Press), a sartorial chap called Dr James, who has already been primed.

November 27. Have begun the second redraft. Principal problem here is to invent fictitious names. What's required is a balance, of the real and bizarre. Incidentally Merle, who was here this weekend and only a few hours ago caught the London train back, has told me that Snell is more enthusiastic over Zob than ever—is pressing for that million. This, she was sure (with a smile), is because a recent campaign—TV, street hoardings, every bookshop window— proclaims Simms, her own Justin Simms, 'the number one bestseller'. I am told bookmakers make *All That Glory* clear favourite for that peculiarly English accolade, Best-novel-to-be-published (this decade). Although I, the unassailable Alistair Wye, know better than that.

Such a bleak glorious stroll we had, this afternoon over the moor.

Christmas Day. A capon I brought up from Riverford Farm is in Merle's oven. We are at her kitchen table, whose centre-piece is the manuscript she completed her first full read of only last night.

'Fine, Al,' she says (uplifting tone), 'though I don't much recognise this 'Merle'.' Today her yellow hair is in a tight coil at her nape. 'Also I think it needs a foreword.'

'To say what?'

'Something anticipatory.'

'How about, *The Guilt That is Hampstead's*, third act, in which the first gardener Adam is granted new life—fairer, more meaningful employment ...'

My job to peel potatoes. Though I cannot first resist a mild gin and tonic.

'Merle' says, 'Now seriously, Al ...'

Well now, let me think. In my memoir of social decay, which has been after all the catalyst of artistic regeneration, I shall start I suppose with a fatality. The corpse—which is my wont—is symbolic. Some time hence its transmogrified mulch is the moving ground that the grandeur of a renascent literature flourishes in. It shan't be compacted—not by those clumsy hobnails our many Marshall Zobs tramp in our world of printed pages in.

Why yes, Merle (or 'Merle'). I shall do that this afternoon. Probably after lunch. What we're talking here is best novel to be published, this, and the next, and the next decade.

Allow me to raise my glass (that gin, that long cool something), and drink your health (that is to you, genteel reader). While I—well, I *shall* remain, as you'll see, your faithful and phenomenal Alistair Wye ...

... and. I *shall* return. Promise. (Yes I certainly shall smile for the camera.)

Click!